About the Aut

Evelyn Walsh lives and works in Swords, Co. Dublin, Ireland and has been writing for a number of years. She was nominated for a Hennessey Award for First Fiction in 2007 and ghost wrote *His Name is Rebecca*, Rebecca de Havalland's memoir, which was published by Poolbeg Press in 2010.

ISBN-13: 978-1463765910
ISBN-10: 1463765916

Copyright © Evelyn Walsh 2011

All rights reserved.
No part of this publication may be reproduced, stored in a retrieval system, or transmitted, in any form or by any means, without the proper permission in writing of the author, nor be otherwise circulated in any form of binding or cover other than that in which it is published and without a similar condition including this condition being imposed on the purchaser.

All characters in this novel are fictional and any resemblance to anyone person/persons living or dead is coincidental.
Tibraden in Leitrim is also a fictional location.

Cover design by www.designforwriters.com
Photography by Kenneth Walsh

www.ev-allthisandheaventoo.blogspot.com

EVELYN WALSH

The Heron's Flood

For Anne Griffith – a very special lady

Chapter One

October 2005

She sits on a kitchen chair, staring through the open door into the utility room. The room's normal spotless sterility – white tiled walls, washing machine and drier, white melamine presses housing all her cleaning products – is now marred by the crumpled body of her husband, his chest leaking blood and other matter onto her well-scrubbed linoleum.

She worries a little about the pool of blood. At first there had been so much bright red stickiness. Then the flow had trailed off to a trickle. Just as well, she thinks, if it leaks under the washing machine the whole thing would have to be shifted.

Norah sighs, she has never felt so tired and there is so much to do. She would like to sit here forever. Another while and then she will see to it all. She studies the hands in her lap, turns them this way and that. There are a few flecks of dried blood stuck in the cracked skin of her right index finger. She picks at it to dislodge it. His or hers? His, she thinks

The house seems so quiet. No banging doors or blaring telly, no noisy whistling or barging maleness. Nothing but an off the station buzzing from the radio lying face down beside Tom's body.

She looks up at the kitchen clock. 10.30pm. Where

have the hours gone? No point ringing the station house, Denis Bradley will be long gone home.

She has to ring somebody though. She can't leave Tom lying in a heap on the floor until morning. She stands up, cold and stiff. Her skirt, pants and tights are still damp. She realises without surprise that she has been sitting for over three hours, thinking, not thinking. She walks to the phone on the kitchen counter and lifts the receiver.

999.

How easy it is to press the same button three times, she thinks. That's probably why they use it as the emergency number.

'Emergency services, which service please.'

Norah can't find her voice and when she manages to croak out 'Gardai. Ambulance. No – Gardai. Yes. Definitely,' it doesn't sound like her. The words seem to have come from far away, a tiny childlike voice. She can hear her seven-year old self in that voice. There is a clicking and a whirring then:

'Gardai?'

'It's my husband. I think. No. He is...he's dead. I need someone to come..., to tell me what to do.'

'Alright love. What's your name?' The steady male voice speaks slowly.

'Norah. Norah Furlong.'

'Are you alright Norah? Are you hurt? Hurt in any way? Is there anyone else there?'

'No. We're on our own. I. No... I'm alright. It's him.'

'That's good, Norah. Good. Now, where are you Norah? And can you tell me what happened to your husband?'

'Tibraden. We live in Tibraden. There was a terrible row. Terrible. He.. I..'

'Where exactly is Tibraden, Norah? Tell me the nearest big town.'

'Mohill, about ten miles from Mohill, on the Carrick road. Leitrim. Our house is about five miles west of the village.'

As she describes the location of her house and the easiest way to it, she can feel herself reconnecting, becoming more self-aware. She feels as if she has been hovering over the room for the last few hours, abstractedly watching her physical self.

'Ok, Norah. Norah? Are you still there?'

Norah can hear activity and the crackle of other voices behind the voice in her ear.

'Yes. Yes I'm here.'

'Norah, are you sure your husband is dead? Can you go and check, make sure he's not breathing? Can you do that for me Norah?' He sounds so concerned. His voice reminds Norah of Uncle Frank, the way Uncle Frank would say her name frequently as he talked to her. Frank always gave her name weight, importance, reminding both of them who she was.

'Yes. Yes, I'll do that.'

'Don't hang up now Norah,' the voice rises a little. 'Just go to your husband and see if there is any sign of life. It's important. Will you do that, Norah?' His voice has more urgency now and Norah wants to do the right thing for him.

'Yes, yes, I'll check for a pulse, will I? Under the jawbone – isn't it? Or the wrist – aren't they the best places?' Her voice childish again.

'That's it Norah. You go and see now, then come back and tell me, alright? Don't hang up, just go and see and come back and tell me.'

Norah puts the receiver on the counter and walks to the open door between the kitchen and the utility. Her stockinged feet feel cold and she stands at the door for a moment before she steps down into the utility room. It feels like the biggest step she has ever taken.

He has settled into classic recovery position. On his right side, right arm trapped under his body, left hand curled around the handle of the garden shears that is lodged half-way into his chest. His head tilts slightly downwards, chin towards chest, eyes open, blank and staring at the brownish stain starting to crust on his shirt. The slight bend of his knees reminds Norah of a picture she saw once of a child sleeping.

Norah bends and puts her hand in front of his mouth, ready to run if there is any breath, then she places her fingers under his chin to feel for a pulse beneath the stubble. She draws back quickly. He's so cold. It's not normal, that coldness. She notices the bluish-grey hue of the skin on his face and arms. There is no life here.

She steps back quickly into the kitchen and pulls the door closed behind her, feeling a momentary terror that he – or his spirit, soul, remaining malingering stubborn himness, whatever – will grab her by the ankle, pull her down, punish her.

'No. No. There's no pulse. He's dead.' Her eyes fill and she can feel all the little veins around her nose and mouth pulsing with imminent tears.

'Ok, Norah. Is there anyone with you or anyone you can call?'

Norah pauses.

'No, no. There's no one. We've no family. Just me and him.'

'Norah, a car is already on its way and an ambulance will be with you very shortly.' He sounds so organised. Norah is glad someone is looking after things for her.

'Alright, will I just stay here?'

'Yes Norah. Can you put on all the lights at the front of the house, so the driver knows which house to go to? I'm hanging up now but I'll ring you back in ten minutes to check you're okay.'

'Wait, wait. What's your name?' Norah panics, she needs to keep him talking, she wants him to look after her.

'I'm Cathal, Norah. Cathal Tierney – I'll talk to you soon.' Then a click and the buzz of the disengaged line.

Norah replaces the receiver and notices a dirty brown smudge on it from her hand. She goes to the kitchen sink for a dishcloth to wipe away the mess.

Then she stops. Maybe she shouldn't. What about

forensics and things? All those shows on TV, people in white suits and boots, dressed like that so they wouldn't – what was the word? – contaminate, yes, contaminate the scene.

But she's not trying to hide anything, so surely they won't be annoyed if she just cleans up a little. Her hands anyway. She has to wash her hands. She hates her hands being dirty. She doesn't mind in the garden, she likes the feel of the earth in her hands there. But not indoors, dirty hands have no place indoors. She's sure it will be alright.

Then she has to put on the lights in the hall and living room so Cathal, the gardai and the forensic people and the ambulance can find her. She turns on the tap and presses the nailbrush into the soap. She starts scrubbing at her hands. The swishing of the nailbrush and the splashing of the water soothes. She starts to hum, then stops. She shouldn't hum. She dries her hands thoroughly and then the sink, automatically polishing behind the taps. Tom likes the sink to shine.

Replacing the towel on its hook she turns and peers through the patterned glass of the utility door at the distorted pile that is her husband. She half expects him to sit up. Her legs feel weak , they tremble as if she has been ill in bed for a long time.

Supporting herself by placing her hands along the wall she makes her way down the hallway. She switches on the lights in the living room and pulls back the net curtains, illuminating the gravelled driveway outside. She hears the sirens in the distance.

Why the sirens she wonders? There isn't any traffic worth blasting out of the way. Probably a young garda. Excited by the thought of his first murder.

Murder.

She stands and waits, staring through her mirrored image in the window to the black October night.

March 1975

The child in the camel-coloured coat stood at the school gates and stared up the quiet road with fierce concentration. She banged her schoolbag against her knees and counted under her breath.

'One, two, three, four,...she'll be here before I get to twenty,' she thought.

But twenty came and went and six or seven more twenties too. The road was so quiet it was scary. It was normally filled with the colour and noise of over five hundred primary school girls, rushing to or from the building. Mothers pushing prams and buggies adding to the commotion, chatting to each other, shouting goodbyes or greetings to daughters at the gates.

The red-bricked building squatted silently behind Norah, dull now that it had disgorged its contents for the day. The black surface of the playground, still glistening from earlier rain, needed running feet and shouting laughter to give it meaning. Norah was dwarfed by the big black gates which creaked in the wind. She glanced nervously about; she wondered had a spell been put on the school and the road, perhaps everybody was sleeping or dead.

'That mother is never late,' thought Sr. Pascal as she approached the heavy gates to lock them.

'Norah Breslin. Are you alright?'

Norah jumped.

'Oh! Sister, Mammy is late.' Her eyes filled with tears.

'Don't cry child. I'm sure she'll be here in a moment, I'll wait with you.'

Norah looked up at the nun, her kindly words didn't soften the severity of her normally stern face. She wasn't nicknamed Sr. Pascal the Rascal for nothing.

'She looks okay,' thought Norah. But the Rascal's temper and her quickness to mete out slaps with the ruler were legend. Fear of rousing this anger by a misplaced word overcame Norah's fear of walking home alone.

'Oh! I just remembered Sister. Mammy said to come home on my own. She had to take my baby sister to the clinic.'

'Aren't you the silly goose, forgetting an important thing like that and getting all upset for nothing!' Sr. Pascal clanged shut the gates and started to apply the padlock. 'Off home with you now as quickly as you can. Your mother will be waiting for you.'

Norah walked slowly up the road, squinting in a sudden burst of spring sunshine. She was sure that any moment she would see Mammy running towards her, pushing Louise in the pram.

Her bag was heavy, it banged against her bottom; she normally put it into the pram where Louise could bite on the straps.

'Mammy, Mammy where are you?' She thought, her plain, plump little face scrunched up with anxiety.

She glanced back at the deserted school gates. If she went back there to wait The Rascal might come out again. She would be really cross if she knew Norah had told a lie.

It was only a white lie though, not a mortaller.

They had learned all about the different types of lies and sins for their First Holy Communion in May. Norah had her dress and shoes already.

She stopped, smiling, the frown lifting from her face and showing that magical internal brightness that shines so easily from children.

That's where Mammy was!

She'd gone into town to get Norah's Communion bag and medal. Daddy had waited for her this morning and given her a lift in. She must have been delayed or missed the bus home. Or maybe the bus broke down and they had to wait for another. Relieved and pleased that she had worked out where her mother was, Norah started to skip up the lane that led to the main road.

The lane was as deserted as the area around the school had been. Set between the convent wall and the back gardens of a terrace of houses, it was used daily as a short cut by large numbers of school children and their parents.

It looked awfully long and grey to Norah. She had never noticed that before. The high grey wall of the convent on one side blocked much of the light. Set into a six-foot wall on the other side were the wooden back gates to the terrace of houses. To chase away her fears Norah started to run and count the gates as she passed. There were sixteen gates to the end of the lane. She knew that. She used to count them with her friend Valerie as they ran along ahead of Mammy and Valerie's Mam.

'One, two, three, four, five...'

She stopped. Outside the second-last gate stood the formidable figure of Prince – the bulldog who terrorised all passers-by. If Norah's mother was with her she would have said,

'Don't look at him, keep walking. Ignore him if he barks.'

But Norah always noticed Mammy gripping the pram handle a little tighter if she had to pass Prince.

Norah heard a whimpering noise and realised the sound had come from her throat. She couldn't go back to the school and face the irritation of Sr. Pascal. Maybe she should wait awhile and see if a grown-up would come along. Then Norah would be able to follow them up the lane.

She stood uncertainly, her brain buzzing, heart pounding.

Prince stared at her. Then he scuttled forward a few feet rolling his shoulders. He growled, a low threatening rumble. Norah jumped with fright and she shouted,

'Go away, go away.'

She moved back to the nearest gate and started to bang her bag against it. Prince was galloping the short distance towards her. She screamed at him again,

'Go away, go home.'

She turned her face away from the advancing dog, closed her eyes and huddling against the flaking red paint of the gate she banged frantically, screaming,

'Help, Help, Oh! Please, please somebody help me.'

Prince was upon her. Barking ferociously. A taut bundle of muscle, his whole body a coiled spring bouncing at her heels. The noise of him barking and the blood rushing in her head was deafening.

'G'wan, get out of it,' a woman's voice shrieked. She banged a dustbin lid against the wall and stamped her foot at the brute. Prince retreated a few steps, still snarling.

Norah's arm was grasped and she was yanked quickly through the red gate which was then slammed shut behind her.

'You're alright, love. Listen, listen, you're alright.' A grey-haired woman hunkered down in front of Norah, still holding her firmly by the upper arm, watery blue eyes gazing kindly at the distressed face of the child.

'Bloody nuisance that he is! Listen to me, now. Listen. You're alright. He just barks and makes a lot of noise. Stand up to him and he backs off.'

Then she stood up and muttered,

'Not that that's much good to you when you're petrified, you poor divil.'

'Oh! Oh!' Norah couldn't speak, she even found it hard to breathe. Tears were coursing down her face and all she wanted to do was hug the woman and howl with relief.

'Come on in pet, you can go out through my front door onto the road. Where do you live?'

The woman brought Norah up a narrow garden path into the kitchen of the house. Norah's legs were shaking and to her horror she realised she had wet herself. The wee had spread down through her navy wool tights and left them wet, heavy and uncomfortable.

'45 Willow Park Crescent,' she managed to snuffle out.

'That's off the road up past the post office, isn't it?' queried the woman.

Norah nodded. The woman glanced at her watch then handed Norah a biscuit from a tin on the counter.

'I'd walk up with you, but...well, you're alright now aren't you? I'll go down to Matt Brown about that bloody dog again this evening. You tell your Daddy to call into him too. Maybe they'll learn to keep that back gate shut one of these days. Now, here – wipe your eyes and nose. Are you okay?'

Norah took the proffered tissue and nodded again, the biscuit stuffed into her mouth. The crumbs fell from her lips and she swiped at her tears and runny nose with the tissue. She sniffed and looked at the woman who laughed and patted her on the head.

'You poor thing, you'll be alright before you're twice married. C'mon with me now.'

Norah was led through the kitchen and a narrow hallway and out the front door. The woman pointed up the road.

'See where the lane comes out, love'

Norah nodded again, peering timidly up the road in case Prince decided to emerge this side of the lane.

'Don't worry, he never comes out this way. Off you go now. I'll watch until you get to the other side of the zebra crossing.'

Norah moved away from the safety of the woman's front door. Her wet tights made walking uncomfortable and to the fear of meeting Prince was added the fear of meeting any of her classmates. They might notice and laugh at her.

'Oh, Mammy! Mammy. Why don't you come?' She prayed fiercely as she stood waiting to cross the road.

'Go on now, it's safe,' shouted her saviour from the doorstep.

Norah ran across the road then turned and waved her thanks. At the post office she turned the corner and walked slowly up the three hundred yard stretch that was Grove Road. At the top of Grove Road she turned right into the crescent of bungalows where she lived.

It was a pleasant little housing estate; thirty-three semi-detached bungalows set around a small green open space. The Breslin home unremarkable among its neighbours. Safe, ordinary, comfortable.

Norah went up her driveway and around to the back of the house. She tried the back door but it was locked. She moved back into the garden and stood up on the swing seat to see if her mother was moving around in the kitchen. But the blank kitchen window stared back at her, empty and silent.

She returned to the porch at the side of the house. If she stood on her tip-toes she could just about reach the door knocker. She banged it up and down several times, face flattened against the half-moon patterned glass. But no shadowy figure appeared on the other side of the door to welcome her home.

Eventually Norah stopped knocking and curled herself into a ball in a corner of the porch. Nobody could see her. She would be safe until Mammy came. She cried and cried until sleep blessedly overtook her.

As dusk settled on the suburban housing estate, two Gardái walked in uncomfortable silence up the driveway of the Breslin home. Their duty to break bad news to those at this house. A dreadful car accident that morning had taken the lives of all three occupants of Dan Breslin's car.

A lump came to the younger man's throat when they discovered a cold, scared child. She looked like an abandoned teddy-bear, and the garda could not but cry when he realised she was to be the recipient of the news.

Chapter Two

October 2005

I first heard of Tom Furlong's death – without knowing who he was – on the car radio as I snailed my way through tedious Dublin traffic. A man found dead in suspicious circumstances. Another person being held for questioning. The fact that the death was in county Leitrim, in an area bordering my home county of Sligo, did register the death more firmly in my consciousness. Enough for me to comment to work colleagues about the remoteness of the area when the topic came up for discussion at tea-break.

Tea-break in the civil service. Seed bed of malicious gossip. Breeding ground for all discontent. Desultory conversation about the goings-on of various soap characters turns to reflection (wildly generalised) on the mental and physical make-up of one or another of our colleagues. Someone will always have a gripe about the shortcomings of the canteen menu, which will lead to a free-for-all of aggrieved complaints about the conditions we work in – the lack of car-parking, the cold, the heat, the lack of air, the draughts, etcetera, etcetera.

Of course it always finishes (ten minutes later than it ought) with mutinous mutterings against 'them'. 'They' never listen to anything we say, hence the state of the office, the section, the department, the government and of course the country. 'They' will always let you down.

Thankfully, 'they' will also always be there to blame for everything that goes wrong, within or outside our sphere of influence.

Apparently this phenomenon is not exclusive to the civil service, it exists in every organisation, large and small. People will find the lowest common denominator, identify a common enemy and unite in opposition. To our immense satisfaction we can vent our grievances without having to propose any solutions. Where would the world be without tea-breaks?

Three days after I had heard of the death in Leitrim, Rob greeted my customary late arrival into the office with a waving yellow post-it.

'Sinead Lateeveryday – your Ma rang. Twice. And you left your mobile here last night and it's been driving me mad with 'I Will Survive' at regular intervals. It is SO naff, will you P..L..L..EASE change it!'

'Thanks Rob,' I grinned at him. 'Did Mother say what she wanted? Never, ever let her hear you calling her 'Ma'. Based on the brief phone conversations she has had with you she seems to consider you a good influence on me. She always asks after that 'nice young man'. I think she may be considering you as possible marriageable material for her deeply disappointing daughter.' I laughed at his horrified face.

'She didn't say what she wanted. Ugh! Jesus, I'll definitely call her 'Ma Breslin' next time I'm talking to her. Married to you! My skin's gone all cold and clammy.' He walked away with an exaggerated shiver.

He's a good person, Rob. A great friend. He torments some of the more priggish members of staff and camps up his homosexuality to upset their sensibilities. Rob is incredibly smart. Smart enough to know when not to overplay his hand in the bureaucratic straitjacket that is our civil service; he knows when to back off and eventually win the game. He's brilliant at his job, ploughing through more cases than most of us in a day and he deals with each file even-handedly. He has a highly tuned bullshit detector for the lie that some of our taxpayers seem to think it their duty to tell. He is well regarded by management and loved by most of the staff. If he wasn't collecting money from them most of the taxpayers he comes into contact with would also rate him as a 'decent skin'.

I checked my mobile, four missed calls. All from Mother. I sighed and punched in her number. She answered on the fifth ring. She once told me she always waits until the fifth ring.

'Never let people know you're waiting for them, Sinead. Never let people think that you're not busy.' She has lived her life hiding behind hundreds of little rituals, routines and timetables. Nothing impetuous or even vaguely out of sync with the picture she likes to portray of herself. A stately respectable widow of a bank manager.

Sometimes I ring and deliberately hang up after the fourth ring. Then I feel guilty and won't ring for a day or two so she won't guess it was me that had hung up earlier. If she ever gets number recognition on her phone I'm shagged. It's horrible. I can't help it, she brings out the worst in me. I liked the thought of her wondering who had rung. She would never think it was a wrong number. She doesn't make mistakes like that and so assumes neither does anyone else.

'Hello Mother, you were looking for me?' My voice, I thought (as always when talking to her), sounded a little strangled.

'Sinead, thank goodness. I've been trying to get you since last night! Why aren't you answering your mobile? I left messages,' her tone aggrieved.

I bristled immediately.

'I left my mobile behind me yesterday. I'm very busy here Mother, is this important?'

'Of course it's important. I can't understand why you won't get a landline in the apartment. And there's no need to sound so impatient. My goodness, Sinead, you know I wouldn't disturb you in work unless it was important. I hope I know my place in your life at this stage.' I could hear the suppressed sniff. I gritted my teeth. I had to submit; the fallout wouldn't be worth it.

'Sorry, Mother. Of course you wouldn't, just a bad morning here. What's up?'

'Did you hear the news?' Temporarily mollified, her voice dropped to a confidential tone.

'Which news? The TV? Radio? Anything in particular?' I wasn't that interested. I had long fallen out of the habit of buying the 'Sligo Champion' for news of the inhabitants of the rural parish I'd been reared in.

'Do you remember Norah Breslin? Well, she's been Norah Furlong for about fifteen years now.'

'Norah?' I couldn't place the name amongst any of the immediate neighbours. 'Don't think I know her, do I?'

'You should! She's your second cousin. Her father was Dan Breslin, son of your father's Uncle Jack so her father and your father were first cousins. Maybe she's not a second cousin, is she a first once removed?'

'No, second cousins I think.' I still couldn't place the woman.

'You met her at least once, maybe more. Remember! Her parents died and your great Uncle Frank and his wife Teasie took her in. We went to visit them the summer after she came to them. We thought we should show them some support.' She gave a saintly little sigh.

I did vaguely remember a pasty-faced little girl in a tartan kilt and frilly white ankle socks. She had been a year or two older than me. I remembered the socks. I had been enamoured of those socks. I pleaded for a pair of them, to no avail. Eventually resorted to asking Santa for them; he didn't deliver. Frilly ankle socks weren't for muck magnet six-year-old me.

'I do remember. Wasn't their place a small one, around Mohill somewhere? Uncle Frank had goats, didn't he?'

'That's him. He had asthma, couldn't take cows milk hence the goats. Himself and Teasie were very good to Norah. Took her in when she had no one. Her mother hadn't any family; well, none able to care for a young child. The grandparents on Dan's side were long dead when he and the wife were killed. Very tragic, a car crash. I think there was another child that died in the accident. Frank and Teasie immediately offered to take Norah in although they were well into their fifties at the time. They had no children of their own, I suppose they felt it a blessing to get the gift of a child that late in their lives.' My mother was enjoying this, lots of death, drama and tragedy. However, she was keeping the best to last.

'I couldn't believe it when John O' rang me today. Norah's the woman who has been arrested in connection with the death of that man in Tibraden!'

'Hold it, Mother, hold it! How on earth is John O' involved?' John O' – John O'Sullivan, an ex-boyfriend of mine whose name caused a stir of interest in me that I preferred not to acknowledge.

'Well, apparently the legal aid people in Carrick contacted him. Norah told her solicitor the only family she had left was your father – Lord rest him. All she could remember was Sean's name and that he had been bank manager in one of the banks in Sligo. This solicitor fellow had been in college with John and they had kept in touch; he knew John was from hereabouts so he rang John to see if he could trace the family. But – wait 'til you hear Sinead – John rang me to see if I would be prepared to talk to Norah!' She paused for breath, the drama quite wearing her out.

'And?' I prompted.

'And what?'

'When are you going to meet her? What does she want? More importantly did she do it?' I was speaking very softly now; the tea-breakers would love this.

'I'm afraid it looks like she did. She was on her own in the house with him and 'twas her called the police and said she thought he was dead. When the ambulance arrived he was pronounced dead at the scene,' her voice dropped to a whisper although I knew she was on her own in the house.

'He died from blood loss – wounds from a garden

shears stuck in his chest. Imagine! And she seems to have admitted killing him. But she has clammed up since then, shock or something according to John O', and the guards and psychiatrists think maybe a family member could draw her out – get her to explain.' Mother's voice had risen in pitch and volume as she drew the story to a close. Nothing this out of the ordinary had happened to her in years, or ever I'd imagine.

'So when are you going? Ask John O. to go with you, he'll make sure all the legal p's and q's are minded.' I knew damn well she wasn't going but I wasn't going to make it easy for her.

'Goodness Sinead, I can't possibly go. I've never even been in a police station. Besides, she's your father's relative not mine.' That sniff again; inference being that none of the noble Fitzgerald clan into which she had been born would dare to be related to a murderer, or, if they had a misfortunate murderer in the family, said murderer would be smart enough never to be caught.

'What about Rachel?' I knew the answer to this one as well. My sister was assistant principal in the local national school. Mother's 'my daughter, the assistant principal' could not be sullied by even the slightest hint of infamy.

'Don't be ridiculous, Sinead. Rachel can't go. What about her position?' A tiny dismissive laugh at my naive suggestion.

I laughed myself. I had to – otherwise I would have screamed. This may all appear to be a perfectly normal exchange (albeit about an extraordinary situation) between two human beings. But it wasn't – it was for us a battleground. An old, scarred battleground. Lots of history and hidden meaning; old wounds to be attacked, re-opened and licked clean again. Every conversation I had with my mother from the time I was capable of independent thought was like this.

I'm entirely to blame for reacting the way I do. She had always been quick to point out my inadequacies and I always reacted in a certain way, fighting against her but deep down believing the negativity and filing the throwaway comments to be taken out, re-examined and brooded over. She was my bête noir and I had let her play the role.

I had eventually accepted that, yes, my mother was a problem but she needn't necessarily be THE problem. I could let my reactions to her rule my life or I could just accept and ignore them.

It's hard though. When you have fallen into a certain pattern of thinking and behaviour that you have used for a long time it is resistant to change. I had seen less of Mother once I left college and that helped, but I couldn't completely cut ties. My childhood home and the area I was reared in hold too many strong, happy memories for me to cut it from my life. I would learn to cope with Mother, because if I didn't, she would have won. And that would never do.

'Mother, is there absolutely no one else? I can't believe this woman has lived in a vacuum all these years. Surely there must be friends? Has she no children? What about his family? Although I suppose they're not particularly well-disposed towards Norah if she's accused of killing him.'

As I spoke I wondered about the Breslin genes. The family hadn't reproduced much and those who had managed to be born didn't seem to last very long. My father had been an only child – as had Norah's father. Those two were, unusually in an Ireland of huge families at the time, the only issue of the previous generation. And of those, all, barring Frank, had died before they reached sixty. Dan died in the accident before he was thirty; my father had a massive coronary three days short of his fifty-fifth birthday. Norah, myself and Rachel were all that remained of the family, all females so the name would probably die with us.

'I don't know anything about his people. They were butchers by trade, I think.' She paused, a tradesman's family didn't figure on her social radar. 'I suppose they are unlikely to be willing to talk to Norah until they find out what happened. There are no children, so there's that to be thankful for. What do you think we should do?' Her voice had become querulous, although I had not yet agreed to row.

'I don't know Mother. John O' asked for your help so you better let him know you can't – you don't know the woman and as you say you've never been in a police station and you hardly want to start trotting up to one now.' I was being a bitch I knew, but I had to make her ask – not wait for me to suggest.

'Oh dear! Would I not be letting John down? He's such a good man.'

An expectant pause. I said nothing so she had to continue.

'And then, well, the poor woman. I mean, she must be desperate if the only family she can think of are distant cousins she's met at most twice in her life. If Sean was alive he'd go immediately. Always a fool for the underdog Sean was,' the sniff again, 'indeed that's why he never moved out of the smallest bank branch in Sligo.' It was an old complaint but she read me right. I immediately rushed to Dad's defence and found myself agreeing to ring John O' that evening to see if I would do as Dad's emissary on earth.

Mother had gotten her own way again so we parted on cordial terms with me promising to let her know everything as soon as I could.

I was annoyed with myself when I got off the phone. Not only for letting Mother use me but for putting myself in the position of having to talk to John again. We had been an on-again off-again item for about five years in the period between the last years of school and the first few years of college. First loves. The last two years of it had been very much on and we had lived together. John had been studying law in UCD and I had been struggling with accountancy. I had what could euphemistically be called a breakdown and John had nursed me through the six blackest months of my life. I dropped out of college, almost out of life. I applied for Executive Officer in the Civil Service in a brief fit of energy, got the job despite my best efforts, and was assigned to Revenue.

There I have stayed ever since. I even managed to move up a grade in the intervening years, more by accident than design. I didn't let my parents know for eighteen months that 'my daughter, the accountant' was not going to be a phrase they could throw into conversation.

My mother has never, ever forgiven me this transgression. I never told her of the depression, something over which John and I argued, but I couldn't have borne Mother's sympathy any more than I could her disapproval. Depression does not need sympathy. Empathy, yes. Mother is still known, ten years later, to wail into her gin and tonic over her daughter with 'one of the highest IQ's in the county spending her time totting up the taxes of shopkeepers'.

John had been such a constant in my life during that time that later I found it hard to be anything other than dependant around him. I admired and loved him for his support but I think a part of me possibly resented him for being stronger than me and I pushed him away. He had returned home to practice law in his father's business.

That was the final nail. I felt at the time that there was no way I could ever live in rural Sligo again, I thought it would have suffocated me and John loved it, the countryside, the practice, the people; even the bloody constant rain. I was content in Dublin, in the anonymity of my two-bedroomed apartment in Glasnevin. Mother grumbled that I couldn't even buy property right, choosing the northside over the ultimately preferable even number of a south Dublin postal code.

I never sought him out when I went home but Mullaghadone is a small village and I inevitably ran into him if I left my mother's house at all. He was always pleasant, friendly and warm. Always John O', everyone's rock, nobody's enemy. He was highly involved in the local community, in raising funds for the GAA club, the church and the national school. His sister was principal of the school Rachel taught in and Rachel claims he's unbelievable – the energy he puts into projects he comes up with to squeeze money both out of the local populace and the cash-strapped Department of Education.

He doesn't have kids or a wife, although he's considered a local catch and had been pursued as such. He laughs off any suggestion he should 'settle down'. John is your original community activist but he hates being called that; he has no interest in politics – just in people. He believes firmly that the local school provides the community's lifes blood and is its future. He is determined to give every local child the opportunities they should have.

Given my background with John I needed to psych myself up for a conversation with him about a distant cousin I barely remembered who had, apparently, murdered her husband. I left work early to avoid the worst of the traffic. I wanted to have a run whilst the light was still with me.

I never listen to music while I run. I prefer to listen to the rhythm of my heart and feet, to see the traffic snarl and flow, catch brief glimpses of faces as I jog past and wonder at lives encased for two or more hours a day in stalled cars. People over the age of about twelve never look happy; they make the most extraordinary faces as they drive, particularly if they are alone in the car. Some appear to be having full-blown arguments with themselves.

The winter was coming. Soon I would have to run at lunchtime if I wanted to run in daylight at all. I hated running in the dark.

I arrived back to the apartment as the late October sun was being pulled down into the horizon. Yellow and orange and red were streaked across a few low clouds. The trees scattered throughout the apartment complex were already almost bare, enough curled-up dead leaves on the path to make a satisfying crunch underfoot. The air was cool and sharp but missing the smell of peat fires that I always got in Sligo. Delicious autumnal weather.

Gloria Gaynor was belting out 'As long as I know how to live' as I walked in the door. I laughed, Rob was right – it was naff.

'Sinead.'

I always loved the way John said my name. It was both a greeting and an endearment.

'John. I was just about to ring you.'

Chapter Three

He laughed.

'A step ahead of you my dear.' It was an old joke, John always got to things before I did. I didn't have to remember for myself when we lived together, he did it for me. We never ran out of anything and if we were late paying any bill it was because we were broke, not because we had forgotten about the payment due, but even that was unusual. John was great at budgeting and at keeping things clean and organised. At my most vicious I sneered at him for this trait, made it out as an irritant – which it can be if one is less organised.

'As always, John, as always.' I laughed at his joke, the banter familiar and comfortable.

'Mother told me about Norah Breslin, or rather Furlong. Tell me how you got roped into this. By the time Mother had explained my convoluted relationship to the woman I could scarcely take in anything else.'

'It's not that unusual really, given Ireland's small island syndrome. The legal profession in it is even smaller. The solicitor appointed to Norah was a year ahead of me in college. You may have met him – Liam Nulty?' John described the man and mentioned a few different events where we might have met. But I couldn't place him. A lifetime had passed in the years since college.

'When this woman said she thought she still had relatives in Mullaghadone Liam remembered that I was from here. So he decided to get in touch, see if I could help. She has clammed up, refuses to help herself at all. Just says, 'I did it. I killed him.' She was the only one in the house, there were signs of a huge struggle and there is no indication of anyone else having been there. He's dead. Full stop dead so it's open and shut on the face of it.'

'Jesus.' It was like something from a film, far outside of anything I'd ever experienced. 'If that's the case John, what do you think we can do for her? I mean, I only ever met her once as a small child. I can't imagine a character reference from me would be of much use. I wouldn't recognise the woman if she stood in front of me.'

'The medical examination on her showed that she has been beaten, probably quite often and it appears over a long period of time.'

'Jesus,' I said again, this time sitting down on a kitchen chair.

'There's evidence of broken bones, some which never set properly. Some very severe bruising, some of it quite recent. If Liam could pin the damage on her body to the husband then he should be able to put in a plea of manslaughter. There are a number of defences to be considered – provocation, diminished responsibility or self-defence. But Norah refuses to say anything more than 'I killed him. I killed Tom'.

'My God! I thought that sort of thing was over in this country. There's so much about domestic violence on TV, in the papers. So much help out there now. I mean, there isn't the same stigma attached to it surely. It sounds like one of those horror stories of married life years ago. Mother said there were no kids. She's relatively young. Why on earth did she stay with him, let alone murder him? Is she suffering some mental illness?' I couldn't understand it.

'I think the question should be not so much why did she stay but why did he treat her like that. Your initial reaction is much the same as mine was. We all do it, make the woman culpable even though she is the victim. I talked to Liam, he has dealt with a fair few domestic abuse cases. Christ Sinead,' John's voice changed from the business-like tone he had used until now. 'He told me some awful tales. Really...it made me feel sick, I can't believe that human beings are capable of hurting and demeaning one another in such ways...not people ...people we might live with...people we know...I...,' he paused, I could almost hear him shaking his head in disbelief. 'There is no obvious mental illness in Norah. I would imagine there must be some mental instability caused by living in an abusive marriage. If so it will reduce her moral culpability but she's not opening up to the psychiatrists either. She's been referred to St Teresa's for assessment. The medics say she's in shock but there doesn't appear to be any psychosis, nothing in fact to indicate any kind of mental illness. Liam explained something to me that I found hard to believe. He says – this is according to the books – he says in a lot of the cases the abuser assumes the victim is either excited by or enjoys the abuse and – in quotes – "related behaviour". They use it to justify their behaviour, 'she likes it' sort of attitude.'

'Christ. Jesus, John... That's some leap of the imagination.'

'It's not rational of course. Is it ever by anyone else's lights? A tough one to get the head around, but apparently that's the way a lot of these characters think. They are totally egotistical. Above and beyond the normal boundaries of egoism. The psychiatrists are saying that because there is evidence of abuse over a long period of time Norah's mental state is probably more fragile than it appears. This is really where your family comes in. They've suggested that if she had something, or more properly someone, that could makes her feel she still belongs – is a part of family for example – that it might mean something to her, break her out of her silence. Look, I know it's a long shot, but Liam would be grateful for any help.' This was a long speech for John and he took a deep breath and paused, a question in the air.

'A really long shot, John. I doubt she'll even remember me.' I thought for a moment.

'I suppose it can't do any harm, and if she's had as bad a time as you say she has I'd like to help. Have to say I'm a bit apprehensive about it, I wouldn't be alone with her would I?'

He promised both he and Liam Nulty would be with me all the time and we made arrangements for John to pick me up at Mother's on Saturday morning. I was due a trip home anyway. We chatted for a while, he filled me in on local news, recent engagements, births, etcetera; I filled him in on the news of some old college friends he had lost sight of. It was good. Comfortable.

I rang home after I'd talked to him, Rachel answered on the second ring,

'Rachie! The second ring! Mother is obviously out or you never would have dared to be so bold,' I teased.

'Bridge! Her lifeline and mine! House to myself three evenings a week, pump up the music, let the dogs in, put the fire half-way up the chimney. I'm very rebellious in fact.' She laughed.

I can always see Rachel's face when I hear her relaxed lazy laugh. She's beautiful, our Rachel. Not in any classic sense, she is a little heavy for her small frame and she claims she'll run to fat when she gets older but for the moment she's quite luscious, lovely sallow skin and these enormous hazel eyes in a face best described as giggly and topped by a mad tangle of dark curls.

Rachel has this aura though – I don't know – life and contentment and goodness shine out of her. Make her special. One of those people who light up a room when they come in and who leave a huge gap when they leave. Like Dad in temperament. I claim sainthood for both of them; they put up with all of Mother's foibles with rarely a murmur of dissent.

'Let's pray she doesn't fall out with any of the bridge club or you'll have to move out!' I half joked.

'Hmm, that could be a blessing in disguise. I can't ever

see her letting me go without marrying me off. Not that I mind,' she added quickly.

'We mulloch along fine together most of the time. I don't take in half of what she says; I use Dad's old technique of nodding and saying 'Really?' every so often. It passes for conversation.'

We laughed like conspiring kids. Which we were of course.

'Seriously Rachel, you should think about getting out. What about applying for a principal's post somewhere else?' I hated thinking that she might be putting her life on hold simply because she happened to be the one living at home when Dad died.

'Look, I don't mind, honestly. She's not so bad.' She laughed at my harrumph of disgust.

'There is some compensation to living at home. It's cheaper for a start and I've managed to buy – wait for it – a camper van!'

'Really! One of those R.V. things? You hippy-in-waiting you.'

'It's brilliant Sinead, wait until you see it. Myself and Eoin have already booked the ferry for France for Easter next year. Then come the summer, who knows where we'll end up. We're going to take her out around the country weekends before that. So you see, I do have my own place! I can run away to the garden and hide in my RV if Mother gets on my nerves.' She was so excited.

'One thing is certain,' I laughed. 'Mother will never ever spend a night in it. I can hear her already.'

'"Really, Rachel. I didn't bring you up to travel the countryside in a caravan. Goodness, even travellers have stopped travelling!"'

Rachel roared with laughter.

'Oh God, Sinead you have her to a 't'. The poor auld snob. Where on earth does she get it from?'

'God knows. Listen, I assume she's talked to you about this Norah Breslin Furlong woman.'

'She did. It's ridiculous her asking you to do the visit. I

can easily do it, not drag you down.... unless you want an excuse to see John O' again?' Rachel was sharp, must be all the dealing she does with devious kids.

'I don't need an excuse Lady, all that's in the past. But yes, it will be good to spend time with him this weekend, catch up and so on. And what about your 'position in the community'?'

'Mother still thinks no whiff of anything other than possibly sighting moving statues should touch me.' She sighed then laughed. 'It's just as well she doesn't see the camper van rocking on the nights Eoin stays over. Did I mention how unutterably irresistible he is?'

Rachel and Eoin, her wiry, bouncy boyfriend. Like two teenagers. But these were teenagers without the angst, all froth and bubbles and underneath warm comforting latte.

'Fair play LADY! Enjoy it as often and as long as you can! Let Mother know I'll be down Friday night will you? She can kill the fatted calf. You can tell her I'll be going over to see Norah on Saturday.'

We chatted for a while longer then hung up. I ran myself a bath and luxuriated in it for an hour wondering about Norah, reliving times with John O' and planning what I should wear for the weekend. I was as bad as Mother really, 'keeping up appearances' intensely important to both our psyches.

Chapter Four

Norah sits in a fireside chair, gazing through a barred and rain-streaked window at the lawn rolling down to a small stream.

From the main gate a long driveway leads up to the imposing stone-faced building of St. Teresa's Psychiatric Facility. The main building is stern and quiet as you approach it. A hotchpotch of smaller extensions and prefabricated buildings to the rear, used as offices and treatment rooms, do little to enhance the building's beauty but their clutter softens somewhat its severity of aspect. Built in the late 1800s on the outskirts of Drumsna by an absentee landlord, the estate was bequeathed to the Mercy Sisters in the 1940s to be used as an institution for 'the mentally ill'. It had been adapted as such and is capable – at a pinch – of housing seventy beds. Originally called St Teresa's Mental Hospital and run by the Mercy nuns, it's referred to locally as 'the Mental'. It had passed into ownership of the State in the late 1970s and most of its residents were long-stay patients.

Some beds are generally kept available for those requiring short-term treatment and Norah had been lucky to be granted one of these beds in an empty two-bedded room. It is peaceful and she needs peace.

The door to her room opens and a care assistant breezes in with a tray.

'Now Norah, c'mon a stór. Try to eat a little something;

we're getting worried about you.' She bustles to the trolley table at the end of the bed and places the tray on it, wheels the table to Norah and smiles at her.

Norah smiles back weakly. The 'a stór' reminds her of Teasie's encouragements to her as a child, attempts to hurry her along when she might not be doing something fast enough.

'I'll try. But I just don't feel like eating.' Her voice is quavery, tearful; she can't rid herself of the childish whinge in it.

'Do try, like a good woman, you'll be getting me into trouble if I keep bringing back full trays to Cook. He'll think you don't like him!' The woman gives a little laugh.

'I'll try.' Norah pours herself tea, adds milk and sits with her hands around the cup. She turns her attention to the view from the window again.

The care assistant sighs and sits on the vacant bed.

'Draw her out' the senior staff had said. She is enthusiastic about this job, thinks she may be able to make a difference.

'Lovely view, isn't it Norah? Not as good today with the rain and all – but Lord on a good day it can be beautiful. I often wander down as far as the river at break time and just sit there taking it all in. There is a heron down there quite often, sometimes he takes off and flies upriver. He's amazing, those enormous wings and the long spindly legs trailing after him,' she shakes her head, laughs a little again.

Norah doesn't react, just continues staring. The woman stands up, straightens the coverlet and moves over to Norah. She places her hand gently on her patient's shoulder.

'You try and eat now. I'll be back in a little while.'

Norah nods and the other woman leaves the room.

Norah scours the river bank but cannot see the heron from her vantage point.

'Maybe he's gone upriver... Upriver to take down a flood,' she thinks and she smiles, the saying brings Frank to mind.

Frank Breslin had been a great man for predicting the weather by watching the actions of animals. For years a beautiful grey heron had hunted in the shallow water of the stream that ran through his smallholding. Norah loved to watch it. Its grey-blue plumage as sleek as fish scales along its body. It would carefully lift and place its spindly legs, stalk through the shallows, neck muscles tensing when it spotted its prey. Then it would stand motionless until the prey was within striking distance……. and when it struck………oh!......... such speed and skill and fright and glory.

Norah never tired of it. Sometimes she felt sorry for the fish or frog being hunted. But mostly she just marvelled at the heron. Some days Frank would take time out from his work about the land and watch with her, they might chat about the heron. Frank said there had always been herons in or about the stream, at least always in his memory. He had never managed to find their nest though. Norah the child had believed him. Now she wonders.

Frank always said that herons knew when heavy rain was on the way, that their flight upriver was a warning that a flood was coming. They would only fly downriver again when the levels had returned to normal and their fishing spot was once more tranquil.

'Animals have more sense than us, Norah. They know when danger is on the way, they will always protect themselves in the best way they can.'

The house Tom had been born into was upriver from Frank Breslin's cottage. An old two-storey country house, it had been built in the early 1930s for the doctor of the time.

Local lore had it that a relative of the Furlongs had won the house in a hand of cards, a royal flush it was said had beat the doctor's full house. The first time Norah remembered seeing the house was shortly after her arrival in Tibraden, some six weeks after her family had been buried.

Those weeks had been long and strange and frightening.

There was a social worker – her name was Maeve. She had a nice face but she wasn't there all the time. Sister Pascal came to visit Norah twice in the foster home. So had Mrs Corrigan, one of the neighbours, but she'd just cried all the time and kept hugging Norah until it hurt. One day Maeve came and told Norah that she would be going to live in the countryside, with an uncle and aunt.

'But I don't have any uncles or aunties. I know that because Mammy and Daddy didn't have any brothers or sisters.'

Maeve told her these were a 'GREAT' aunty and uncle and that Frank had been Daddy's uncle and Teasie was Frank's wife.

'Can't I stay here and go back to school and maybe see you sometimes and maybe Mrs. Corrigan or some of the other people on my road?'

Maeve said no, Uncle Frank and Auntie Teasie really, really wanted her to go. They were delighted to have her, they had no children of their own and Norah would be like a daughter for them.

'But I'm not their daughter. I'm not even their real niece just a stupid great-niece or whatever you said. I don't want to go to the country. I'm afraid of cows,' she had bawled.

Maeve had promised that she would bring Norah all the way to the house in the country, that she would stay with her for a few hours, then go and stay in the town near the house and would come back to see her there every day for three days. Then Maeve would come back to Dublin and pack up all the rest of Norah's clothes and toys and books and bring them down to Frank and Teasie's after one week. If Norah was still unhappy then she and Maeve could sit down and talk about it.

Norah had to believe her, even though it was stupid saying 'if she was still unhappy'; Norah knew she would never be happy again.

Frank and Teasie were standing at the door of the cottage when Norah and Maeve arrived in Maeve's car. Frank lifted his cap and bending down he had opened the car door and thrust his head inside,

'Welcome, welcome Norah Breslin. You are truly welcome to this house.'

Frank had very little hair left on top of his head, the odd crinkly tuft, but there was a perfect semicircle of thick wavy grey hair ringing the back of his head from ear to ear; this hair extended into extraordinarily bushy sideburns. He was a tall, slim man, slightly stooped. His face was brown and crinkly and kind and he had big blue laughing eyes. He stretched his big hand into the car to grasp Norah's and he shook it vigorously.

'Let the child be Frank, you'll break the poor craithers little fingers!'

Teasie's voice floated in over Frank's head. Frank immediately withdrew both hands and face and gave himself a nasty bump on the car door frame in retreat. He let out such a yelp that Norah scrambled from the car with a start.

'Are you alright, please say you're alright!' Her eyes had filled with anxious tears.

'Of course he is, the old eejit! One thing you'll learn, child, Frank is always bumping and tipping into things, aren't you, a stór?' Teasie smiled at Frank and placed her hand lightly on Norah's shoulder,

'I'm a bit careless alright. I'm sorry if I frightened you,' Frank laughed and rubbed his head. 'I knew I shouldn't have taken off my cap. A cap is a great thing, Norah Breslin, to keep your brains in place.'

Norah grinned as the big man carefully placed the dubious-looking cap back on his head. Then she shook his hand and Teasie's the way Maeve had asked her to do.

The kitchen they went into was warm and brown and red and cosy. There was a sheepdog nursing two pups in a straw-filled cardboard box by the range. Norah stopped and took a step or two backwards.

'Do they bite?' she asked.

'Not if we don't disturb them while they're drinking from their mammy. When they're done she'll clean them and then Frank will help you play with them.' Teasie said.

'They're great fun, pups. We kept these two especially for you. You can name them if you want.' Frank smiled at the child's wide eyes.

'Really?'

'Really.'

And that was it, as simple as that. Maeve had kept her promise and stayed for a few days and then returned a week later. By that stage Norah was as settled as a child who has lost everything could be. She spent her days playing with Smut and Fluff, the pups, and going 'for adventures' with Frank, he proudly showing all twelve acres of his kingdom.

He showed where you could cross the stream without getting wet, where you could find birds nests and the spot where the old brown hen liked to lay her eggs under the hedge. They searched for and found what they thought would be the best place to build a tree house, and he promised to do that for her. She quickly got over the fear of cows and goats, for if she wanted to be out and about with Frank she had to put up with animals. He showed her how silly cows could be and how stubborn and smart goats could be.

Some days it was very wet and they couldn't go out much so Teasie let her help making bread and stirring the soup and once she even let Norah make an apple pie all by herself, even down to slicing the bitter cooking apples with a sharp little kitchen knife. Frank declared Teasie could retire, that there was a new cook in the house now. Norah almost burst with pride, and they had all laughed at him when he bit into the pastry and some oozing apple dripped onto his stubbled chin.

Then Norah had started to cry and she had wished, oh so hard, that Mammy and Daddy and Louise could be there. To meet Frank and Teasie and to taste her apple tart and tell her how good it was.

But Teasie had scooped her up onto her floury apron and dried her tears and snot with a corner of it and told her it was alright to be sad. Once she knew that Frank and Teasie would try to always be there to hold her when she needed to cry, and that they knew it wasn't the same as having a Mammy and a Daddy and a baby sister, but they would do their very, very best. Eventually the tears dried and her body just shook with dry, heaving sobs.

She fell asleep on Teasie's lap that evening and it wasn't the last evening she did that. Many evenings over that long summer she spent crying for things past. Silly things would set her off, mostly things she hadn't seen before and immediately thought 'Wait 'til I show Mammy or Daddy'.

One evening in late August Frank said, 'Come with me now child and we'll check on the sheep in the top field.'

'Put on your wellies now Norah, it can be boggy up there,' Teasie had fussed.

Norah felt a bit nervous, sheep weren't animals she was comfortable with yet.

'Will they be locked up?' she asked.

Frank laughed. 'No, but don't worry. Sheep are very nervous creatures, they'll always move away from us. I won't let any harm come to you,' he said, smiling at her scared face 'But if you're worried you shall have a big stick, we'll get one in the field on the way up. A stout stick is the best protector against allcomers Norah Breslin.'

They set off through the fields, Frank pointing out this and that to her, demonstrating the best way to use the stick against a silly animal. When they got to the top field Norah decided to stay on the house side of the hedge, she wasn't ready to move among the sheep, stick or no stick.

From here she had a good view of Furlong's back yard, bikes and toys scattered about and they had a proper swing. Not a tyre on a rope like Frank had put around the ash tree for her yesterday but a real metal framed swing with metal link chains and a wooden seat. It was red.

'Look Uncle Frank, just like the one in my old house.' Then she had burst into tears.

Frank had lifted the little girl in his arms and crooning to her he carried her back to the house. Teasie saw them coming from the kitchen window and ran to meet them, thinking Norah must have hurt herself badly to be carried so. Frank shook his head at her when she ran up.

'She's alright, alright, just worn out with the sorrow and letting it flow from her'.

Norah sighs now, thinking of the safety she had felt then in Frank's arms. She wishes she had never seen the Furlong house, the heron had certainly flown upriver and from there brought down a flood of troubles on her.

The door opens again, Dr Fitzgerald and Liam Nulty, her solicitor, come in. They are accompanied by a strange man and woman. Norah looks at them without much curiosity, she assumes they are either doctors or the police.

Dr Fitzgerald comes to her and places his hand on her arm.

'Norah, you may not remember her, but this is Sinead Breslin. She's a cousin of yours, a daughter of the Sean Breslin you told us about who lived in Sligo.'

The woman moves forward and extends her hand.

'Hi Norah, I remember you. We were very small though so you might not remember me.'

The woman is tall and slim, successful looking in a pair of well-cut trousers and high heeled boots. Her red coat looks expensive. Her fair hair is cut short, chopped, highlighted and spiky, eyes blue and sharp. Norah searches her face looking for some resemblance to Uncle Frank.

She nods in greeting and takes Sinead's hand. Sinead's grip is firm, determined. Norah smiles and Sinead returns the smile.

'I remember meeting you once alright. You were with your sister, a cute little thing she was. She had a head of gorgeous curly hair.'

'Yes, yes that's Rachel and she still has the gorgeous curly hair. She's even still horribly cute.' Sinead laughs, she seems pleased that Norah remembers her and her sister.

'I don't remember meeting you again after that, I remember your Dad though. He visited a few times over the years. He had a really deep long laugh didn't he?' Norah laughs a little herself as if she can hear Sean Breslin laughing.

'That's him alright!' exclaims Sinead. 'And he wasn't a big man, my mother used to say his laugh was too big for the rest of him! I used to think up silly things to tell him just to make him laugh, we would all laugh when Dad laughed.'

Dr Fitzgerald smiles,

'Norah, this is John O'Sullivan, another solicitor. He is a friend of Sinead's and Liam's. John would like to help you too - if you will let them.'

Norah accepts the third man's warm handshake. He's tall too, taller than Sinead and Liam. A handsome man, dark wavy hair and a strong face. In his mid-thirties she guesses, well-groomed and confident looking.

'It's stopped raining,' she says. 'I wonder, could I walk in the grounds?'

'Of course Norah, as soon as your visitors are gone I'll arrange for that.' Dr Fitzgerald checks his watch.

'Look, unless you both need to take notes why don't we all go for a walk with Norah? If that's alright with the Doctor and Norah of course.' Sinead looks from the men to Norah.

'I'd like that,' Norah says.

All three men nod assent.

'Come and find me before you leave,' Dr Fitzgerald says to Liam.

Chapter Five

I travelled to Sligo the following Friday evening, spent the night chatting to Mother and Rachel about the goings on in Mullaghadone. Mother and I managed to avoid squabbling and when she went to bed at 11pm, Rachel and I settled into a detailed gossip about all the local romantic or otherwise news, plus we gave her relationship with her beloved Eoin a good girly dissection. We talked for hours and when I eventually looked at the clock I stretched my arms up and backwards.

'Jesus Rachie, it's three o' clock and I've to be up at eight to go to visit this poor creature.'

' Hmmm,' she stretched too. 'You're lucky, you've only to spend time with your 'perhaps not to be ex-boyfriend' and a mad distant relative. I've to take a squad of under tens for football training.'

I laughed.

'Don't, Rachel. Not the mad relative bit, the 'perhaps not to be ex-boyfriend' bit.' I was genuinely more nervous about that. I would have John and Liam to help me with Norah, but who would help me with John? Particularly as I didn't know exactly how I felt. I couldn't go back to the way things were, didn't want to – that whole period was clouded with the depression I had suffered at the end. But I couldn't see a future either, not with the new me in the context of a new or different John. I stood up, gathered the cups and plates from the coffee table and brought them to the kitchen. Rachel put the fire guard up and followed me to the kitchen finishing off a story about something Eoin had said to Mother, charmingly disarming her in the process and thus succeeding in becoming 'the most civilised young man in the parish'.

We tittered together, juveniles in conspiracy against our elders. I hugged her.

'You're great Rachel, really great.'

'Hey big sis, you're not so bad yourself.' Holding onto my upper arms she pushed me back, studied me.

'Seriously, mind yourself tomorrow. Don't get hurt.' Her caring eyes, framed with eyelashes to die for, looked intently at me. When we were at school the nuns used to accuse her of wearing mascara but she never did, never wore a screed of make-up apart from a little lipstick occasionally to highlight her gorgeous full lips. 'Kissable' lips John used to call them, making me slightly jealous of course.

'I'll try,' I sighed.

I didn't sleep well that night, worrying about spending time with John. When I did eventually doze off I dreamed of the shower scene from 'Psycho'. None of this predisposed me to be anything other than nervous the following morning.

John collected me and we drove to the hospital where we met Liam and were shown to Norah's room.

I don't know what I had expected – a hideous woman with sly eyes capable of killing? Someone I could instantly dislike and wash my hands of? Maybe someone odd and strange and frightening? Or if half of what John had told me on the way up was true someone so damaged after almost two decades of living in a destructive marriage that she could never be normal.

But what struck me most at that first meeting was her normality. I knew she probably had lots of irritating quirks like everyone else but we could have been meeting at some family occasion after a gap of thirty years. Not a wedding or anything joyful, a funeral perhaps. The dead person gone and once condolences are offered conversation concentrates on discussing what the still living have been up to in the intervening years.

Norah's doctor introduced us to her and we chatted for a moment. Then we went out into the grounds of the 'Mental' for a walk. It had been wet when we were driving up but the rain had cleared away and it had turned into a fine soft afternoon. I inhaled deeply, could smell winter coming, but for that day it had granted us a reprieve.

Norah had a look of my Dad about her, which naturally drew me to her. She's slim, thin almost to the point of scrawniness – a tiny waist and hardly any chest – she was dressed in an old-fashioned way, a long navy skirt and a pinkish blouse. She wore dark tights and flat slip-on shoes. The blouse was pretty, flecked with little flowers but she had ruined it by topping it with a mannish grey cardigan, complete with pockets into which her hands were crammed. Her clothing could most kindly be described as dull. And although she's only three years older than me, she looked more like someone in her late forties for whom life has been particularly difficult.

Smaller than me, she stood about 5 foot 6'', her hair a similar colour to my own but faded and dull, pulled back into a childish pony tail that day. Her face wasn't made up and her skin looked tired and undernourished. I noticed a mole on her collar bone in a similar spot to one Rachel has. Despite the dullness of her clothing and skin she had something. She just escaped being beautiful. There was something about her face, each feature on its own was pleasing enough; large Malteaser-brown eyes, pupils dilated – probably from shock or medication – her nose was a little too large and slightly crooked, her eyebrows unplucked. She had a thin upper lip but was blessed with high cheekbones. She was pale, but not a sickly pale, and had a smattering of attractive little freckles over her nose. But the features together just didn't seem to fit properly, her face seemed unformed. Perhaps it was her eyelashes that caused that effect. They were the strangest thing about her face, made you look twice because you assumed you had made a mistake on your first glance. The eyelashes on the right eye were dark and the ones on the left were fair. I mentioned it.

'It's nearly always the first thing about me that people notice.' She gave a self- deprecating shrug. 'Although I suppose now it'll be 'Norah Furlong? Oh – are you the woman who killed her husband?''

She glanced at me then redirected her gaze back to the river.

I was a bit startled by the speed with which she had raised the subject.

'Names can be changed Norah,' I said lamely.

'That still won't change the fact I killed him. I can never change that, get away from that.'

I looked behind me, Liam and John had fallen back a little, arguing some point of law I supposed – or more likely the finer points of some golf shot or who was going to win an upcoming GAA match.

John caught my eye and smiled. I pointed to the little bridge spanning the little stream and Liam nodded for myself and Norah to cross.

As we strolled over the bridge Norah pointed out a heron standing still in the shallows upstream. She told me of a saying Frank Breslin had, about the heron flying upriver to take down a flood. We walked in silence for a minute or two.

'The house my husband – Tom – was born and raised in was upstream of our house. I suppose the heron flew up there and took down a flood of troubles on me and mine when I married him.' She studied her feet as we walked, arms wrapped about herself.

'I heard.' I said. 'I mean... John told me Tom used to hit... abuse you.'

'Abuse me.' She exhaled a sharp breath. 'Funny. I suppose that's what it is, was. I mean, I never thought of it like that, not really. Certainly not in the beginning. It was just Tom. Being in a bad mood – or me annoying him –

getting on his nerves, not giving him enough attention... or sometimes too much.'

'Sounds like there was no pleasing him. It's not your fault Norah.' I almost barked.

'What do you mean? I killed him, of course it's my fault,' she retorted, voice sharper than it had been.

'No. I mean the beating, the abuse – none of that was your fault.' She had moved slightly ahead of me and I put my hand on her shoulder. She stopped, turned to face me.

'Wasn't it? I keep thinking I should have known how to handle him better. Every marriage has its own problems doesn't it? You hear about it all the time, newspapers, books, radio, TV.' She gave a little smile. 'In fact it's a wonder anyone ever gets married. Are you married Sinead?'

'No, no. Old maid me. Never found Mr. Right. Or if I did I lost him!' I coloured slightly as John and Liam caught up with us. I thought she noticed my discomfort but she didn't say anything.

'Can we swap places Sinead?' Liam asked, 'I need to discuss a few things with Norah.'

He took Norah's elbow and gently guided her a few steps ahead.

'Well?' John nodded his head towards them. 'What do you think?'

'She seems really nice. Gentle, quiet. And she's so thin, slight even though she's not small. I mean, it's hard to imagine her having the strength to even slap anyone, let alone drive a gardening shears into them. Was he a big man?'

'I don't know. I haven't seen the files yet and Liam didn't mention it. But I agree, it doesn't seem possible.'

We moved on slowly in silence. A weak November sun hung low in the sky, creating tiny sparkles in the drops of rain still dripping from the bare-branched trees lining the path.

'Will you see the file? Or is this as far as it goes for you? I still don't know what I'm supposed to do for her.

She's a nice woman and I'd like to help but what good can I be to her?' I loosened the top button of my coat and removed my scarf, wrapping it around the shoulder strap of my bag.

'I don't know. Liam has asked me to stay involved if I can. I'll have a look at the work load in the office at the moment. I've taken on a junior, business has been good, mostly house and land purchases though, wills – so it doesn't take too much brain power, just methodical administration.' He made a face.

'Is it boring? Not like you John, you're a methodical person anyway. Would you not just fly through something like that?' I couldn't imagine John being bored, he was always so enthusiastic about anything he got involved in.

'Not boring. Just… workaday I suppose. There's not much of a challenge in most of the stuff we handle. The odd interesting case. I shouldn't complain, I do love the work generally, I particularly enjoy having my own practise. I couldn't imagine being a cog in a wheel in a big company. Look!' He pointed as the heron flew upriver. He seemed to move in slow motion, the flap of his great wings audible.

'Isn't he magnificent!' I told him Norah's story about her heron flying upriver and taking down the flood of Tom Furlong on her.

'The poor divil, by all accounts describing what descended on her as a flood is a fairly good analogy,' he said.

'You know, I think I'll let Liam know I will give him a dig out. Maybe I could even take her on if she can part fund some of my hours. He's fairly swamped with legal aid stuff and I can afford take her at reduced rates – regard it as partly pro bono.'

I was pleased. John was a good man, a good solicitor. He would do his best for Norah. I also had a fleeting moment of wondering if he had any other reasons for deciding to take her on. In all honesty it was a moment of hoping there was.

Liam and Norah had stopped, waiting for us.

'Okay folks? Norah and I are finished here. I just need to go back and get my briefcase, she needs to sign some documents. Sinead, Norah would like some clothes and toiletries from her house.' Liam looked at me as Norah blushed and looked down at the damp path. 'I could get them but I think she might prefer a woman's touch. Any chance you could...?'

How could I refuse?

'Sure. No problem – if you'll give me directions I could go now, that's if it's okay with John?'

John nodded assent.

'No good,' said Liam. 'I'll have to arrange access to the house. Are you free tomorrow?'

'I'll still be in Sligo but I could do it in the evening, drop back here with a bag and head off to Dublin then.' That was agreed.

Norah looked relieved. I imagined that she was the type of woman who would be extremely uncomfortable with any man going through her clothing. Funny that those sort of hang-ups still linger, even when your life seems to lie about you in shreds.

'I'm sorry Norah. I have to get back to Sligo now. I'll help out in any way I can.' John touched her shoulder and she flinched, stepped back slightly.

'You've all been so kind. Honestly. I don't deserve it. I'm sure you all have busy lives.' She turned back towards the hospital and we fell into step around her, 'I feel so tired, I could just sleep and sleep and sleep. And I don't dream at all. Isn't that odd? Just this really, really deep dead sleep. But when I wake up my eyes are so heavy and I feel as if I haven't slept for a week.' Her voice was fainter, more childish than it had been. 'I think I should go back for a rest now.'

'That's alright Norah. You need to rest. You have a long and difficult time ahead of you and you'll need all your strength. You have my mobile and office numbers, ring me at any stage, particularly if you think of anything in connection with what we discussed.' Liam's voice was businesslike but I noticed a gentle undercurrent in it. John had told me Liam had daughters; perhaps that explained his slightly fatherly tone with Norah.

We returned to Norah's room and she gave me directions to her house, Liam was to ring me later with arrangements. John and I waited in the lobby while Liam got Norah to sign papers. We asked the receptionist to page Dr Fitzgerald for us.

'Will you be alright going to that house tomorrow? It won't spook you or anything?' John raised his eyebrow as he asked me.

'You must have forgotten. I don't spook easily.'

He faux smothered a laugh, 'I seem to remember a bit of a drama about a mouse on one occasion! Also, remember when you thought you were being followed home one night?'

'I was considerably younger! Although I must admit I'm still a bit of a drama queen when it comes to mice.' I was surprised and slightly chuffed that he remembered the incident when I thought there was someone following me. It must have been a dozen years ago.

'No, I'll be fine. There'll probably be a policeman outside anyway. You can give me a ring tomorrow night if you're worried about me.'

The flippant words were out of my mouth before I thought about them. We both smiled, nervously on my side and I may have even blushed slightly. I could have kicked myself. I was behaving like a teenager. Mind you, so was he.

Liam and Dr Fitzgerald both arrived at the same time. The doctor took us to his office and discussed Norah's condition briefly. She was depressed and very distressed at times, needed plenty of rest, counselling and some medication. Eventually she would need some new focus in her life. Tom's death had relieved a huge area of stress in her life but had at the same time also taken away her whole world. They had a psychotherapist working with her and would set in train some specific counselling for victims of domestic abuse plus grief counselling.

She really needed a reduction in stress but that wasn't going to be possible as the case gathered momentum. Basically he said that there was little more the hospital could do for her, they had her on some short-term medication and once she was stabilised on that they would be discharging her. Liam thanked him and asked that he be notified a couple of days before that happened.

We left the hospital in the early afternoon and stopped in Carrick-On-Shannon for a late lunch after which we took our leave of Liam. By the time we got on the road to Mullaghadone the winter evening was already drawing in. The dark clouds and rain of the early morning had cleared completely, leaving a beautiful mackerel sky, ribbed light cloud streaked salmon pink. John and I sat in companionable silence, enjoying the sunset and the passing countryside. John dropped me home with a peck on the cheek and a promise to contact me the following evening.

Chapter Six

Norah lies on her back on the bed, the nursing staff have given her something to relax her. She feels anxious, she thinks it's anxiety – it's something strange anyway, not fear, she knows fear, the way she feels is something akin to fear. The discussions with her solicitor and her newly-found cousin have turned her thoughts to the future. She can't think about any future. She has no future. Not now. Maybe sometime, a long time away. But not just now.

She is drowsy. The volume of the radio is down, just a low burble of voices and music. She feels herself drifting. Tom's face, not that last grey face but a younger Tom, slips into mind.

A smiling Tom. He didn't smile often. Not a real smile, the one that got to his eyes and made them crinkle up. He had this cheesy smile for customers in the shop along with a big blustery greeting. She used to tease him about it before they married.

'You're like that fella on the telly, the one that used to be the butcher in 'Coronation Street'. All shouting and laughing and fooling the customers into buying stuff they don't need.'

'Exactly!' He put his arm about her, 'the more steak and chicken and chops they buy the more money in the bank for us.'

That day had been a good day. A beautiful soft spring

day by the lake. It was the day he had asked her to marry him. And she had said 'yes,' of course she would, not today or tomorrow but in the future. A happy day. A day of kisses and cuddles and hand holding and talking of being together always. They hadn't told anyone, not then, not even Frank. And Norah always told Frank everything.

'He'll not be happy.' Tom said, face hard. 'He doesn't like me, doesn't like my family. Auld fool.'

'Don't, Tom.' Hating it when he spoke badly of Frank. 'He doesn't hate you. Frank doesn't know how to hate. I think it's just because of your mother, you know the way she is, poking fun at them being poor. It upsets Teasie and Frank just probably doesn't trust your family because of that. And he'll think we're too young to be thinking of getting married, although he married at eighteen years himself. He wants for me to go on after the Leaving Cert, do another qualification, have the opportunities he and Teasie didn't. He thinks I have brains, God knows why, you know how hard I find learning. He just wants what's best for me. If I work hard I might get enough marks to get the grant.'

'You won't leave me will you Norah? I couldn't bear it if you went away.' He held her tightly, staring fiercely at her.

'I'll never go too far. Galway at the farthest,' she had said. 'And I'll always come back. You're the boy for me Tom Furlong – always.'

'The only one?' His grip tightening.

'Of course. Stop Tom, you're hurting me!'

He had loosened his grip and kissed her.

Norah turns on her side and stares at the grubby cream wall. She has no more tears; she feels she has been crying all her life. Too many tears.

'I will never cry again,' she thinks. 'Never.'

She closes her eyes and this time sleep does come. Deep, dreamless sleep.

Later they wake her, suggest she goes to the television room to mix with some of the other patients. She tells the nurse she's tired and wants to rest.

'No nonsense now Norah, 'tisn't good to be on your own all the time,' says the night nurse sharply. She has a cross little face, lips thin and determined. She is quite small, petite almost, and Norah thought she might be in her fifties. Her skin was tired and well-lined with a crinkle of tiny little lines pulling down her eyes and mouth; she has a scraggly head of badly pinned-back greying hair. Norah cannot help but notice the off-white grubbiness of the woman's uniform. She decides she won't be bullied. Not anymore.

'I may get used to it,' she retorts just as sharply. 'Amn't I likely to be spending a fair few years in a cell?'

The nurse opens her mouth to snap back, revealing a smear of pink lipstick on crooked teeth. Norah tightens her own face and the nurse sees her determination so bustles, muttering, from the room.

Norah feels weak after the little confrontation and plops into the chair by the window. It's very dark outside, but the moon, when it slips from behind sporadic cloud, casts a cold, bright light over the countryside. The evening star is clearly visible.

'Star light, Star bright
First star I see tonight
Wish I may, Wish I might
Have the wish I wish to night

All the little songs and rhymes of childhood. Talismans against the night. Safely indoors, warm and not scared, looking out, fearing not what cannot be seen.

'What would I wish for? Where would I wish to be? What time, what place? What difference would it make? Where did I take the road that got me here? What could I have changed to prevent...everything? That hour when I gripped him and talked to him and tried not to breathe in that foul stench – what if I hadn't heard him? Or heard him and kept running?'

On her first day at her new school Norah had raised her hand after an hour or two. 'An bhfuil cead agam dul go dti an leitreas?' The Irish chant, familiar to every child, asking permission to go to the bathroom.

Eileen Hanrahan nodded and pointed Norah towards a stone-built shed at the rear of the school building. When Norah had opened the shed door she could see no toilet and went back to the classroom.

'Muinteoir, I can't find the toilet.'

The teacher laughed, took the child by the hand and brought her outside again. Explained how the dry toilet worked. Norah was disgusted.

'I don't need to go now' she said quickly.

'Are you sure, child?' Miss Hanrahan was sympathetic. A dry toilet was an anachronism then, Tibraden having the last one in operation publicly in the county, possibly in the country. The schoolhouse, built in 1886, showed its years. A large new school was supposed to have been had been opened that September and three small rural schools within a twenty mile radius were to amalgamate into it, but both planning and construction had been slow so the opening was much delayed.

Throughout the years of the planning and construction process supplying an indoor toilet in the old schoolhouse had been deemed an unnecessary expenditure. It was a constant source of aggravation to children, teachers and parents. The parents had been schooled here too, but had no misplaced fond reminiscences about the dry toilet. Even children in the most isolated homes all now had indoor plumbing. In general the children relieved themselves at break times behind a bush or tree and retained larger deposits for home. The toilets were only used in dire emergencies.

Norah's reaction reminded the teacher that Paudge Mc Kenna, the local man who came once a month to clear away the slurry, hadn't been replaced after his death last March. She made a mental note to remind the Board of Management that someone needed to be contracted to continue the job until the toilets became obsolete. The stench around them just then was unbearable. The toilet was situated at the end of a steep slope and when it rained heavily – which it did often – rainwater seeped into the trench and that, combined with what was in it, created a dark oily looking sludge and an indescribable stench. Even the hardiest of children noticed it.

When Norah went home that evening she had rushed past Frank, exclaiming,

'Hurry, hurry, please, please.' And into the bathroom with her.

'Holding onto it all day were you?' Teasie laughed when a relieved Norah came out after a few minutes.

'Oh Teasie! It was terrible. You have to sit on this plank with a hole it and pee or poo in this dark hole and you can't flush or anything and it's even smellier than the cow's poo in there. I'm never, ever going to the toilet in school again. Never!'

Frank and Teasie rocked with laughter at the indignant tone and flushed face of the child.

'We should have warned you. Not to worry, it'll not be for too much longer.' Frank tousled her hair. 'There'll be a brand new school with nice white toilets in it for you all next year. Let's hope ye don't get the skitters in school in the meantime!'

Teasie explained the expression to Norah who giggled and turned almost green at the thought.

One day early in the following year Norah came home and discovered she was missing a schoolbook. She was a conscientious child, anxious to please.

'I know I put it in my bag,' she said. 'It must have fallen out. Remember Teasie, my bag was flapping open when I came in.' She put her coat on. 'I'm going to walk back along the way, see if I can find it. It's not been raining so it'll be alright.'

'Wait a while and Frank will walk with you, he's just off milking the goats.'

'No. I better go now. It's a bit windy, the book might blow away,' said Norah, pulling on perennially necessary wellies.

Teasie smiled at the child's eagerness.

'Off you go then, aren't you quite the scholar, so worried about your schoolwork!'

Leaving the farmyard Norah ran along by the riverbank towards the school. She found spring in the countryside to be very different to spring in Dublin. Trees and hedgerows in bud, everything bursting with new growth and lots of wildlife about. Frank had taught Norah the names of nearly all the birds that nested in the area. In Dublin she could only remember ever seeing crows and sparrows, robins and sometimes seagulls. Here she had seen blackbirds, jackdaws, tits, magpies, wagtails, a heron, she had heard the cuckoo but hadn't seen him yet, larks and even a hawk. An owl could be heard at night hooting from his nest at the back of the shed.

Sometimes she had found it hard to remember what her house and garden in Dublin had been like and she couldn't picture the things she knew she should remember there. She would never forget her mammy and daddy and Louise. Never. Teasie said if you kept people in your thoughts in a way it meant they never died. Every night Norah would say a prayer for them and kiss their photograph.

Climbing over the ditch into the field sloping down towards school Norah started to sing her favourite song of that moment.

'Bye, Bye Baby
Baby, Bye Bye'

She stopped and looked behind her. She thought she had heard someone calling. She couldn't see anyone so shrugged and resumed her singing. Then again, a cry, definitely.

'Help, help. Please.'

It was a child's voice. Norah moved down towards the school where the voice seemed to be coming from.

'Hello, hello. Where are you?'

'I'm here. Carmel, Carmel get Daddy. Please, please.'

'I'm not Carmel,' the shouts were coming from the shed that housed the toilet. Opening the door and pinching her nose against the smell Norah stepped into the dimness, the only light coming from the two smallish holes that served as windows high up in the wall.

'It's Norah. Who's that? Where are you? I can't see you.'

A muffled splashing and then she spotted in the murky light a figure in the pit.

Norah and the figure both screamed.

'What! What, what is it Norah? Why are you screaming.' The voice sounded terrified.

Taking a step forward in the gloom Norah saw that the plank that served as toilet seat had split in two, half was gone and the other half was in the slurry caked hands of a child. Norah realised they must be hands but they looked like two moving little piles of wet seaweed. She thought it was a boy because he had short hair that was plastered against his skull. His face, apart from the whites of his eyes, were unrecognisable as anything human. The parts of his body she could see were covered in liquid shit.

Shrinking back, Norah whimpered

'Who are you? Who are you?'

The figure had started to cry again.

'Tom Furlong. I'm Tom Furlong. Please Norah, please get me out. I ..I...needed to go. I couldn't wait and Carmel ran off without me. It just broke. It just broke and I fell in. Please help me. Please. Get me out, Norah.'

Carmel was Tom's older sister, she was in Norah's class. A bully that Norah had already fallen foul of. Tom was only in senior infants, two years behind them.

'Hold on Tom. I'll help you. Oh the smell. Poor Tom.'

Norah took hold of the plank that Tom was gripping and started to pull. But the weight of the child in sodden clothing meant she was only able to pull him out a few inches before the plank slipped out of her hands and he disappeared down into the hole again.

'Tom!' she screamed peering into the murk. With a flailing splash Tom's head re-emerged and he struggled to his feet coughing and spluttering then retching through the foul liquid.

'I've tried and tried……..I keep trying to climb out and then I just slip. The sides of the hole are all wet and slippery. Help me, please help me. I'm really scared.'

On a heaving stomach, Norah stretched into the pit. She pushed her arms under Tom's armpits, her head to the side of his, recoiling as the wet sludge on his hair and face came into contact with her skin. He gripped fiercely onto her shoulders and Norah tried to pull him out, but he was too heavy for her, a dead weight and her body slithered forward. She was more likely to tumble in too so she loosened her hold around him and pulled back slightly. Moving his hands up Tom quickly locked them around her neck, screaming again.

'Stop, Tom stop! You'll pull me in too. Let go! Let go!'

His hands slipped from around her neck and he stumbled back a step but this time didn't fall. Tears cleared two little rivulets down his filthy face. His sobbing grew louder and he didn't speak, just let out moans Norah had never heard the like of before, except maybe when the cow was calving. They didn't sound human. He didn't look human.

'Stop it!' She shouted sharply. 'Stop it Tom! Try to stop and we'll think of something. Here..,' she had thrust her hand towards him '…hold my hand. Hold my hand while we think of a way to get you out.'

Tom's sobs subsided, his cold slippery hand a fish in Norah's own.

'You'll never get me out, I'm too heavy. It's starting to get dark. What if we get stuck here in the dark?'

They had tried several more ways to get Tom out of the

pit but all failed. Eventually Norah said,

'Tom, I'm going to have to go and get a grown up. We'll never get you out on our own.'

'No, no, no Norah. Don't leave me on my own here. It'll be dark and scary. I'll die if you go. Please stay with me, please oh please oh please,' he was frantic, squeezing her hand in his.

'But Tom…. Alright, alright don't be scared Tom. I won't go. I'll stay with you all the time. Someone will come. Let's shout. My Uncle Frank will come. Auntie Teasie will tell him where I went and he'll come looking for me. Especially now it's getting dark. He knows I'm frightened outside in the dark.'

Now that they had stopped their physical efforts to get Tom out they noticed the stench more. It was unbearable. They could taste the excrement in the air, both of them gagging and coughing occasionally.

'Help, help. Anyone. We're here. In the toilet. Help us!' They shouted together, Tom's voice tremulous and weak. He reminded Norah of the little lamb that had been born to one of Frank's ewes at the weekend he was shivering so. He had been in the pit now for almost three hours.

But no one came. Eventually they stopped, the only sounds their strangled breathing as they tried to avoid inhaling.

'I'm so tired'. Tom's eyes started to close and his legs gave way and he slipped down again.

'Tom, Tom! You mustn't fall asleep. You'll slip in and drown. I'll sing, Tom. Sing with me so you stay awake.' Norah yanked at his hand.

They both sang the Bay City Rollers hit over and over.

'Stop, stop,' Norah said half way through the chorus. 'Listen.'

'Norah. Norah,' a voice not too far away

They started to scream. When the door had opened and Frank's lanky frame appeared in the doorway both children cried with relief.

Frank lifted Tom out and carrying him in his arms and Norah on his back he brought both children back to Teasie. Teasie ran baths for both of them and afterwards dressed Tom in clothes belonging to Norah. The child was exhausted after his ordeal.

'Now Tom, poor little man, come – the two of you – a big feed of boxty for you, that'll set you right. Frank's walked up to your house to get Daddy to drive down to bring you home.' Teasie sat the children up to the table and served them up the popular potato dish.

When Frank returned with Seamus and Eileen Furlong, Tom was sound asleep at the table, head on folded arms.

Norah stands and readies herself for bed. Who would have thought that remembering could be so tiring. She remembers Eileen Furlong's disparaging look around Teasie's spotless but sparsely furnished kitchen. Even then, even after Frank and Norah having rescued Tom, Eileen could not resist lording it and trilled about how cosy the 'little house' was and how hard it was to heat her big house. Norah smiles, remembers Teasie's mouth setting in a straight line, her 'Minnie Brennan' face Frank called it, after a popular character in a tv soap opera of the time.

Tom's father had been quiet as always, lifting the sleeping child and taking him out to the car. Seamus Furlong always kept his own counsel. Norah never heard him utter more than one or two words in all the years she knew him. Eileen ruled the roost aided and abetted by Carmel and Fidelma, the daughters, as they grew older. Seamus and Tom had merely been endured, abided because Seamus and eventually Tom were the wage earners.

There was no respect for them and precious little liking even.

Norah felt that Seamus was, at best, ambivalent in his feelings towards her. If he got as far as contemplating her at all. It was more likely that he had been as indifferent to her as he was about all his own children. Bullied all his adult life by his wife, Seamus had just ambled through as best he could, avoiding rows and conversation at all costs. Norah had read somewhere that you marry your mother or father, recognising in your partner something of your parent that made you love them.

Why had Tom married her? She was totally unlike either of his parents, she was timid but not uncaring as Sean had appeared to be and she bore none of Eileen's domineering traits. Why had she picked Tom? Perhaps she hadn't. He pursued her from her early teens and he was always there. His constant presence never let her consider that there could be another boy for her.

'He was the only one who asked.' Norah speaks aloud, startling herself. 'Why didn't I say 'No'?'

Chapter Seven

Mother was out when I got back to the house. Rachel and I joined Eoin and friends for a meal in Sligo that night so I didn't see her until I tumbled from the bed about twelve o'clock the following day. She was just in from Mass, best coat and shoes, handbag and gloves to match.

'There you are. Do you get up a while everyday! I'm making coffee, do you want one?' She was fussing with coffee grounds and filters.

'Please. Exactly what I need. I slept too much.' I stretched. 'Why do I always sleep so much when I'm here? Do you put drugs in the milk or something?' I plonked myself down at the kitchen table.

'Fresh country air! Or maybe too much wine with dinner?' She raised her eyebrows at me.

'Not guilty. I was the designated driver, so it was one glass for me and coffee after that.' I poured myself some orange juice.

'Now, tell me all about yesterday. Nobody at the bridge club has mentioned it to me, so us being relatives is obviously not common knowledge.' She sat too.

'Mother, you're going to have to get used to the fact that we are related to Norah because it's bound to get out.' Sometimes she was exasperating.

'Well, I suppose it will. But I won't be the one telling people.' She pursed her lips.

The kitchen filled with the smell of brewing coffee as I

told her all about my visit to the hospital. When she heard I was to meet the police that afternoon at Norah's house in Tibraden she shrieked.

'Sinead, the scene of the crime. Lord! That's terrible, aren't you nervous?'

I put bread in the toaster and poured coffee for us both.

'No, why should I be nervous? There's no one in the house and I'm sure there'll be a garda with me all the time, noting what I take.'

I placed the cups on the red and white chequered oilcloth covering the table and got milk and butter from the fridge.

I love my mother's kitchen, a big rectangular room, dominated by an old farmhouse table and chairs. The kitchen units are a rustic pine and she has a fabulous distressed pine dresser filled with pretty floral delph. She always seems to have fresh wild flowers in a glass vase on the low deep window sill overlooking the garden, even down to sprigs of holly in winter. It was cosy, homely – I thought it at odds with her personality. To one side of the large black-leaded range that she still uses for cooking is a big wooden ladderbacked armchair with several cushions on its wide seat. My father's chair. I cannot walk into that room without picturing him in that chair, glasses perched at the end of his nose as he rustled through a newspaper.

We chatted for a while. Both of us trying not to irritate the other. At least I was trying. Mother thinks she's perfect, therefore any fault I found with her was my problem not hers.

I had never tried to discuss our uncomfortable relationship with her. Perhaps she didn't see it as uncomfortable? Rachel claims we are too alike, each convinced of the rightness of our own point of view.

It was a lovely day, so after I showered I dressed in jeans and jumper and pulled on my boots. I was sorry I hadn't brought my running gear but settled for a brisk walk down to the village to buy the paper. I took a brief stop at the lake to admire it. It's tiny by lake standards I suppose, cupped in the palm of the hand that the series of little hills around it make. As a child I wanted one day to build my own house down there, that way I would have constant access to all of the lake's pleasures. Swimming, boating and fishing plus glorious views – all on my own doorstep.

I got a big greeting in the small local grocery cum newsagents cum hardware cum whatever you happened to need. The name over the shop is Coughlan's, but it's called Jimmy's by everyone. It's owned by Joe Coughlan. His father, long dead, had been Matt and it was the grandfather who had been the Jimmy who started the business. I chatted with Joe about local news, old times and of course the weather. This was what I both missed in Dublin and hated in Mullaghadone. This knowing all about you, your seed, breed and generation. The belonging. Tainted by the fact that if you sneezed everyone within a ten-mile radius would have heard about it within an hour and would talk about the terrible cold you had. It is both a comfort and an aggravation.

My mobile rang as I walked back towards home. Liam, with details of the time the Gardai would meet me at the house plus contact numbers, etcetera, which he said he would text to me.

'Thanks a lot for doing this Sinead. It will mean a lot to her knowing she has some family looking out for her. I know you don't want to get too involved….'

'Having met her Liam, I can honestly say I don't mind. It doesn't seem a lot to do for someone who has been through all the things Norah has – despite how it ended.'

Liam sounded relieved to have secured some support for her – however shaky it was.

We hung up with promises of texts.

Mother had the dinner ready when I got back. Or Sunday lunch as she called it, I referred to it as 'the dinner' to irritate her. Poor devil – she'll never civilise me!

After washing up I repacked my weekend bag and bid Mother and Rachel goodbye. Mother stood at the front door as I threw my bag into the boot. She moved forward when I opened the car door and laid her hand on my arm.

'Drive carefully now. I know you think I'm silly but be careful at that house.'

I opened my mouth to laugh at her but was surprised to see a glitter of tears in her eyes so I just smiled and nodded. Then I surprised us both and gave her a hug, which had the unfortunate effect of encouraging the tears.

'Mam, what's wrong?'

'I'm sorry, I'm such an old fool. But I do worry you know. And I see so little of you. It's silly, but every time you leave the house I wonder will it be the last time I'll see you.' She had unearthed a crumpled up tissue from somewhere and was using it to dab at her face.

I was taken aback; I'd never even considered she might feel like that. For the first time in ages I really looked at her and despite the well-groomed hair and the make-up I could see the old woman she would become.

She was sixty-eight. Not old in today's world and she was active, enjoyed a good social life. But realistically old age and all the horrors it can foist on you were not far away. Normally I wouldn't have visited again until Christmas but I reconsidered as I chivvied Mother into a weak smile with some lame remark about not getting rid of me that easily. After I was in the car, belted up and engine running, I rolled down the window and said:

'Look, I'm going to come home again in a fortnight. I think I might visit Norah if she is still in the hospital. I feel sorry for her. She has absolutely no-one, and as you said it's what Dad would have done.' The last bit to stem her protestations at becoming any more involved with Norah.

'That would be lovely Sinead. I'll make sure to have a bread and butter pudding made for you this time!'

We laughed. Bread and butter pudding with a dollop of custard, a childhood favourite. And nobody could make it like Mother.

'Bags I scrape the custard pot.' I said, tooted the horn and reversed down the driveway.

She stood at the door waving. She looked small and lonely.

'Watch it, Breslin. You're getting sentimental,' I muttered as I fiddled with the radio dial to find something other than sports programmes. I eventually gave up and slotted in a Tom Waites CD. His gravely voice could keep me company on the N4.

Traffic was light except around Carrick-on-Shannon and I left the N4 at Annaduff, taking the road for Mohill as instructed. I missed the turn for Tibraden initially and had to stop to consult Norah's directions before reversing and finally finding the turn that led me to her house.

It was an isolated spot. Norah's place was the first building I came to and it was at least two miles in from the main road. The bungalow itself wasn't visible from the lane, the plot of land surrounded by well-matured spruce and pine, but once you turned in and clattered over the cattle guard it came into view quickly enough. I glanced at the car clock. I was fifteen minutes early so no police car yet didn't surprise me.

I sat in the car for a few minutes and decided that a little nosiness would be okay. I surely couldn't interfere with any evidence. If the authorities hadn't taken whatever they wanted from outside the house at this stage then they should have.

The first thing that struck me when I got out of the car was the silence. I'm well used to countryside but even where I had been brought up you would hear sounds of activity. Dogs barking, the odd car or tractor passing on the road, birds, sheep, even the sound of more distant traffic. But the silence here was thick, you could almost taste it. Whether the oppressive wall of dense bluish-green foliage around the plot caused this or my overactive imagination, the silence was unnerving.

Norah's home itself was ordinary enough looking, neither particularly new or big. There was a bay window on the room to the left of the front door and two other windows to the right overlooking the gravelled drive. The curtains were drawn in all rooms – to prevent nosey people like me mooching about I suppose. I could see net curtains as well through a gap in the drapes.

Net curtains aren't the norm in rural areas. In the absence of constant foot traffic past your house there is no need to block any of the precious natural light from it. Even Mother, who is almost paranoid about her privacy, has only venetian blinds in the front rooms and they were mainly to combat the late evening sun from shining on the television in the living room. All other rooms only have drapes and the ones in the kitchen are never closed.

I walked towards the back of the bungalow and noticed the sharp lines at the edges of the grass you normally associate with people who like to garden. The grass was a little long. The bulk of the plot was to the back of the house and apart from a small tarmac area immediately outside the back door was lawn with various flower and shrub beds set into it. Or they had been. The garden was like a bomb site.

Large spruce trees bounded this as well; it was gloomy and depressing in the half light. Maybe the trees had been planned to protect plants from damaging wind but they hadn't been able to protect them against a mad man on a digger.

On the day he was killed Tom Furlong had found out that a man, an old friend who shared Norah's interest in gardening, had visited her. Tom went mad over this. He borrowed a mini digger from a nearby farmer and tore the garden to pieces. Then he tried to kill her by trapping her in the shed and knocking it down around her. It must have been hellish. John thought the case would never go to court. The coroner and the DPP would rule death by misadventure or self-defence. Except Norah insisted on saying she had murdered him.

I heard a car pulling in to the front of the house and walked back around. A large Garda in his mid-fifties was getting out of his car.

'Sinead Breslin? Sergeant Denis Bradley.'

'That's me.' I shook his extended hand. 'Thanks for this, Norah would like some clothes and toiletries from the house.'

I handed him the list and the permission note Liam had asked Norah to give me.

He studied it for a minute before nodding.

'I'll just note what you actually do take and get you to sign for them. Grand day wasn't it?'

I agreed. The light was already almost gone and between that and the dimness the trees around the place added the hallway into which we stepped was dark. The sergeant found the light switch and turned it on.

'Do you know where this stuff is?'

'Norah has it on the note. Most of it in the bedroom at the back of the house, some in the bathroom and she thinks the books and the papers she wants are in the cabinet in the sitting room.'

Sergeant Bradley nodded. 'You know I have to stay with you the whole time?'

'Sure, no problem. Although I don't think there's anything sinister on the list.' I could have bit my caustic tongue. The man was only doing his job and was doing it humanely too. 'Sorry, didn't mean to be smart.'

He laughed. 'Don't worry about it Miss Breslin, you develop a thick skin in this job.'

We walked into the bedroom and Sergeant Bradley found the light switch. I wish I could remember the room to describe it now but there was just nothing memorable in it. I'm not particularly into interior design but usually in most houses there will be one or two things that put the owner's stamp on it. Later when I tried to recall the house I only had a vague overall impression of blandness. I took the holdall from the bottom of the built-in wardrobe Norah had described and tried to find the clothes she had asked for. Not that there were too many to choose from and they were of poor quality. I felt mean even noticing this, clothes obviously weren't important to Norah. I found the underwear and nightdresses she wanted and took the fleece dressing gown from the back of the door. I consulted the list again.

'That seems to be everything from here'

The sergeant stood back to allow me out of the room then switched off the light and pointed out the bathroom to me.

It was immaculate. That much I do remember. My own bathroom is a bit chaotic, given that I seem to hoard half-used jars of various creams and lotions without any real storage space for them. But this. It was like a bathroom in a bed and breakfast – spotless and without any indication that it was used on a regular basis. I found the toothbrush, toothpaste, deodorant and the moisturising cream Norah had asked for in the cabinet.

'The last few things here are apparently in the sitting room.'

'Right so.'

Sergeant Bradley led the way back through the hallway towards the sitting room.

This was the room with the bay window, now covered in long mustard-coloured velvet curtains. The carpet was horrendous, one of those awful seventies ones, great big swirls of various shades of green lightened by touches of cream. I felt dizzy just looking at it. I went to the built-in unit and found the books Norah wanted, one of them a Dickens – 'The Old Curiosity Shop', a Thomas Hardy and a book by Mary Webb called 'Precious Bane'.

Norah had described these books as old friends, ones she almost knew by heart.

'I read them at times I find it hard to concentrate,' she had said. 'It's soothing when you know what's happening next. And it's funny, I still always find something new in them. Something I hadn't noticed the last time I read them.'

I had a look.

I remembered reading the Dickens years ago and was familiar with the Hardy from TV adaptations but I'd never heard of the other one. I made a mental note to get it, interested to find out what it was that attracted her to it.

Seargeant Bradley had to give me a hand looking for the legal documents, one an agreement with a local farmer about using land for grazing and the others birth and marriage certificates. We found them in an old red and white biscuit tin at the bottom of the cabinet.

'Funny how lives always seem to end up in biscuit tins,' he laughed. 'My mother kept every picture taken and document in relation to all of us in various biscuit tins. I was in a very old and battered 'Mikado' tin. When she died we had a great night of tears and laughter going through our boxes. Probably old fashioned now, what with computers and everything, but you'll always need to store the original somewhere. I suppose as a garda I should be recommending a bank or at least a locked safe for valuable documents. Still….'

I knew what he meant. As children we had loved going through the old boxes of photographs, getting Mother or Dad to tell us who was who, finding out what they had meant in their lives and seeing the birth and marriage certs, official documents with 'fancy handwriting' recording the moments of importance in their lives.

There were precious few photographs in Norah's box. Perhaps she kept them on a computer. Although the little I knew of her so far didn't make me think so. I closed the box and replaced it and handed the holdall to the Sergeant so he could make his own list of what I was taking.

I sat back on the gold-coloured velour of the chair I was in and looked about the room. It was so old-fashioned. Spotless. You would think it had been specially cleaned for new tenants or something. That was it! That's what it reminded me of. Different houses I had shared and rented over the years before I finally bought the apartment. Everything serviceable, but no touches to make it a home. No ornaments or gee-gaws on the mantelpiece or about the TV unit. I stood up to look at the couple of framed photographs that were on the walls. One was an aerial shot of an old two-storied house by a river. I knew it wasn't

Frank Breslin's house, I remembered that as a bungalow, so this was probably the house 'up the river' that Tom Furlong had come from. The photograph on the wall behind the television was a wedding photo of a much younger and happier looking Norah and a young man I assumed was the deceased Tom. He was taller than Norah, although not by much and was quite thin. Weedy I would have called him. His wedding suit looked slightly too big and sat uneasily on him. I'd love to be able to say I could see meanness in his face, some sign in his eyes that he would turn into a wife beater. I couldn't see anything. He looked like most young men do on their wedding day, slightly nervous and happy.

'Bet they never saw that day ending in this,' I said to the Sergeant who was repacking the bag with the now noted items. 'Isn't it terrible that love can end like this?'

'Precious little love here, if you ask me,' he said shortly. 'Only power and fear.'

I was surprised, until then he had been careful not to mention what had happened. I opened my mouth to ask what he meant but his face had closed in again and I realised he knew he had overstepped some mark. I signed his form and thanked him for his help and we left the house to its darkness and stillness again.

As I pulled away from the house I wondered what would happen to it. Would Norah ever want to live in it again? And who would buy it? Knowing what I knew about the lives that had been led in it and the death that occurred in it would definitely put me off, even if its isolation and drabness didn't.

I was back at the hospital within half an hour and asked to see Norah.

The nurse went to get her but returned alone a few minutes later. 'She's asleep and I really don't want to wake her. She was very distressed all day and didn't sleep well last night. Do you mind?'

'God, no. Let her sleep. I'll just leave this bag for her. Will you tell her Sinead called and I'll see her soon.' I pulled an old envelope from my bag and scribbled a message for her.

I was back in Dublin shortly after nine and gladly closed the apartment door. I booted up the heating by several degrees and put the kettle on. I opened a packet of chocolate digestives; comfort was definitely on the agenda this evening. I looked around the apartment with new eyes, as one often tends to do after being away. But I particularly noticed it after the shabbiness of the hospital and the sparseness of the furnishings in Norah's house.

I really love my apartment. It was the location that had sold it to me first, convenience to the city meaning I didn't have to drive in if I didn't want to. My block was set well in off the main road so traffic noise was minimal. The whole complex is set on grounds that originally belonged to the convent of a nearby school. This meant that the trees and green spaces around it were mature. The main room had a big window and I rarely pulled the curtains from April until October. Enjoying the natural light for as long as I could and then at night the lights of the nearby city.

There was a message on my phone from Rob about a meeting of the musical society next week. I have always loved musicals, have a decent enough voice, but dancing is not my strong point so I tend to take a backstage role a lot of the time, joining in when choruses, etcetera, are required. Panto season was nearly upon us and the society had started rehearsals for 'Babes in the Wood'. Rob was directing and was pleading for me to throw my hat in the ring.

'I need you Breslin – the hand the holds the props rules the world.'

I laughed, even at a distance that man could make me laugh. I set about texting him but was interrupted by Gloria Gaynor. John O'.

'Hey, how are you?'

'Are you back in Dublin?'

'Yes, here safe and sound. Didn't get spirited off by the

ghost of Tom Furlong. The house was a bit creepy though,' I admitted.

'See, I knew you were a wuss,' he laughed.

'No, not like that. Just...I can't really describe it. Gloomy because of all these big trees around it and then that wrecked garden. When you think of what she must have gone through that night. Then indoors, the décor was really... dull. It's like nobody has lived in that house for a long, long time. Like a really old person's house. Something like that. Do you know what I mean?'

'Sort of. Although I probably wouldn't notice the décor.'

'That's true. Remember,' I laughed, 'when we were living in that second flat for about six months and I asked you what colour the bedroom carpet was, you hadn't a clue! I think you got it right on the fourth guess.'

'Aw c'mon, the only reason I didn't know the colour was because it was usually covered with the clutter of two students' lives!'

I suppose we could have gone on reminiscing but neither of us were ready. Not at that stage anyway.

I told him about the visit to the house and the hospital.

'Listen, I think I'll drop down again next weekend to see her. Will you be around?' I held my breath.

'Sure. I could even go to the hospital with you if you like.' I think there was breath holding on his side too.

'Great. I'll text before I leave Dublin. It might be Saturday morning.'

After a little more chat I hung up and looked at the packet of biscuits. I'd only have one. Not so much comfort as congratulatory. I really was a teenager again.

Chapter Eight

The phone on my desk rang and I picked it up, still checking the column of figures on the screen in front of me.

'Sinead Breslin, Revenue.'

'Sinead, thank God, Sinead.' It was Mother. Crying. Mother never cried, I had only ever seen her cry three or four times in my life. I had induced those tears once, when I told her I had dropped out of college. Even when Dad died she had cried only briefly, then went through the rest of the experience with a blank look on her face.

'Mam?' I hadn't called her that for years.

'Oh Sinead, it was awful. Awful! And Rachel is in class and I can't reach her,' she gulped.

'Are you on your own? Are you alright?' I was panicking now and stood up as if that would somehow help. Rob threw me a look across the room, I shook my head at him.

'I'm on my own now. But I don't know what to do. There's no one to help, no one here I can tell.' She was sobbing like a child.

'Mam, Mam, please... you're scaring me. Calm down and try to tell me. Are you hurt?'

'No. No,' her breathing calmed a little as she blew her nose and tried to take a deep breath.

I could picture her, standing in the hall, looking at

herself in the mirror over the hall table. My eyes pricked with tears thinking of her normally guarded face distraught.

'Good. Now try to tell me. Are you frightened?'

'Yes, of course I'm frightened. She's mad. Completely mad!' A note of irritation at my lack of understanding.

'Who's mad? Are the doors locked. Are you safe in the house?'

'Yes. No. Hold on.' Sounds of the receiver clattering to the table, footsteps, a door somewhere banging, footsteps again then a snuffled 'Now. It's all locked up.'

'Ok. Good. Now tell me what happened. No. Get a chair, sit down and tell me what happened.'

Another clatter and footsteps. If I had stopped to think about it, it was the first time my mother had ever done anything I suggested without an argument.

'I'm back,' she said unnecessarily.

'Start at the beginning, try to tell me it all and then we'll decide what to do.' I had been thinking and rooted my mobile from my bag when she was gone. I started a text to John O' as she spoke.

'It was that Carmel one. That Carmel Furlong. His sister. The Tom fella. She was here, just arrived and I got such a fright at her arriving that I let her in. Lord save us Sinead, you should have heard her, the terrible things she said.' She started to cry again.

'Mam, Mam, it's okay. She's gone now, you're safe.' I sent the text.

'I don't feel safe!' she almost shouted. 'I just don't. That woman. She had such a look.'

'Why did you let her in?' I regretted the words the minute I said them.

'Sure I didn't know she was mad! I didn't even know what she wanted. She seemed normal. A bit. Different. And I didn't really let her in, she just came in. Next thing I know she was in the kitchen and sitting in Sean's chair. Imagine Sinead, your father's chair!'

I almost laughed, whatever had happened to frighten

her so, the scandal of some unwanted guest sitting in Dad's chair was putting things back into perspective for her.

My mobile beeped. A text – John O. *'On way'*.

'Start at the beginning, leave nothing out.' Rob's hand appeared on my forearm, a mug of tea materialised in front of me. I grinned and mouthed a 'thank you' to him. He blew me a kiss and retreated. Thank God for friends.

'I was just about to leave, to go and get my hair done when the doorbell rang.' Her voice had calmed a little. The doorbell going would be a surprise. Only hawkers or people looking for directions rang the doorbell. Anyone else visiting the house would open the door after a brief tap on it and walk in with a shouted 'Hello'. It was just the way of things in the country. Even Mother's pretensions couldn't overcome that one.

'It was this woman – 'Are you Sean Breslin's widow?' she asked.

'Yes I'm Catherine Breslin, and who might you be?' I said and then she stepped into the porch.

'"Well then, I'm a sort of relative of yours," she said and she went, no, she pushed past me into the hall, looking all around as if she owned the place.'

Mother's voice had steadied a little and a tinge of anger came into it.

'I should have known then and not gone in after her. I should have just gotten into the car and driven away.'

I made some soothing noise.

'But she was a woman and younger than me but not so very young that I felt afraid, not then. I was just annoyed that she had barged in past me.

'"Excuse me," I said to her, 'but I was just going out. Can I help you?" That's when she marched into the kitchen and plonked herself into Sean's chair, starts foostering in her bag for something, prattling on as if this was some sort of a social call.'

'"I'm Carmel Furlong," she said, and she gave me this look. That was when I started to feel a bit afraid.'

"You don't know me. I'm sister of the poor Tom Furlong that was murdered in cold blood by that ..that sleeven bitch of a wife. That cousin of your husband's." She still had her hand in her bag. Lord God Almighty Sinead – she sounded so vicious when she said about Norah murdering Tom that for an awful minute I thought maybe she had a knife or something in her bag.'

'Mother! You poor thing!' Although the situation would once have seemed ludicrous in sleepy Mullaghadone, after listening to some of the stories about Norah and Tom's relationship in an even more sleepy Tibraden over the last few weeks nothing would surprise me when it came to the Furlong family.

Mother's voice was steadier at this stage, her indignation overcoming her fear.

'I sort of backed away from her a little. Jesus Mary and Holy Saint Joseph, then I screeched and banged into the door.

'Where are you going?' Carmel asked me and she looked surprised. There was only an envelope in her hand. Honestly my heart nearly stopped with relief and then I got all flustered and felt bad for misjudging and all.' Mother gave a high-pitched hysterical giggle, 'Oh Lord I know it's not funny but....'

'Mam, you poor thing. Was that it?' I was smiling my end too.

Her voice sobered.

'If only. That was the easy bit.' She started to cry again. 'Sinead, it was horrible, disgusting. She said such awful, awful things, such terrible accusations about Norah. How Tom had been a saint for putting up with her and 'that grabbing auld bitch Teasie Breslin'. And that all Norah wanted was control of the land and the money and to sell out Carmel's home from under her.' She stopped again. 'Did you know that Tom Furlong owned the old homeplace and the land as well as his own place? And three butchers' shops through the county and had lots of cattle and land set?'

I was surprised. 'No, Norah never mentioned money either time I've seen her. I assumed by the way she dresses and by the house when I visited it that there wasn't too much money. I did ask once the last time was she okay for cash and she just nodded. It never occurred to me, but I suppose it should have.'

'Well, according to this Carmel one, Norah is a very wealthy woman. Or will be. That's what the letter was. It's for Norah. I suppose there's hateful stuff in it. She's going to challenge Norah's rights to the house she lives in, the homeplace. At least I think that's what she came to say. There was so much other stuff, rambling stories about years ago and her father and his business interests that I wasn't sure. I just sat there and nodded and prayed she would go. She shouldn't be able to do that, come here and frighten me.'

Mother was getting angry again, which I felt more comfortable dealing with.

'Oh Lord, there's the doorbell again,' her voice raised on a hysterical note

'Don't worry, look through the living room window. I asked John O' to drop in, make sure you were okay.'

She clattered away from the phone again. I made a mental note to replace it with a walk-around one next time I was home. I heard footsteps back, an opening door and voices. Mother came back to the phone, her social voice half-assumed again.

'Yes, yes, it's John, will I put him onto you?' She didn't wait for an answer and John's voice replaced hers.

'Hey, everything okay?' It was relief to hear his calm tone.

I quickly explained what had happened and how he had been the only one near enough I could think of who wouldn't make a drama out of a crisis.

'Don't worry, I'll talk to your Mother. Make sure she's okay and I'll have a look at the letter. I'll pass it on to Liam and we'll decide what to do. Liam mentioned this woman before. She's bit of a nutcase apparently. We might think about an injunction. The very least we'll do is send a solicitor's letter.' John always in control and wasn't I glad of it now.

'Might that not just add fuel to the woman's annoyance?'

'Perhaps. But that's her problem. She has to be warned off. We'll talk to the Gardai here and in Tibraden, get their advice. I'm in Dublin on Thursday. Can we meet up? Lunch? Or a drink after work? Just for a quick chat face to face, without Norah or Liam about.'

My heart did – what – I'm not sure if it plummeted or soared. What did he want to talk about?

'Oh! Right. Yes. Of course. How about Ryan's in Queen Street, about six-thirty?

He agreed and put me back onto Mother. She was regaining her composure, fussing about John having come out.

'Give him a mug of coffee and some of your sponge cake and he'll consider himself compensated.' I laughed, John could always wheedle Mother around.

I promised I would be down the weekend after next. Mullaghadone hadn't seen so much of me for years.

Work was busy and there were rehearsals most nights now for the show. So the few days to Thursday flew in.

'Looking good, Miss B. Somewhere or one nice after work?' Rob's eagle eye.

'Meeting an old friend for a drink. John O'Sullivan. The solicitor who is helping out in my cousin's case.' I had confided in Rob, knowing it would go no further. If I mentioned it to any of my other colleagues I would have had the tabloid press stalking me within forty-eight hours. I have never, ever seen gossip travel as fast as it does in Revenue. And imagine what could be done with a juicy murder!

'Hmmm! Old friend about to become more perhaps?'

'Rob! Leave me alone, I'm confused enough.' I laughed him away.

The level of interest John had taken in Norah's case

had surprised me. Initially I assumed he was just doing Liam Nulty a favour, putting Norah in contact with distant family, but he had gotten totally involved in the case and was in regular contact with us all.

We met at six in Ryan's. He looked good; he always did. John is extraordinarily comfortable in his own body (and a very nice one it is too), could fit into his surroundings very quickly; he looks as at home in a well-cut pinstripe suit as he does in jeans and sweater. The conversation had quickly turned to Norah and the case. John had been to see her with Liam earlier in the week. She was being discharged from the hospital next week and Liam was trying to put in place some sort of accommodation for her. She didn't want, naturally enough, to go back to Tibraden.

'I was on my own with her for about half an hour whilst Liam went looking for the doctor. She was really tense that day, I think she's even thinner than the last time I saw her, if that was possible. There's something about her. A vulnerability that's not irritating, more like a child's vulnerability. You'd know to look at her that she's been through a lot, but she's not sorry for herself. She's still here.' John stopped, gripped his tumbler of whiskey and stared into it, swirling the contents around before taking a large mouthful, sucking on the peaty taste of the Laphroaig.

'I asked her how she felt. At first she didn't speak, just kept shaking her head. Then she got up and walked over to the window, wrapping that awful bloody cardigan she's always wearing around herself.'

He sat back in the chair and shook his head, opened his mouth to speak then closed it again. He looked around the busy lounge of the pub, people sitting in groups talking and laughing.

'Look at them,' he said.

'What?'

'All of them, their lives. Since I met Norah I keep looking at people wondering what dirty little secrets they're hiding. Most of my work is in-house, land sales or commercial law, the boring stuff. I'm not naïve, I know you only ever see the tip of people when you meet them. But I've always stayed away from family or criminal law. Even when I was studying I knew I didn't have the bottle for it. I would have got too involved, burned out too quickly.' He paused again.

I waited. John, the original stoical, unemotional man. Used to dealing with hard facts, laying them out in their natural sequence and watching people twist and turn these facts into the story they wished to tell. Untangling the web of lies they will build to extricate themselves from the predicament that required his advice in the first place. People driven by motives of greed, lies told in the pursuit of money, property, power.

He was obviously finding dealing with Norah hard. She seemed to have an innate acceptance of her predicament; neither of us could understand her apparent reluctance to save herself, to vindicate Tom's death in any way. It was like she couldn't feel sorry for herself so others had to feel that for her. He was bewildered.

'She said she felt like the littlest Russian doll. Frank had given her one of those little sets of Russian dolls for her eleventh birthday. Matryshuka dolls – and every day after school she would play with them. But when she married and packed up all her belongings to move into the house with Tom, the second smallest doll was missing. So the littlest one rattled about inside. And she felt they were never right after that. If she laid them out the littlest one looked all wrong, out of place. And that was how she felt. Like the littlest doll. Hidden but not fully protected because her first shell was gone. She just didn't feel right.'

John finished his drink, looked at me.

'I didn't know what to say, it was the most she's ever said to me, I was bloody useless. I just walked over to her and took her hands, squeezed them a little.' His voice had thickened, he looked down at his own hands as if he expected to see the answer there.

I could feel myself filling up.

'You did exactly the right thing John. That's what Norah needs more than anything right now. People to hold her hand. Accept her.' I leaned over the little pub table, took one of his square hands. I'd forgotten how big they were.

'Bullshit!' John banged his glass down on the table. I jumped, it was totally out of character.

'What Norah needs is a bloody good barrister and a cracking case showing evidence of consistent physical and mental domestic abuse that will vindicate reducing the charge to manslaughter in self-defence. You can do the hand-holding, Sinead, I'm going to do my damndest to help Liam provide the rest.'

I felt like cheering, then like crying. If only the bloody man had been half as impassioned when it came to us, or rather I had let him be impassioned, maybe we would been at a different stage in our lives right now. I had to leave him that evening, I had a rehearsal at eight-thirty; but I think in retrospect I'm glad I had to leave. I would have said too much. It would have ended in a 'you said, I said' row, me getting hot under the collar and frustrated, expecting him to have done things he couldn't have possibly done at the time. He would have become cooler and more distant, and the progress we were making in our friendship would have been put back a couple of years again. Older, although probably no wiser, I walked away.

Chapter Nine

Norah walks the grounds in weak late-November sunshine. Tears run down her face; there are too many to check. Semi-blind, she paces the route she has taken every day for the past month. A difficult session with a psychologist or grief counsellor or whatever title he gave himself has turned on the taps.

'Everyone belonging to me dies. Always dies. If they don't leave me I just get rid of them.' The silence stretched as he waited for her to continue.

'Poor Tom. Why did I do it? Why? It mightn't have been as bad as I thought. I'd survived before. No matter what, he didn't deserve that.' Then he had confused her with his talk, 'psychobabble' Tom would call it. But it was too hard; all the ones who died. Gone, all gone.

It is Frank's death she is reliving as she stops on the bridge, wondering why she doesn't just throw herself in the river. If there is a heaven at least she would meet Frank again. Frank would make it all better. She half laughs at the thought of Frank trying to lift full-grown spirit her on his knee. She blows her nose fiercely with a well worn tissue, wipes away the tears and takes back the thought of suicide.

'Frank, Teasie, Mammy, Daddy and Louise. What wouldn't they give for one more day on earth, one more day. Even just to say goodbye. Teasie was the only one I got to care for, say goodbye properly to. I can't take the one thing I have that they don't and waste it. There has to be a reason I'm left. There has to be. I just don't know it yet,' she admonishes herself fiercely.

She's also afraid to die just yet. Just in case there is another side. Tom might be waiting for her there. He would be still very angry with her. She isn't ready to face him yet.

Norah leans on the little bridge railing. There has been heavy rain most of the week and the stream is swollen and moving fast. Churning, rushing peaty water foaming slightly in dips and hollows. It was a day like this that Frank had died. But in February. Saturday February 19th 1983.

'It's stopped raining thank God, will you go looking for Frank, a stór?' Teasie stood up from her chair by the range and placed her knitting on the seat. Norah was sitting at the kitchen table trying to study but actually dozing off in the heat from the range.

'I will. It might wake me up. I stayed out too late last night and I can't make this stupid geography stick in my head. I think I read this page three times and I still can't list the layers that make up the Earth's crust.' Norah stood and stretched, shaking her head to clear the wooliness in it.

'Lord save us! Do you need to know that for geography? I thought geography was all about different countries, capitals and industries, rivers and mountains, things like that. Aren't you the great scholar to be learning such things?' Teasie shook her head of snow-white newly set curls in admiration at the knowledge her charge had.

'Oh Teasie! I wish I was a scholar! It's so hard to study and then when I do think I know it I seem to make an awful mess in answering the questions.'

'Now, now. You're a great girleen. Don't you always pass your tests and didn't you do well in your Inter. Sure it doesn't matter once you try your hardest and do your best. That old Leaving Cert will be no problem for you.'

Teasie's face crinkled as she smiled and patted the head Norah lay on her shoulders.

'Listen, tell that man his dinner will be all dried up if he doesn't come in. It's sitting over that pot for the past half hour. Not like Frank to miss the dinner. He must've run into someone, is chatting away.'

'Where was he heading this morning?' Norah asked as she pulled on her coat and wellies.

'He was talking about the fencing in the top field – he thought there might be a fox about so he was going to check the usual spots.' Teasie folded her arms across her chest and shook her head, looking out the window for the errant Frank.

Norah stepped out into the damp February morning. It was really a miserable day.

'Where's the bloody spring?' she muttered as she buttoned her coat up and pulled on her gloves. Still, the cold air did blow away the cobwebs as she squelched through rain sodden ground.

She wondered had Tom a hangover. He should have. He had been drinking whiskey and nearly got in a fight with Stephen Cunningham. All because he suspected Stephen might be the one that had sent her a Valentine's card earlier in the week.

'Big eejit' she tutted. It was typical Tom. Overreacting to something small. They had had a lovely Valentine's celebration. Had gone into Boyle for a meal and all. Really romantic. She had felt like an adult for the first time. Tom gave her a beautiful watch. She shook it down her coat sleeve to admire it again. A tiny oval face on a gold linked chain. With a tiny, tiny sparkly diamond on the creamy face. She gasped with delight when she opened the box.

'Tom. It must've cost so much but it's.... oh Tom! It's so beautiful!'

'Nothing but the best for my woman.' He had been so pleased with her reaction.

'And on top of that great big card and the flowers earlier on. You must've spent more than two weeks wages on me. I feel so bad now, only that skittery little card and the Freddie White tape. If only I was working, I'd have a few more bob.' Norah had twisted her wrist left and right admiring the way the light caught on the diamond.

'Not to worry. I've enough money for the two of us.'

Tom was six months into his butcher's apprenticeship. But of course as his father was the butcher Tom was paid above normal apprentice wages – his father gave him a cut of the profits instead and it was an incentive to keep his head down and push the business on.

The meal had gone well, until over dessert Norah stupidly let slip that she had received two more cards. One of course from Frank, but she wasn't sure about the second one.

It was one of the really soppy ones, roses on the front with *'Be my Valentine'* in gold old-fashioned lettering. Inside there had been none of the usual crude rhymes. Just a 'Guess Who?' Norah didn't recognise the writing. Her telling Tom about this had immediately changed the atmosphere between them. She knew he was jealous, why on earth had she told him?

He couldn't rest easy until they got back to the house and he got to look at the miscreant card. He had turned it this way and that looking for clues. He had even asked to see the envelope.

'Tom, that's gone into the range hours ago!'

'If you think anything of me that's what you'll do with this as well.' He had flapped the offending card at her.

'Here, give it to me,' she had lifted the cover of the range and threw in the pink and cream card, poking at it until it caught fire in the dying embers. 'I don't know who sent that and I don't care. Whoever it was is messin'; everyone knows we're going together and have been forever.'

'I suppose. Some fool trying to raise trouble,' he had muttered.

Then she had kissed away his fears, or so she thought. But with whiskey in him at last night's disco he had made some excuse and gone for Stephen Cunningham over some imagined slight at the bar.

Then he insisted they leave the disco immediately and he drove like a lunatic all the way home ranting and raving. She kept quiet in the car, only agreeing with him in a soft voice if he insisted on an answer. There was no point in arguing with him when he had drink taken. He had to shout the anger out of him – it was the only way; sometimes she thought he should have steam coming from his ears like a cartoon character when he got angry. He was like a pressure cooker coming to pressure – and it had to be released or he would explode. Stephen must think Tom was a right bowsie.

It probably was Stephen who had sent the card she thought. She had noticed that Stephen's attitude to her had changed lately, from being someone who had laughed with her and teased like all the lads, he had avoided her a lot in the last couple of months. She had caught him staring at her once or twice and then he had blushed and turned away. She wouldn't be surprised if he did like her. Or maybe she was imagining it. It didn't matter anyway. Tom was her boy, he would call tonight and nothing more would be said about it. She just wished he wouldn't drink whiskey. It made him so angry and was such an old man's drink.

She stood in the top field and looked over the river to Furlong's. Tom's car wasn't there. He must have managed to haul himself out of the bed for work. She couldn't see Eileen leaving him sleep in anyway, she was a terrible tyrant Eileen. Sometimes Norah thought Tom exaggerated how horrible she was. How could anyone's mother be so mean and spiteful?

No sign of Frank but she could see the new chicken wire was up so the fence was mended.

'Looking for foxes he is,' she laughed. Frank hated foxes. For a man that loved all nature his feeling in regards to the fox were extreme. The first time Norah had seen one for any length of time she had been so excited. Watching him from a distance as he stood still, head up sniffing the air, cream-tipped tail erect, one paw half raised. Ready to run. His reddish-brown fur and that creamy underbelly stunning against the greenness of the hedge.

She had run home to tell Frank of course and he immediately went looking for his shotgun.

'What are you doing Uncle Frank?' She was horrified, couldn't believe it.

'I'm sorry peata, foxes are bad news. They'll get into the hen house and what they don't kill they'll scare into non-laying. I've known a pack of them to attack newborn lambs. You wouldn't like that would you? You love the little lambs don't you? We have to look out for them, help the ewes to keep them safe.'

'But Uncle Frank! He's so beautiful. Maybe he's not a bad fox. Couldn't we capture him and tame him, have him like a pet. The dogs would love him I think.'

Norah laughed, thinking of her childish innocence. Frank didn't get the fox that day and her admiration for the fox had declined when next morning she saw where the animal had tried to get into the henhouse. The hens had been in an awful flap and there were only two broken eggs for collection.

She had wondered if the fox Frank was looking for now was related to the fox then? Probably all the foxes in the area down the years were related. She had passed the spot where there had been a set two years ago but there was no sign of activity around it.

Walking towards the hedge field to the left of her current spot she thought she could see a run through the undergrowth where vegetation was greener. Sure sign of a fox, their leavings fertilised the soil. She had slowed her step the nearer she got.

It was too early for cubs but the vixen was probably pregnant and around the den more. Norah thought she might spot her or the male if Frank hadn't caught or scared him off. Ten feet nearer she saw a bundle of old clothes half buried.

'Frank'll be raging,' she muttered, 'some townie fool dumping again.'

Nearer again and there was Frank's shovel and shotgun lying near the entrance to the run.

'Where is he? Frank, Frank!' She called, her voice deadened in the damp still air. Then she screamed as the bundle of clothes slowly moved and Frank's face appeared, so white his moving lips didn't even stand out against it.

'Jesus. Jesus. Frank, what's wrong Frank, what.. what?' Running to him, bending, trying to pull him up. His breath was harsh and laboured, he tried to speak again but couldn't.

'I'll go, get Teasie. No, the doctor and Teasie. Or a car, someone with a car...' She was wild, heart hammering, blood pounding in her ears.

'Help, help....!' Shouting for the help no one was near enough to deliver.

Frank's hand suddenly curled around her wrist and he had looked into her face and his head shook. Then a rattling exhalation and Norah saw the pain and the gaze go out of his eyes.

'Noooooooooooo! No! Don't. Don't you dare! Frank. Frank. Your dinner is ready, you have to come home now. Teasie will be so annoyed if it dries up. Frank. Frank. Come on.' She shook him. But he didn't move.

Then she ran, as fast and hard as she ever could, sobbing and shrieking, 'Frank, Frank'.

She had run to the house, slipping and sliding on boggy slopes. Screaming, 'Teasie. Teasie. Help, help!'

Nearing the house Teasie had come to the back door wiping her hands on her ever-present apron. She ran towards Norah as soon as the girl's distress registered. Norah, sobbing and incoherent, had half-pulled Teasie up through the fields, Teasie discarding her sodden slippers within minutes, scrambling partly on hands and knees to embrace the cold bundle of clothes and skin and bones that had been her husband.

Norah heard a noise from Teasie that she had never heard before or since. A roar that caused a flock of birds to scatter from the hedge. A roar of pain and terror and anger which gave way to a low moaning keening. His name said over and over. She didn't even seem to be aware of Norah.

'I have to mind her.' Norah's thoughts sharpened and suddenly a new way of looking at the world became clear to her. 'Teasie. Listen, listen. I'm going to Furlongs, it's nearer. To use the phone, get help. Alright. Do you understand? Teasie, alright?'

Teasie hadn't replied, just continued kneeling by Frank, her body stretched over his, her arms alternating between hitting him and hugging him. And that low moaning from her, over and over. 'Frank. No. Frank. Not yet. No.'

'He was too young.' Norah says now, slapping her hand on the bridge railing.

Life had never been the same after he was gone. Never as safe.

'Jesus, barring Teasie everyone I ever loved died young. Is there some kind of jinx on me?'

Sixty-six Frank had been. Sixty-six in a rural area where one wasn't considered old until you passed your eighty-fifth year. Frank had seemed hale and hearty apart from his asthma, which was generally well under control. Or so they had all thought.

A massive heart attack. The doctor said Frank wouldn't have been in pain for long. Norah didn't believe the doctor. She had seen Frank's face. His eyes. Once Frank had to put down a dog that was old and had broken a leg. He told her to say goodbye to the animal before he shot it. The tears spring to her eyes again. She remembers stroking the whimpering Smut's ears, and the look in the animal's eyes. She had seen the same look in Frank's eyes those few moments before he died. The pain. The knowledge.

Teasie. The capable, stoic Teasie went to pieces. Inconsolable. Tom had been brilliant, a rock, that time. Only just turned seventeen but he had arranged everything.

Wake, funeral and even got a solicitor to talk to Teasie later about her entitlements and how to re-register the land in her name. Organised other farmers to look after stock, to lease Teasie's few acres for grazing. He had been a great organiser, Tom.

Norah walks back towards the hospital. Doctor Fitzgerald told her that morning that she will have to leave soon. They will see her in outpatients for a while but she doesn't need to be an inpatient any more. He has suggested various counsellors and wants her to stay on medication for at least six months.

But where will she go? She can't go back to Tibraden. Not yet. She couldn't face the house. The loneliness. Her destroyed garden. Then she'd have to learn to drive and to do all the things Tom had always done for her, for them. All the things that needed to be done only for her now. On her own.

And then there was other people. Everyone would know, turn away from her, maybe even refuse to serve her in the shops. The priest. She couldn't face him. The biggest sin of all and she had committed it. She knows she will also have to face Carmel, and that is not a meeting she looks forward too.

But where else can she go from here? She can't leave the country or even the county without telling the Gardai. She never had a passport anyway so she wouldn't get very far if she ran away. But Norah doesn't want to run. She deserves to be – needs to be – punished. She knows that.

Norah stands and looks at the grim hospital front. It has been such a place of safety for her; she has felt safe this last fortnight behind those stone walls. What lay ahead? Would she ever know peace again, feel comfort? More to the point, she shook her head and climbed the steps to the door, would she ever deserve it?

Chapter Ten

Norah sits in the lobby of the small hotel on the outskirts of Longford town. It's too warm and she removes her cardigan, rearranging her blouse. She's nervous. Carmel had written to her. A rant really, as was Carmel's wont. Norah had tried not to read it, Liam said she shouldn't. But it held a strange fascination for her and she had read it, then re-read it again and again, searching through the ream of all the things Carmel had listed that the Furlong family had done for Norah – looking for something to connect to, something to make Norah feel part of that fractured family still. It was mad and she knew it was mad. But she needed badly to belong somewhere. Not this horrible weightless drifting that reminded her of the way she had felt those first months after her parents had died.

Carmel ranted for pages about Tom. How he had been a good man, a good provider and there was no way Carmel was going to let Norah walk away with the Furlong money. Her pen had gouged through the paper in spots – Norah actually trembled reading some of her vicious threats. Talk of solicitors and a court case to demand Carmel's rights to Tom's estate.

Liam hadn't wanted her to even open the letter. He told her how Carmel had barged into Kate Breslin's house looking for Norah. Typical Carmel. No thought that she might frighten an old woman living on her own, intent on getting her own way.

'I don't want the bloody Furlong house,' she had told Liam. She smiles now, Liam had been surprised by her sharp reaction. He explained how it would be hers, all of it and the land and the shops, although in the circumstances Carmel and Fidelma, Tom's other sister, were likely to try and claim part of it, contest Norah's rights to it.

'It doesn't seem right. That I should profit from his death. Is there no law against that?'

'There's the law and then there's justice.' Liam sighed. 'You killed Tom in self-defence, we agreed that would be your plea. You're his widow. You're entitled to his estate.'

It all seemed so cold. Her whole life, hers and Tom's, brought down to a bank balance.

It was Liam who had suggested the hotel. It was far enough away from Tibraden that she wouldn't be bumping constantly into people who knew her. She thanked God now for the isolation in which Tom had kept her. His paranoia had been such that in the last few years he had ensured that the post for the house had been delivered to one of the shops.

Since Teasie's death three years ago the only trips Norah had made out of the house had been to hospital to have a broken arm set and one to a funeral of an aunt of Tom's. He had ushered her into and out of the church so quickly she hadn't even been able to shake the hands of the dead woman's family.

She glances at her watch again. Sinead is coming to visit and Norah likes Sinead, likes her bright and bubbly personality. She wonders about Sinead and John O'Sullivan. There is definitely something there. Norah had caught him looking at Sinead once. Sinead had been recounting some comic incident that had occurred and they had all been laughing. But John had laughed a little too loudly. He never seemed to look at Sinead without some anxiety in his glance. Norah thinks him a gentleman, in every sense of the word.

Norah knows how lucky she has been to have these lovely people looking out for her. Good people. Genuine.

Frank would have approved. Not of what she had done. No. Not that. But of the people who had come into her life since. Frank would have liked them all.

Sinead walks into the lobby and Norah raises her hand to catch her attention. Sinead smiles and walks across the room; she seems so sure of herself, a quick, confident step – she leans down and pecks Norah on the cheek.

'You look well. How is the accommodation?'

'Fine. My room is lovely. It overlooks the river. The staff are all very nice.' Norah feels a bit uneasy. It seems strange seeing Sinead away from the hospital. 'Will I order some coffee? Or maybe you would prefer a drink?'

'I think I'll have a white wine actually. Then we can have a walk about the town. Have a look in some of the shops, what do you think?' Sinead waves to attract the lounge girl's attention.

'Goodness, it's so long since I've been shopping! I've probably forgotten how.' Norah smiles

'Nonsense, it's inbuilt into your female DNA. You'll relearn it quickly enough.'

Sinead always manages to make Norah smile. They chat for a while about Longford. Norah apologises for Carmel's behaviour.

'Your mother was very upset I hear. Typical Carmel. Their mother Eileen was exactly the same. What they wanted was all that mattered. They all gave Tom's father a terrible time and then Tom after Seamus died. Always wanting more. It was never enough; they moaned constantly about what they didn't have to him and Tom and then bragged about what they did have to everyone else.' Norah paused and they ordered from the lounge girl.

'When I think of it I can see how they sucked the life from him and he worked so hard. We had – have – four shops you know. Tom leased out three of them; only kept the one in Tibraden and only opened it three days a week. Plenty really. There was plenty of money to go round, keep everyone. He kept and butchered his own cattle and sheep. We had pigs too at one stage. He said he didn't want to be away from home as much as his father had been, wanted some kind of a life apart from work and making money.' The lounge girl returns with their drinks and Norah pays her.

'Is Tom's mother still living?' Sinead sips on the wine, its coldness causing slight condensation on the outside of the glass. Norah sees Sinead's fingerprints on the glass when she puts it down.

'No! Thank God!' She couldn't help it. It burst out of her. 'Sorry, I've shocked you. It's just that I've been thinking a lot about her lately. Looking for reasons I suppose. Reasons for the way Tom was. Eileen Furlong was a horrible woman. She didn't make life easy for anyone.'

Sinead leans forward and touches Norah's arm. 'You haven't shocked me. And don't apologise for Carmel. She's responsible for herself. She sounds like a mad bitch!'

Norah grins, bites her lower lip to try to stop a giggle. 'I shouldn't laugh but that's exactly what she is. If you're ever misfortunate enough to meet her you'll see that madness in her; it's in the way she dresses, her hair is a statement to madness,' Norah pauses as Sinead laughs, 'and in particular her eyes. Carmel's eyes can look dull, seem slow and sleepy but then you see this gleam in them and she comes out with some vicious comment. She's unbelievable. Even Tom used to say if she was an animal you would put her out of her misery! He could say it, but no one else. The number of times he got into rows over things she had done or said. A small area, you know yourself,' she shakes her head.

'I can imagine,' Sinead twirls the stem of the wine glass. But we're not going to worry about Carmel or any of them today. Shopping requires P.M.A.'

'What's that?'

'Positive Mental Attitude. Very important!'

They both laugh and when they finish their drinks they set out.

Their foray into the damp day is foreshortened however when within their first hour out Norah spots two different people in two different shops that she knows.

Norah almost runs back to the hotel and only feels she can breathe again when Sinead in her wake closes the door behind them in the stuffy bedroom. Norah bursts into hysterical tears. Sinead puts her arms around her and guides her to sit on the edge of the bed.

'Ssssh, Norah. It's alright. Listen to me. Listen. You're safe now.'

'Safe! Did you see the way Sean McAllister looked at me and then looked away all flustered. And that young Cunningham one in the book shop. Did you see her and the friend staring? I can't stay here. I'll have to go somewhere else. Carmel will know before tomorrow I'm in Longford and she won't rest easy until she finds me.'

'Pack your bag. You're coming home with me.' Sinead stands and opens the wardrobe, pulls out Norah's bag.

'What? I can't. Your poor mother. I mean, she'll have a heart attack. And then there's the police. I have to sign in every morning here.' Norah is flustered but has automatically obeyed Sinead's command, gathering her few belongings together and bundling them into the bag. Sinead nods, she's already on the phone to Liam.

Within an hour Norah is checked out of the hotel and in Sinead's car on the road to Mullaghadone. They sit in silence for the first twenty minutes.

'Sinead, this is very kind. But I don't think it's a good idea. Mullaghadone is too small. Your mother...'

'Norah, please. It's all arranged and you don't have to worry. Yes, it's a small place but it's only for a day or two until Liam can get something organised. You can just stay in the house, or we can bundle you up in scarves and hats and big sunglasses. Like a celeb in disguise. A few little changes and I swear your Uncle Frank wouldn't know you if you ran into him down the town.'

Norah nods, she's afraid she's going to cry again. She doesn't think Frank would recognise the person she has become anyway.

When they reach the house in Mullaghadone all is quiet.

'I talked to Rachel. Herself and Mother will be home in an hour or two. They're in Sligo doing a little Christmas shopping.' Sinead leads the way into a big warm kitchen.

'What a lovely room!' Norah feels comfortable for the first time today.

Sinead smiles. 'Yes, isn't it? It's the best room in the house. Come on – I'll show you your bedroom. Then I'll make something for us to eat. I don't know about you but I'm starving.' She shows Norah around the house and leaves her to settle into a pretty, floral-themed pink and white bedroom.

Norah decides not to unpack. She can't stay here. Not for longer than a night or two. She already feels more secure than she has done since she left the safety of the hospital but she knows this can't last. It's not safe or fair for anyone. The tears well up and she fights them back.

'Stop! Stop! What about your resolution?' she mutters. 'You've spent your whole bloody life crying and it never got you anywhere. Look where tears have landed you.' She goes to the bathroom and splashes water on her face, takes one of the mild tranquilisers they gave her in the hospital.

Sinead is in the kitchen singing to herself as she makes omelettes.

'Can I do anything?' Norah tries to look bright, knows she's failing.

'You can cut some bread, lay the table and I'll make a pot of tea.'

Norah moves about the kitchen under direction and relaxes enough to hum along to the chorus of the song Sinead is singing.

'Hey, sounds like you can hold a tune Norah. Do you sing much?'

'I'm no singer. I'm not tone deaf but I'd never sing in public.'

'You'd be surprised at some of those that think they can sing in public!' Sinead laughs. 'I'm in a musical society in Dublin, mostly backstage, occasionally in the chorus or as an understudy. Some of the people that join up can barely sing a scale but think they should be getting leading roles. It's hilarious at auditions. X Factor has nothing on some of the oddballs that turn up.'

'Oh, we love that show! We would laugh so much at all the funny bits. Then I feel so sorry when the judges are being hard on some of them. Tom says I'm too soft......' Sinead is looking at her.

'Sorry, I just forget. I know I... but it doesn't seem real.' Norah flushes. 'None of it. None of anything that has happened in the last two months. God, sometimes I think the last four years weren't real. Since Teasie died. It's been... I feel as if I've been in a trance since then.' The hand holding the bread knife is shaking so she puts it quietly on the bread board and places her hands in her arm pits, shakes her head fiercely to forbid the tears.

'It's over now. Whatever is to come, will come. But that's all over. What is it they say? "The past is another country". Come on. Sit and we'll eat.'

Sinead brings the plates with the omelettes to the table and starts telling Norah funny stories about different shows she's been in.

'Sounds like you have a great social life. Do you like Dublin?' Norah can't eat much but the tea is lovely. Made with tea leaves, good and strong.

'Do I like it? I don't know. It's my life. I love my little apartment and I really enjoy the musical society. Then I have a few really good friends. Some of them are married with kids now so socialising isn't as easy as it used to be for them. I like having access to the shops but the traffic drives me mad. The jobs okay, pays the bills and most of my colleagues are good fun.' Sinead cups her hands around her mug, smiles at Norah through the steam.

'Have you a boyfriend or... sorry, I'm being nosey.' Norah blushes.

'I don't mind,' Sinead grins, 'No, no-one special. I have had a few but nothing ever really worked out. Old maid I told you!'

'I'm sorry. Not about being an old maid I mean, about being nosey... oh God I'm babbling.' Norah laughs along with Sinead.

'Don't worry. Listen there's Mother and Rachel' Sinead calls out 'Hello! We're in the kitchen.' She adds a rider to Norah 'Just do me a favour, don't mention my lack of a man in front of my mother. I like to keep her guessing!'

Two women come into the kitchen and Norah stands up. The younger woman drops her bags onto the table and extends her hand.

'Hi, Norah. I'm Rachel, Sinead's baby sister.'

She's beautiful thinks Norah. Completely different to Sinead, dark to her fair. But with the same warmth and softer than Sinead in some way.

'Norah, this is my mother Kate,' Sinead gestures and the neat little older woman with the well-coiffed hair nods.

'I remember you Kate. Although it's over twenty years. You haven't changed much. Yourself and Sean came to Frank's funeral. Teasie was very touched that you both came.'

'Well, goodness of course we would have come. Has Sinead looked after you alright?' Kate bustles towards the kettle. 'Sinead, did you not heat up some apple tart?'

'I didn't, but I will now. You two sit down and I'll make fresh tea.'

Rachel starts chatting to Sinead about the purchases she made and tries to draw her mother and Norah into the conversation. Norah can see Kate is uncomfortable.

'I was right,' Norah thinks, 'this isn't going to work.' Then Kate asks about Teasie and is soon engrossed as Norah tells of Teasie's long battle with a series of mini strokes and her eventual death three years ago, four years after a massive stroke left her immobile and with no speech.

'Weren't you very good. Nursing her all those years. These two will throw me into a home at the first sign of ill-health.' Kate wryly indicates her daughters.

'Mam! We will not. Don't say things like that' Rachel plops steaming apple tart with a blob of melting ice cream in front of her mother.

'Oh, you wait and see! Bette Davis said, 'Old age ain't for sissies' and she's right.' Kate waved her fork at her daughters.

'Mother! You're not old and you're hale and hearty. You'll outlive us all,' Sinead laughs.

The atmosphere is easier now and Norah relaxes a little. She watches the mother and daughters tease each other. Envies them.

She helps clean up and then follows to Kate into the sitting room to look at some photos she has of Frank and Teasie. She even has a photo of Norah's father as a boy in a family wedding photo. Norah shakes her head looking at the bright, cheeky face of the child.

'I often wonder. That morning. Did they ever think? Did he know or she know even for a little while, that they were dying? I was too young, I never asked. I was just told they were killed in a car crash.'

'You poor thing.' Kate rubs her hand along Norah's arm. 'If it's any consolation Sean told me at the time that they were killed outright. Wouldn't have had time to know anything. It was a lorry jack-knifed onto them wasn't it?'

'So I believe. Thanks Kate. Thanks for everything.' Norah pecks Kate on the cheek 'You've all been so good to me and it can't be easy, you hardly know me, owe me nothing.'

'Well now,' Kate stands, replaces the photo album and pokes at the fire. 'If we can't help out a family member in trouble we wouldn't be up to much. I'm only sorry we didn't stay in touch over the years. But when Frank died and then Sean…..well, you know what I mean. Will I turn on the TV?'

'Sure… yes, that would be nice.' Norah is relieved and

she can see Kate is too.
    Neither of them ready to talk about Tom Furlong.

Chapter Eleven

Neither Norah nor Mother were going to feel completely comfortable being left alone together in Mullaghadone. I had to get back to Dublin and Rachel would be out working for most of the day. I had a chat with Norah before I left. She was great, not a mention of where she would go to stay, completely understanding of Mother's fears. Liam was coming to see her in the early afternoon to take her to sign in at the police station and try to come up with some accommodation arrangements for her.

An idea had been formulating that I had bounced off Rachel the night before but wanted to discuss it with John before I put it to Norah. I had a spare room in the apartment and I was rarely there. She could have the run of the place in the anonymity of Dublin. I imagined she should be easily able to register with Gardai there. Rachel, although admiring my good intentions, was a little worried that I was becoming too involved with Norah.

'How can I not be. Jesus, she's like a little pup that's been mistreated.' We had been in our usual 'big chat' positions, backs against the sofa legs stretched across the mat in front of the fire, bottle of half-finished wine between us, Norah and Mother long gone to bed.

'Sinead, I know. I feel for her too. She's so shy, polite. She seems afraid of her own shadow. But she's not a pup. And Christ, don't forget she murdered her husband!'

'What are you saying? 'A Norah's not for Christmas but for life'?' I laughed and she joined in, albeit nervously.

'Look , I really can't see her as a danger to anyone except herself. And even then, she doesn't strike me as suicidal, she doesn't have that panicky desperation. I'm convinced I'm perfectly safe with her, as are you and Mother. Jesus I wouldn't have brought her here otherwise. I don't know whether killing Tom Furlong took the only bit of aggression she ever had in her out of her but I can't believe the woman I have spent time with is capable of hurting a fly.'

'Oh Lord! Don't say that! Isn't that what Anthony Perkins says about him/herself at the end of 'Psycho'?' Rachel fake shivered. 'Seriously Sinead. Just mind yourself. Okay?'

I had nodded and squeezed her arm. Then changed the subject.

My mind was whirring on the drive back to Dublin, thinking about Norah and Dublin, about John and me. How we had gone bad. I let my mind drift to Rachel's warning about minding myself.

I had suffered (and suffered is the only almost-correct word) a bout of severe depression in the mid-'90s. It was the reason I dropped out of college; I had almost dropped out of life. John was there of course. Coping. And Rachel knew a little of it; we had needed an ally at home to put Mother and Dad off the scent. Although she had only been in her late teens so we, or rather John, spared her most of the details. John talked her into covering for my absences from home. I know those absences hurt my parents but I felt, still feel, that I had been sparing them. At the time I couldn't have borne Mother's pinched fussing face in front of Dad's well-meaning worried one, peering over the abyss into my pit. There I lay, curled up like a foetus, unable to escape from the suffocating second skin that entrapped me.

Caul? Shroud? Either would be a good word. I was

lucky, mine turned out to be a caul. My sheer bloodymindedness, that obstinate streak that had caused me so much trouble growing up, was what kept me clinging to the little bit of sanity I had left. I wouldn't let the bastard beat me and I crawled from the pit, leaving it behind. It lies shrivelled in a little box in the back of mind. Occasionally it grows tentacles and pushes against the lid trying to seep through my brain, make mush of me, my thoughts and actions, my self-belief. But it's never succeeded again, not fully. Medication, friends, work, running, music. All my weapons. I keep myself well armed. For years my first thought on waking has been 'how am I today?' The days I didn't feel like throwing up at having to get up and function are the good ones. With at times unbearable slowness I recovered. Sufficiently to live a reasonable life, to savour the good days, the days of contentment, to survive the bad days as passing moments. And they do pass, that much I have learned.

I lost a lot in the process. John and I the first casualty. I still don't know why.

That's a lie. I had pushed, pushed, pushed him away and he kept coming back. I know all he wanted to do was hold me, be there. But I couldn't bear to be held, couldn't bear his sympathy. I couldn't condemn John to a life with me. I needed toughness, a sergeant major, someone to scream at me, shout at me, kick me in the arse. An iron glove. Or so I thought.

I thought about my maternal grandmother as I joined the M1 and cruised towards Dublin, Mother's mother, Elizabeth Fitzgerald. 'Suffers from her nerves' is all we were ever told. She lived about twenty miles from us and we were dragged on a visit once a fortnight. I hated that house. It was always cold and dark. She used to spend most of her time, particularly in the winter, lying in the darkened bedroom, the only light the perennial flickering Sacred Heart lamp over her bed. Her room always smelled, stale breath and dirty knickers. It was a scary place for a child.

Mother and Dad and the aunties would all call, try to chivvy her out of it, make her enjoy us I suppose. But she had no interest. Occasionally she would stop eating so would have to move into our house or one of my aunt's to be fed and nurtured into a fit state to go home again. I can still see her white, white face, skin like crinkly crepe paper, eyes dead, sitting at the table in a maroon quilted dressing gown, grey hair escaping from a hair net. I'd skip in from school.

'How are you, Granny?'

'Down to zero'. And those were the good days. Most days she wouldn't be capable of even acknowledging me. She was hospitalised several times, eventually dying after her last six-month stay when her physical health deteriorated rapidly as she refused to eat. Mother cried, but there was relief in the tears. When I ended up in hospital myself I remembered it all vividly. I was going to relive Granny's life – sit, shuffling my slippers in the cold ashes of the fire. Face, skin, mind grey. I can never understand people talking about feeling blue or even 'the black dog of depression', although that's a slightly better description. For me depression is grey, deep, drab, all-encompassing grey, no lightening at the edges, no sign of the oppressive cloud lifting.

I refused to see John when he came to visit. In the end the staff asked him not to come, not until I was ready. I wrote to him after about three months, told him it was over. He came to see me once more, about a fortnight before I got out of hospital. It was a sad meeting. We both cried. But at the time I was afraid that this was going to be my life, this falling down at frequent intervals.

The medics at the time told me it was unlikely that my depressive bouts would ever to be as severe again. Endogenous depression they called it. What an impressive title, sounds like you should have studied for years to get it. Basically genetic. It skipped my mother and her sisters but caught me. They said I was now in a position to recognise the symptoms and should look for treatment before it took hold. But what if I couldn't manage it? How could I inflict that awful dragging illness on someone I loved? Who would want to come home to that every day? I don't know that I would have if the situations were reversed. I was twenty-one and I thought my life was over. But John's needn't be. I didn't tell him that. Just told him I didn't, couldn't love him enough; lied and said my feelings for him had changed. He told me he loved me, would never stop loving me. I can still hear his final plea at that meeting in the scruffy coffee shop of the hospital.

'Just give me a maybe Sinead. Please, don't do this to us. Just a maybe some day. I can't stop loving you just because you say so.' His voice sounded strangled. All the bloody tears I had shed and now I was making him cry. I shook my head, hugged my body.

'No John. Please. Just go.' He stood up and moved around the table, placed his hands on my shoulders 'I'll leave you be, but I swear Sinead I'll never ever leave you completely. I can't. You're too much a part of me. Promise me, if ever you need me. Promise me you'll come looking for me.'

I cried. Naturally. But I still maintain I did what was best for both of us at the time.

But now? I didn't know. He had moved on and so had I. It was almost fifteen years since that Saturday afternoon in the hospital. We were different people at this stage. I certainly was. After about two years I had eventually been able to have a chat with him, two years of avoiding places he might be when I went home, two years of distant nods and half smiles on the odd occasion we ended up at the same functions.

It was when Dad died that the ice between us thawed. Ice is the wrong word, there was no coldness, not on either side. A sheet of cloudy perspex maybe. Yes, plexiglass scratched and dimmed by the years but glimpses of the people we had been and the people we had become still there. That day, the day we buried my beloved Dad, John came to me as we left the graveyard. He just took both my hands, looked me hard in the face and nodded. Then he hugged me.

'He loved you so much. Always remember that.'

I returned his hug. It gave me a comfort nothing else could do at that time.

'I know, I know. And you John. He was so fond of you.'

'Maybe that's because he thought at one stage I might have you tamed!'

We laughed. Good tears. Dad had been so relieved when John and I became an item in our Leaving Cert year. There had been tears and tantrums about some of the other lads I had been knocking around with. They were harmless but were a bit wild and undisciplined, a laugh at anyone's expense their worst sin. But in John Dad saw something solid. I think he felt I was safe; John would curb my worst excesses. Mother finally approved of one of my friends, good family and all that so that made life easier all round in the Breslin household. Once Mother was happy Dad could lead his quiet life.

Do I make John sound dull? He was, is, anything but. Steady and solid yes but I've never seen anyone with so much energy. And talk about enthusiasm! If John gets an idea into his head it gets done. He never went at anything bald-headed, everything was thought through but by God once he started something he saw it through to conclusion.

And we had laughed together. How we laughed! John's droll sense of humour. A quiet, wry way of looking at the world that could always make me smile. Our physical relationship had been....I don't think wonderful is too big a word to describe it. We learned together. Slowly and gently, with some tears and plenty of laughter and I remember that side of it with a smile as being deeply warm and tender.

I grinned now as I negotiated the thickening traffic flowing into Dublin, thinking about the first time we had made love. I think we were both slightly in shock afterwards. It had been mutual, unintentional, no discussion or agonising. It had just happened, and it was right. We'd been out walking, rambling towards one of our favourite spots, a small crannog overlooking the lake. A sunny Sunday afternoon two weeks before our exam results were due. Our hopes for college, brilliant careers and social life in Dublin resting on the outcome.

'You'll be okay Brainbox.' I had punched him. 'Bet you'll get the highest score in the school, the bloody county!'

'You're no thick yourself. You'll get what you want.'

'It's all a bit scary though, isn't it.' We sat on the grass, I pointed my face towards the sun eyes closed.

'Is it? Yes, I suppose. But isn't it exciting too? I can't wait to get out into real life. No more timetables and teachers and rules and regulations. Get out there, make my own life, my own decisions.'

'Jesus.' I had opened my eyes and looked at him. 'You sound more like me. I didn't think any of that stuff bothered you.'

'Maybe, Sinead Breslin, you don't know all there is to know about me.' He had started to tickle me.

And the tickling led to a tussling which turned to stroking and kissing and cuddling and then something took hold of us both. Something inexplicable that hadn't happened before. None of it mattered, not the open air or fear of discovery, not fears of pregnancy or breaking taboos. Nothing could have stopped us; we had our own momentum. All the restraint we had both felt up to now, all the awkwardness. It just went. It was him and me and the sun on our bodies and the fumbling and the rush and the joy and the specialness of sex for the first time with someone you truly love.

And I'm not saying it was perfect and we both orgasmed and sighed and moaned and swooned with desire. But it was good. Good and right. And after, clothing rearranged and leaning against each other, I remember looking up into his face; he looked like I felt. Pleased as punch, slightly stunned.

'Jesus,' he said.

I laughed 'No – just me! Promise you won't laugh at the only thing that bothered me?'

'What?'

'It's thick, like, really stupid.' I blushed.

'What? After that... well, nothing you ever say or do will be thick or stupid... not to me... everything counts, y'know. Do I sound soppy?'

'You do. But I know what you mean. I feel a bit girly myself!'

He laughed. I was the most ungirly girl in Sligo. My mother reckoned there wasn't a less feminine girl in the whole of the twenty-six counties.

'Well, what is it? What bothered you? Did I do something wrong?'

'No. God no. It's just. Well. The only thing I was worried about was in case a helicopter or a small plane went over. I was looking up at the sky and it was so clear blue and bright and I felt so good. Then suddenly I heard this noise, probably a tractor or slurry spreader or something but I got it into my head that...' But I couldn't finish because I had to punch him as he rolled away from me in hysterical laughter.

Admittedly the number of small planes or helicopters that passed over our tiny area of Sligo was negligible, less than negligible. But still, you never know. And I had envisioned this pilot and these passengers peering down at us, cheering us on.

So of course I had to pounce on John and start beating him up and of course that led to further physicality. And this time was better, different, not as urgent but definitely better.

That was the start of a really compatible physical relationship and we were sensible and took care of contraception early on and as soon as we came to Dublin we moved in together. Kids weren't on the agenda for us, not then, they were mentioned – our wonderful mythical children – but not for then, not for a long time.

But we never had the long time to reconsider. Shit, etcetera.

I rang Mullaghadone as soon as I got into the apartment. Mother answered, after the fourth ring of course.

'Well, is Norah still with you?'

'She is, the poor creature. You know Sinead you're right. She's so quiet. And do you know she's a great cook, she's after making one of the nicest rounds of soda bread I've tasted in many years.' Mother sounded quite cheery.

'So what's the story, did Liam arrive?'

'Yes. They're gone off together to talk to the Gardai.' She paused. 'I would have her here, just for a little while… but that woman, the Carmel one. She'd surely get to hear and I don't think any of us would get any peace.'

'Look Mam, don't worry about it, I have an idea that I want to discuss with John that might solve all those problems. I'll ring you later when Norah is home and let you know if it's worked out.'

She tried to pressurise me into giving her more information but I was determined to get John's imprimatur on my plan before I pursued it any further.

As soon as I had hung up I tried John's number but it went to voicemail. So I left a message and went to run a bath. No sooner had I lowered myself into the tub of hot, hot water with lots and lots of suds, face pack on, glass of wine on the stool beside the bath and trashy novel to hand then the bloody phone rang.

'Hey. Sorry I couldn't take your call earlier. I was talking to Liam trying to sort out something for Norah.' He sounded tired.

'Actually John, that's what I wanted to talk to you about.'

'Yes, I know, your mother. I'm really sorry Sinead, she shouldn't have that stress….'

'No, no listen. Honestly she's warmed to the whole idea, just doesn't think it would work. Too close to the nutty sister-in-law. But John, what about Dublin?'

'What do you mean... a B and B or something?'

'No, here, what do you think? She could have the place to herself all day. Privacy, anonymity and then I'd be here at night. It might be exactly what she needs. Plus I'm sure we could find plenty of counsellors and the like easier up around here.' I was speaking too quickly, as I always did when I got an idea into my head.

There was a silence then a long uncertain 'Yeaahh.'

I could hear the buts that were about to start. So I pre-empted him and outlined what I thought would be a reasonable arrangement re money, guards and so on.

He laughed 'Your organisational skills have improved over the years. I'm impressed, you have all the bases covered. Just two things. Will Norah agree? Dublin might be a step to far. And what about you? How will you feel about living with someone again? How long is it since you've actually shared a place with someone on an ongoing basis?'

'Mind your own business!' I grinned at his nosiness. 'The bishop wouldn't ask me that! You won't get my relationship info out of me that easy, Bud.'

The information was non-existent anyway. Barring a few one-night stands and one man who bored me to tears after three months dating I had been living a spinsterish existence in the six years since I'd bought the apartment. Rob had moved in for two months when his relationship had broken up and he was in the process of buying a place, but apart from that I had been on my own.

And I liked it, I liked not cleaning up for maybe a month at a time and then doing a whirlwind blitz. I liked wandering around in the nip after my shower sipping a glass of wine whilst I decided what to wear if I were going out. I liked being in control of the remote control. All that stuff. But. It probably wasn't good for me – and at the moment I felt Norah needed something from me. I didn't know what or why I felt I had to give to her. But I knew my offer was heartfelt and I had thought it through.

Lying there in the cooling bath water, occasionally

sloshing water across my breasts to stop them getting cold, I explained all this (bar the lack of men or a man in my life) to John. He accepted the offer and said he would ring Liam and Norah immediately.

'What's the noise in the background, it's kind of echoy. Are you washing dishes or something?'

'Not quite. In my beloved bath, that's all.'

'Have you not come around to the concept of the power shower yet, a modern urbanite like yourself? You and your auld bath. Hey, do you remember..?'

I stopped him. Yes I did remember. The baths we had together were great fun – but a long time ago. We were different people and I didn't know that I could bear the thought of John seeing my body in its mid-thirties, however well-maintained I had kept it, whilst he remembered the bloom I had, we all have, from seventeen into our early twenties.

'Go on, make your phone calls and let me know what the story is. There's a room ready for her here at any stage she chooses to take it. And John, if she is going to be more than a day or two in Mullaghadone will you keep an eye on Mother and let the gardaí know. I don't want that mad sister of his upsetting her again.'

John rang off, promising to let me know as soon as something concrete was put together. I got out of the bath and dried myself off; the cooling water had lost its lustre. Maybe it would be nice to share it? No, it never would again. Certainly not with anyone new.

Chapter Twelve

Norah is in Kate's garden in borrowed wellies and a heavy jumper, garden tools about her. She promised Kate she would tidy up the garden for her before she leaves for Dublin.

Dublin! She can hardly believe it. She hasn't been in Dublin since she left it in 1974. At one stage she had talked about it, before Frank died, before Tom became so much a part of her life. Maybe applying for a job in the civil service or working in one of the big stores or if she did well enough in exams maybe train to be a nurse. But it hadn't happened and it hadn't bothered her. Not after Frank was gone; she couldn't have left Teasie. She had been content with her little life. Most of the time anyway.

Secateurs in hand she trims back the rose bushes, pulls away dead foliage and puts some shape on an overgrown pyracantha hedge. She'll come back before the end of February to cut the rose bushes back hard. She tidies away the fallen leaves and thinks about building a compost heap area for Kate. One of the bought tumbler ones maybe. Kate wouldn't be fit for turning compost and she doubted that Rachel and Sinead had much interest. The garden had obviously been much loved at one stage but it been allowed to become overgrown and somewhat choked in recent years.

'It was Sean's greatest pleasure,' Kate had sighed. 'I made him build the shed to leave his mucky boots and tools in. He used to have my kitchen floor destroyed before that. I'm no gardener; I love to look at it and sit in it in the summer but I couldn't tell one plant from another and I'm always afraid to do the wrong thing. A young lad comes in and looks after the grass during the spring and summer. But he's a farmer's son and flowers are outside of his understanding.'

Norah had laughed. She knew exactly what Kate meant. Tom never begrudged her the time or money she spent on her garden in Tibraden but he couldn't understand growing things that couldn't be eaten.

She misses gardening, but she's dreading going to see her home and garden. Liam is going to drive her to Tibraden to pack some more clothes and check for post. Denis Bradley is going to meet them there. Norah is nervous about meeting him. She had always liked Denis, he had called to the house a couple of times over the years, always kindly. He tried to get her to swear a statement against Tom on two different occasions.

After Teasie died Denis came to her, told her he was always there if she needed help. He had reminded her of Frank as he had been when Norah met him first. Kindly and slightly bumbling, but that didn't hide the keen intelligence beneath the quiet exterior.

'Norah!' Kate calls from the back door, 'Liam is here. I have a bit of lunch made for you both.'

Norah waves an acknowledgement and returns the garden tools and wellies to the shed. She has enjoyed her morning in the garden, always does; it's a place where she didn't have to think about anything except what she's doing with her hands. The garden and the kitchen. She loves baking, would have loved a large family to cook meals and bake bread for, apple tarts, fruit cakes. But it wasn't to be. She pulls back on her shoes and washes her hands at the outdoor tap.

Liam has Kate laughing about something one of his children said.

'Kids are great,' said Kate. No sign of those two of

mine producing grandchildren for me to spoil. Particularly Sinead, far too fussy, that one! I've hopes for Rachel and Eoin but I'm afraid to open my mouth. An interfering mother is a danger to any relationship.' Kate places a fry-up in front of Liam and another for Norah. 'Now Norah, sit yourself down and eat up.'

'Thank you Kate. I'll be as fat as a fool if I stay here too much longer!'

'Nonsense, you're far too thin. You need to look after yourself – all you have ahead of you.' Kate blushes, she has avoided all mention of Tom's death and the pending court case with Norah until now.

'Would you listen to that!' She gabbles at a news item on the radio about the lighting up of the Christmas lights in Dublin. 'Don't they start Christmas far too early, ridiculous; all it does is make people spend more money. I'm sure you're looking forward to it Liam what with the children and Santa?'

Liam laughs and tells them about the ever-growing lists that his daughters were writing.

Norah eats in silence, smiling and nodding when she feels it's required. Christmas. So close now. She wonders where she will be this year. It was always a time she held her breath with Tom. An excess of drink and having to spend a longer period of time than normal with his family meant tensions and tempers rose as the day would progress. It always ended with a row. No matter how many times she asked him not to drink, not to react to his sisters' taunting or to let his mother – while she was alive – rile him. Every year he'd say it would be different. Every year it got worse.

After lunch Norah and Liam drive to Tibraden. Liam chats to her, tries to relax her. But she can't. She knows Tom's body is long gone but she knows she'll still see it, still imagine the crusting pool of blood dribbling across the utility room floor.

'Norah, I hate to do this to you but you're going to have to give some us some detail on the incidents of the other times Tom…… hurt you. We've been onto the hospitals and are working on getting your records. Is there anyone, anyone at all that could verify what you're saying? What I mean is, were any of these events ever witnessed?'

'Do you not believe me?'

'Of course we believe you. But this is a court we're going into. It's your word against a dead man who can't tell us his version. There must be someone. Neighbours, local shopkeepers, anyone.'

Norah laughed shortly. Neighbours! After Teasie had died, Tom had kept her so isolated that she could go for months without seeing anyone – even his own family. She never learned to drive so had been dependent on him to get anywhere.

He even stopped going to Mass. She had tried to embarrass him into taking her.

'What about the customers? You know what people are like, they'll start to ask questions.'

'Nobody gives a damn about things like that anymore,' he had sneered, 'you're still living in the dark ages'. He had been drinking that night, only a few pints, but still she ended up bring punched and kicked. She never mentioned Mass again.

'There's Charles Donnelly. He'll remember…..' Norah paused. 'The police have already talked to him because he was at the house earlier that day… the day of…. the day Tom died. Charles might not want to get any more involved though. And why would he – he owes me nothing.'

'He owes you and the courts the truth, as all decent human beings do. He was Teasie's physiotherapist, wasn't he? Did he become friendly with you – or why was he still calling after she died?'

'No, he's an occupational therapist. Yes, he became a friend I suppose. More of Teasie's than mine at first. He works in the hospital in Sligo and she used to attend as an outpatient after the first stroke. Then after the second one

he would call to the house every six weeks or so. We got friendly; he's a nice man, Charles, awfully good to Teasie. I often thought he went above and beyond the call of duty in relation to her. He was so patient and she could be cranky enough on a bad day, but he always got her back into good humour. He came to her funeral and called to see me once or twice after. But then Tom found out.........
I don't know the details, but I know Tom went to see Charles and threatened him. Charles rang me once or twice in the weeks after that, tried to get me to look for help.' She paused.

'Then there's Denis Bradley, he would know a little of what went on. He might remember the one time I left Tom. One Christmas day, must be ten years ago, Denis wasn't Sergeant at that stage, he wasn't that long stationed there actually. Teasie called him, but I wouldn't go any further with it. Back then, I thought I could handle Tom you see. Then after Teasie had her stroke I needed him more than ever. I bent over backwards to avoid a row, a beating.' Norah shakes her head. 'I'm sorry Liam. I can't. I just can't talk about it.'

Liam sighs. 'Norah. You're going to have to help yourself. You don't deserve to go to prison. In my view, what you did, on the basis of what you've told us, was self-defence. But we need to build on that. Build up a picture of your life with Tom. If you can't tell me, could you maybe write it down? No matter what you think of, write it down. Will you try?'

She nods, she'll try.

What a failure. Jesus, she couldn't keep one person, one single person who said he loved her, happy. Maybe she wasn't made for happiness. Maybe she made Tom what he was. If he had been with someone else, someone with more go, better looking, better able to handle him, maybe it would all have been different. He would have wanted her more, wanted to make love to her, wanted her to have his children.

She looks out at the passing countryside, catches sight

of houses glittering with Christmas lights. Looking all jolly; expectant of presents, family, laughter.

The second Christmas after they married Tom insisted they have dinner with his family.

'Mammy will go on and on about it if we don't. Trust me, it's easier.'

'But what about Teasie? I can't leave her on her own. Not on Christmas Day!'

'For fuck's sake. You already spend half your bloody life with her,' he shouted and stormed from the room, slamming the door. So she gave in and was wondering how to tell Teasie when Tom's mother solved it by inviting Teasie to dinner too.

Teasie wasn't the same woman after Frank died, quieter in herself, mourning really; she tended to agree and go along with anything suggested.

The day had been a disaster from the start, Carmel had already been at the Irish coffees when they arrived and Tom proceeded to catch up with her state of inebriation by knocking back whiskey after whiskey. The niggling at each other started and developed into a full-blown row by the time the Christmas pudding was served.

Eileen Furlong didn't help matters, bringing up old grievances, stirring the pot for all it was worth. Fidelma, the youngest, passed out on the sofa courtesy of a bottle and a half of wine with her main course. Teasie put her hand under the table and squeezed Norah's hand. Norah caught her eye and smiled, then grinned. She couldn't help it, the whole thing was ludicrous. Paper hats, fancy table laid and three adults squabbling like a bunch of cranky children. Unfortunately, Tom spotted their conspiratorial smiles.

'We're going,' he snapped, pulling off his green crepe paper crown. 'C'mon, we'll drop Teasie home first.'

'Oh Tom, I thought Teasie could come home with us for a while, have a drop of sherry and maybe a mince pie later on?' Norah stood up and started to clear the table.

'Oh, are we not invited to chez Furlong then?' sneered Carmel. 'You'd want to remember whose family money is keeping you and your aunt in sherry and mince pies.'

'Shut up Carmel. Teasie's tired, she looks like she could do with her bed Norah. Am I right, Teasie?' Tom grunted in Teasie's direction.

One look at Tom's purple face and glinting eyes was enough to make Teasie nod. She squeezed Norah's hand again.

'Thank you Eileen, Carmel, for a lovely meal. Maybe next year we could have dinner in my house.' Teasie glanced at Fidelma's loosely flung limbs on the couch and raised her eyebrows at the faltering snore emanating from the slack mouth. 'Thank Fidelma when she wakes up.'

There was silence in the car down the lane. Tom pulled in at Teasie's first.

'Teasie, are you sure? It's early yet, we could watch the big movie and you could doze off on the couch if you're tired?' Norah pleaded, but Teasie was already out of the car. Norah got out too and walked her to the door. Teasie grasped her forearm and looked into Norah's eyes, her own eyes watery..

'Don't let him bully you, a stór. You always have a place to stay. Once I'm here there is always a safe place.'

'It's only the whiskey, Teasie. That and that bloody family of his. He'll be alright after a sleep. I'll drop down in the morning. We'll go for our St Stephen's Day walk, just like always, okay?' Norah touched Teasie's cheek, felt the dampness of tears.

'It's okay Teasie, don't worry – honestly, he's good really. It's just the whiskey making him cranky.'

Teasie didn't speak, just hugged Norah and went in, closing the door behind her. Norah stood for a minute then Tom shouted from the car.

'Will you come on woman! I'm getting cold.'

She climbed into the car and sat in silence for the three miles to their house while he ranted and raved about Carmel and his mother.

'Bloody bitches. No wonder my father dropped dead of a heart attack. Not a day's work between them and not a word of gratitude to me that looks after them all. And you, why don't you stand up to them?' He removed his left hand from the steering wheel and poked her leg viciously. 'And that bloody stuffing! Why the fuck did you tell her it was nice. And a big bloody tub of it home with you, not even the friggin' dogs will eat that shit.'

Carmel had stuffed the turkey with some sort of a citrus-based stuffing instead of the traditional pork and sage or parsley and thyme in breadcrumbs. It was awful and had tainted the taste of the turkey as well. Hardly anyone touched it but Norah had felt sorry for Carmel and her efforts, so she had tried to be nice about it.

'It's different, zesty is what the celebrity chefs would call it. Very unusual. But nice. Fair play, Carmel. I don't think I would even have thought of experimenting. Teasie and I are real old traditionalists, aren't we?' She had babbled to cover the silence at the table.

Teasie nodded agreement and swallowed the dry, orangey breadcrumbs that made up the stuffing.

'Huh, well if ye like it so much ye can take it with ye. Jaysis Carmel, that's about the first original dish thing you've ever produced. I wouldn't mind only it ruined the bloody turkey as well. And it the finest bird Tom had in the shop. Ye'll not live this one down. I vote Mam goes back to doing the cookin' next year,' Fidelma had waved her half-full glass about, sloshing drips of red wine onto the remains of her dinner.

'Shutupshutupshutup!!' Carmel screamed.

'Lazy cow.' She glared at them all. 'Cows I should say – not one of ye gave a dig out. Well, you can bloody well do the washing up.'

She tried to storm from the room except the sleeve of her sweater got caught in the door and her dramatic exit was diffused as she fumbled to untangle herself.

Tom cackled with glee and Norah felt like she was caught in a bad dream,

'Fuck off, you stupid cow. Norah offered to cook this year and you should have taken up her offer. At least we wouldn't have been half poisoned.'

'You're nothing but a limp wrested, lily-livered, mean little man, Tom Furlong. Just like Da. No gumption. No good for anything except making money. And that string of misery ye married. Didn't bring much with her did she, not even a sign of a son to take over the business. Good job we're still around to keep an eye, make sure she doesn't spend it all on Breslins.' Carmel's face was white and pinched with rage.

'Oh shut up the pair of ye. No wonder nobody wants to spend time with yiz. Not even the bloody Breslins. Squabblin' ferrets – that's all ye ever were.' Eileen threw her napkin onto the table in disgust and stood, grasping a glass and a bottle of wine from the table. 'I'm going to bed and I may stay there until New Year's Day – so keep your rows quiet and don't come looking for me.'

Eileen took regularly to the bed, eventually emerging paler and thinner after a week or ten days, the smell of vodka or gin oozing from her and a black plastic rubbish sack in hand in which the evidence of her binge clinked mournfully.

When they got back to their own house Tom continued to drink. He sat on the couch for a while complaining about programmes on the television as the level in the whiskey bottle went down. Norah left the living room and went to the kitchen to make sandwiches, taking her time, hoping he would fall asleep. But it didn't work. He followed her out, moved about the room behind her muttering to himself. He went in and out of different rooms, paced the house, a caged animal letting the odd roar out of him. Most of the stuff he shouted was garbled nonsense, but then his grievances focused in on the Christmas dinner.

Eventually he came back to the kitchen and banged the bowl of left over stuffing down in front of her. He gripped her neck from behind with fierce determination and forced her face down into the bowl. 'Here, if you like it so much, you can have the lot of it. Stupid cow. All stupid cows. Naw, cows in't as stupid as yiz.'

Norah raises her hand to her face now and rubs at her nose, her eyelids. She shudders, remembering the panic of not being able to breathe, of trying to raise her head as he ground it down into the cold, citrusy breadcrumbs. The vice-like grip he had on the back of her neck, his arms sinewy – strong from years of hauling and cutting dead meat. The crumbs went up her nose and into her mouth, they stuck to her eyelids. Then he pulled her out of the bowl by the hair and flung her against the wall. She curled up in the foetal position, survival her only thought, afraid to think of what was coming. He let fly a few kicks, cursing, a madman. He was so drunk, half the time he would stumble and hit the wall. Eventually he ran out of breath, ranted and raved about stupid fucking bitches, greedy cows.

It wasn't her he was kicking. At least she thought not. It was them. His mother and sisters.

Now Norah releases a shuddering sigh. Christmases. That had been the worst one really. The very worst.

Liam glances at her tense face, the only sound in the car the swish of the windscreen wipers.

'I know it's hard Norah. But the more incidences we have to work with the better our case will be.'

'I don't know Liam. No matter what. I could tell you lots of things. Terrible things. Things I find hard to believe myself. But. I took a human life. The most unforgiveable sin. I did have options, I'm not stupid I know I could have, should have, walked away. Particularly after Teasie died. I always knew I could….go. But to what? And why? He needed me and it wasn't all bad…..or maybe…I don't know. I thought I needed him. I did need him. I just couldn't. I thought….' She stops, stares out the passenger window at the rain drumming down on the countryside. 'I can't explain it to myself Liam. How can I make anyone else understand, live my life as it was then. I didn't think beyond each day to be honest.'

'Norah, I'm a solicitor, I believe in justice and the law. But in this case it was self-defence. You told me you thought he would kill you that night – why should his life be more valuable than yours?'

'But he hadn't before. Maybe he wouldn't have. Oh God.' She covers her face with her hands then thumps them down in fists on her knees.

Liam pulls the car into the side of the road and puts on the hazards.

'Listen to me. Maybe he would have. You have to accept that it was you or him, Norah – if you realise that it will make your own life, your future, more peaceful – from my viewpoint you had little or no choice that evening. I never knew Tom but I know you and I'm glad you're still here. All of us, myself, John, Sinead and her family. Please let us help you Norah, all of us that want to. Let us do for you what your parents and your aunt and uncle would do if they were here. Think about it at least. Write it down, tape it if you feel you can't sit opposite someone and tell them. It might even help you to come to terms with Tom's death.' He puts his left arm about her stiff shoulders and lays his right hand lightly on her clasped hands.

She keeps her head bent.

'I did try to leave once. But...I went back, there was Teasie you see, the strokes, she needed minding and stuff that money was needed for. And he was always in bits afterwards, so sorry, and things would be good for ages, once he just had me things were okay. We had each other. It seemed enough for him and if things were quiet with him it was enough for me too.' She shakes her head, looks at Liam's uncomprehending face.

He sighs, starts up the car again. 'We better go, Sergeant Bradley will be waiting at the house. Just think about what I've said Norah. The more you give us, the stronger your case.'

Norah stares out at hedges and fields briefly illuminated in the car's headlights. They pass the figure of a woman walking on the road, head down against the driving rain, reminding Norah of that night, that Christmas night.

She remembers that night, that Christmas night. Walking, half stumbling those three miles back to Teasie's house after she lay still in a heap in the kitchen and he eventually conked out on the couch. She felt hopeless, for the first time since they had married she felt she couldn't cope. She had to get out. Teasie's was naturally in darkness when she got there for it must have been two or three in the morning. She remembers how confused she felt, as if her head was stuffed with a really bad cold. Maybe she should go back. Teasie was old. Frail now Frank was gone. How could she bring this down on her head?

It was freezing and Norah had no coat, no keys. Nothing. She had walked away from her own house with nothing. She stood in the yard looking at Teasie's cottage, yearned to be cocooned within its walls. She could see the little red light of the Sacred Heart lamp glowing in the kitchen, the dull glow of the light from the bathroom reflected up the hall. She turned towards the road again, then back towards the house. She was exhausted. Whatever she was to do it had to take little or no energy. The hens started to fuss, sensing someone in the yard. Norah walked to the hen house and bending down she let herself in amongst the poultry. They objected for a while but eventually realized she presented no danger and clucked back into fluffed up sleeping positions.

Norah pulled as much straw about her as she could to minimize the cold and had dozed a little until the first fingers of light crept between the cracks of wood. Opening the low door she crawled out into the yard and slipped up to the kitchen window.

Teasie was moving about the kitchen with sticks and bits of turf, lighting the range. Norah's breath had caught in her throat, she was about to bring Teasie's quiet world crashing down.

Norah tapped on the kitchen window and tried to call Teasie's name, but only a croak came out. Her voice sounded like she had a severe sore throat. Teasie screamed, then realising who the creature at the window was, had opened the door. It was one of the rare times Norah heard Teasie curse.

'Jesus, Jesus. What happened?' Teasie looked at the state of the girl she had reared in front of her. 'It's him, isn't it. Norah. Norah. Sit. Sit.' The older woman was trembling, she went to the sink and had filled a bowl of warm water and tried to clean some of the dirt and scratches from Norah's face and hands. She was in almost as shocked a state as Norah was.

'God. Oh Lord, I knew something was wrong. But. Lord, Lord, Norah. This has to stop.' She was crying as she dabbed at Norah's face.

Norah felt so ashamed, bringing it all back to Teasie's door. She had tried so hard with Tom, tried to make it work but he never changed. Every time he'd swear it would be different but then something would go wrong, she'd say the wrong thing or cook the wrong meal or not have the house clean enough. Or something would happen in the shop or up at his mothers and she wouldn't be able to lift his mood.

Teasie picked bits of stuffing and straw from Norah's hair, making soft little comforting noises, asking what had happened and had it happened before. Norah knew she shouldn't, Teasie wasn't able for this but she needed to tell, right then she needed to tell someone. She even told her about the sex – how it was, or rather wasn't. Not unless he was angry. She couldn't meet Teasie's eyes, her face aflame with shame. She knew people wondered why there were no children yet. She prayed that the odd time they managed to complete the act of sex that she would be pregnant. Maybe then it would stop. Maybe if she gave him a family he might stop.

Norah had never seen Teasie so angry.

'Don't dare wish for that. You should be glad there are no childer for him to punch too. Don't dare blame yourself. Tom Furlong is bad. Bad out. You're finished with him Norah. You'll come back here. I'm going to ring Denis Bradley.' The frightened old woman of a few minutes ago had gone. The fiery little Teasie was back. Bristling with the thoughts of a battle to save her precious Norah.

Teasie sent Norah in for a bath. Norah stayed in it until the water was almost cold, thinking, not thinking. When she came out Denis Bradley was in the kitchen. Denis wasn't stationed that long at the Mohill station, which covered Tibraden. As a child he had spent summers in the area with his grandparents and he and had known Frank well. He was sitting at the kitchen table holding the sobbing Teasie's hands in his.

Denis was gentle and kindly, asked Norah about 'her troubles'. Norah wasn't sure about involving the guards and tried to make light of it; reluctant to be disloyal, she made it out to be a drink-fuelled squabble that had gotten rough. Teasie got annoyed with Norah and said Tom was nothing but a violent little bugger. Norah smiles a little now, she had been almost as shocked at Teasie using words she normally reserved for rodents or foxes to describe Tom as she had been at the events of that night. Everything was out of sync.

Denis calmed Teasie down and Norah busied herself making tea. As she stood waiting for the kettle to boil Tom's car had pulled into the yard. She could see his face as he got out of the car and her heart jumped. His whole body was slumped, defeated, the anger gone, that look on his face you sometimes see on those who have heard of a sudden death. Norah couldn't help the pang of deep sympathy that ran through her. She knew how sorry he would be, how upset. Her instincts were, as always, to forgive.

In that moment she knew she shouldn't have left her

home, should have sorted it out herself. With him. For only the two of them could fix it. Or so she thought.

When Teasie heard the car door slamming she knew who it must be and she reacted like a fighting bantam cock.

'That man will not set foot inside this house. Norah. Listen to me. He will never lay a finger on you again. Go tell him, Denis.'

Denis went out and whatever he said Tom went away.

Denis came back and talked to the women for a while. About statements and courts, how Norah could look for a restraining order on Tom. Norah had been horrified. This would ruin Tom completely. Not just him personally, but the businesses, everything.

'Can't you just warn him….tell him to leave us be?' she asked Denis. He stayed a little longer, talking gently to them, then said he'd come back later with another garda to take statements.

When he was gone Norah cried her eyes out. She didn't want to make things worse, bring trouble on Tom's head. She just wanted peace and quiet, things to be the way they should be, to get Tom to a stage where she could manage him most of the time.

Eventually she stopped crying and calmed down. Teasie made soup and they put on the television, watched some silly movie, the dog curled on the old mat in front of the range. Norah had wished to God she had never left the comfort of that little house. Teasie dozed in her chair and Norah's heart ached for her. She had aged so much since Frank died, seemed so frail in comparison to the hardy little woman Norah had known as a child.

A car pulled into the yard again and Norah went to the door and opened it. It was Tom. He sat in the car, had the headlights trained on the door. Norah stood her ground. Then he turned off the engine and lights and still he sat in silence. Norah assumed he was staring at her, but she couldn't see his face. The dog wandered out past her and went towards the car wagging his tail.

Tom stepped out of the car.

He looked awful and was so remorseful. 'Please. Please', he said. 'I don't know what... apart from the whiskey...possessed me. Jesus, Norah, I feel worse than you look. I swear, I swear. One last chance. I'll stop drinking, go for counselling. Anything, anything you want. Don't leave me Norah. I won't survive without you. You know that. You're my whole life. Please just let me show you I can change.'

It was the agreement to counselling that made her think he might be serious, might be ready to try. He'd always laughed at the whole concept of counselling before. 'Fools and their money,' he would snort, 'I don't need to pay someone to listen to me, tell me what to do.'

So Norah took a step or two towards the car.

Jesus, she thinks now, it's always the little steps we take that drop us into the darkest holes.

He had been crying, was crying, leaning against his car his shoulders heaving, great big shudders. Norah had never seen him cry before. Not like this. Not since he was a child.

She went to him, put her arms about him – told him to stop, that they could work it out together.

Then Teasie came out of the door waving the poker shouting at both of them.

'Fool! Foolish, foolish child! Can't you see he's bad through and through, just like his mother and his sisters. Get back in the kitchen now Norah......and stay there while I talk to the big man that is your husband, talk to him with this poker, his language!'

Norah rushed back to the little woman standing there in her Fairisle cardigan, her face fierce, the poker held aloft. Tom lifted both his hands, told Teasie he had done wrong, would never do it again, a bad mistake he said.

'Mistake!' she screamed, 'you call what you did to her a mistake?? A mistake is an accident, Tom Furlong, not something as deliberate and horrid as what you did to her...,' Then suddenly her voice had gone to a gurgle, a choked gargling noise came from her as her face crumpled and she dropped the poker, lifted her hands to her head and stumbled forward. Tom moved quicker than Norah and caught Teasie before she hit the damp ground.

Liam's car pulls into the laneway that leads to Norah's house. The house they had brought Teasie back to after three months in Sligo General Hospital. The house Norah had nursed her beloved aunt in for the three years following that St Stephen's night, through a number of smaller strokes and then through the final one that left her completely incapacitated.

Whatever else, Tom had been great, wonderful, through Teasie's illness. He brought Norah to the hospital almost every morning when Teasie was an inpatient and collected her every night. He never made any demands on Norah at that time and when it came time for Teasie to leave hospital he provided everything that was needed for the house to make Teasie's life easier and more comfortable. Denis Bradley had called back at the time and asked Norah did she want to proceed with the complaint she had thought about making on St Stephen's night – but how could she? Not then, things were better than they'd ever been, Teasie was getting the best of care. Norah had thought all her troubles were over.

Norah knows what Liam thinks, what they all think, because she thinks it too. How stupid, gullible she had been. She feels culpable for what had happened by nature of that stupidity. But she had wanted to believe Tom, wanted so much to believe him.

Chapter Thirteen

I had arranged to meet Norah upstairs in the Winding Stair bookshop and café for lunch the day she arrived in Dublin. When I went into the café she was sitting at a table near the window, looking out at the boardwalk along the quays and the passing crowds of Christmas shoppers. The winter sun streamed through the window, the light catching in her hair

'She can be good looking,' I thought, surprised.

'Hey!' I said, plopping myself into the old wooden school-backed chair opposite, 'You found it! We'll make a city girl of you yet!'

'Liam drove me up, he dropped me in O'Connell Street and pointed me in the right direction. I don't think I could live here full time. Lord save us, so many people! Where are they all going?'

There was a small paper HMV bag on the bare brown table top in front of her

'What's this?' I picked up the bag, slipped out a CD, 'Shopping?'

'I went into a big music shop, passing the time until I met you. I haven't heard these songs in years. It was cheap,' she added as if she thought I might scold her for squandering money.

'Burl Ives!' I chortled, 'I'd say my mother hardly remembers him.' I flipped it over and read the tracks. It was like a step back into a black and white movie. Norah leaned over and tapped on the title of track five.

'See that one? *Leonora*? Uncle Frank used to sing that for me when I was a child. I can still hear him. He had a beautiful voice. Saturday night was always bath night. Teasie would draw my bath and help me wash my hair. After I would sit on a little stool in front of the range, the door open to dry my hair. Teasie would brush it out. It was longer then, so long I could sit on it. It would get fiercely tangled and was a torture to me, but Teasie loved it and loved to brush it "Your crown of rippling sun blushed hair" she'd say. Frank would laugh, call her soft and sing to distract me from the pain of the detangling.' She sang softly herself,

'Leonora, let your hair hang down,
Leonora let your hair hang down,
I'll give you a ring and
A wedding in the Spring............
Leonora let your hair hang down'

She smiled and shook her head. 'He always said Burl Ives must've been thinking of me when he sang that song and my Mam and Dad probably called me Norah after the Leonora of the title. I remember....' she stopped.

'What?' I prompted.

'Oh nothing. It's just... Tom sang too. Not that song, although he knew it because I was always humming it. No, he would sing *Norah*. You know that one?

'When I first said I loved only you Norah
and you said I loved only me', she sang the first few bars under her breath.

'I know the tune but I think I knew the Norah in it as "Maggie".'

'That's the very one! I've heard that version too. Tom has a lovely singing voice too, not as good as Frank's was, but he can hold a tune. He always sings with his eyes closed, beating time on his knee with his hand, palm upwards.' She demonstrated.

I glanced around self-consciously. These matter of fact

comments about her dead husband were a bit unnerving. Particularly when she spoke of him in the present tense.

I also couldn't help having a quick look at all the faces at tables near us, afraid one might be some horrible paparazzi fella who had spotted Norah, recognised her and was trailing her. Our conversations would appear screamed all over the tabloid press. I could see the front page, us sitting at the table under a banner headline 'Vicious husband slayer singing ballads with unknown companion in well-known Dublin café.' How would Mother explain that to the bridge club!

I grinned to myself as I ordered lunch, John always said I had the most lurid imagination of anyone he knew. But with Norah as a 'husband-slayer' in a country as small as Ireland one would think the journos would find it easy to locate her. I also thought the fact that Tom had been a butcher would give the papers delicious headlines to play with. Perhaps the murder of a butcher with a small business in rural Ireland by his timid wife wasn't big enough news in a society hungry for the latest antics of a score of minor celebrities and politicians.

I was feeling quite pleased with my suggested arrangements for Norah. It's easier to get lost in a city. It was also an opportunity for me to see a little more of John and to finally bring amicable closure to whatever feelings I had had for him. I hoped I wouldn't regret it.

Norah was only teasing with her smoked salmon. She crumbled warm, fresh brown bread onto her plate and intently picked at the crumbs with her fingertips.

'Is it not good?' I asked, indicating the salmon.

'No. I mean yes, it's lovely. I'm just not very hungry. Kate made me a big breakfast, then I had the cup of tea with Liam...' She tailed off again, 'To be honest Sinead, I'm too frightened to eat. I think I might throw up I'm so nervous.'

I reached across the table, squeezed her hand. 'Relax, you're with family now. Us Breslins, or what's left of us, must stick together!'

'Family. God I never thought. After Teasie there was only Tom. And he. Well. There was only him.' She raised her serviette to her eyes, dabbed at them, blew her nose. 'Sorry. I'm sick of myself constantly blubbering. The doctor says it's because I'm letting go, grieving and accepting things, all that stuff. Do you know after Teasie died I don't think I cried for years – not unless it was in physical pain and that's different, they're tears wrung from you, you can't stop them.' She pushed the tissue up her sleeve.

'I know it was me that did it like, made him die. And I know it sounds mad but I miss him. Not the beatings and the silences and the rest but the other times, the good times; it wasn't all bad.'

I nodded, tried to understand. 'We're such creatures of habit,' I thought. When you're used to something, no matter how bad or hard it is, I suppose there must be some kind of a void when it's gone. Personally I found it hard to think she missed the bastard, but to each their own.

I ordered tea for us both and apple cake with sticky toffee sauce for myself. Norah teased a little of the sauce onto a teaspoon to taste and remarked how like the caramel sauce for sponge cake Teasie used to make it was. She always relaxed when she spoke of Frank and Teasie. At least she had some good memories of childhood. She told me anecdotes about growing up a city kid in rural Ireland and I swapped them with yarns of my own.

We laughed at her description of her first day at the country school. A little 'jackeen' in what would've been regarded as very fancy clothes and black patent shoes. Black patent shoes! She must've looked exotic to the other children back then. I mentioned my memory of her frilly socks.

'Lord! Those socks! I loved them, but they weren't the most practical thing to wear when you had to scramble over a ditch and through a boggy field to get to the school.' She smiled.

'Would you believe in the end I balled them up and

threw them in the river? When I started in the school Frank used to walk me down and collect me every day. But then the others started to tease – after all I was almost eight – so I asked Frank to stop. He would be standing at the gable end of the house instead, waiting for me to come home; he would wave and beckon to me as soon as he saw me coming over the brow of the hill. I remember missing my friends in Dublin so much, particularly at lunchtime, everyone seemed to have a best friend and the games they played in the yard were slightly different to the ones I knew. I was so nervous I'd blether too much if anyone talked to me and I suppose the Dublin accent put them off.' Norah paused, added milk and sugar to her tea.

'I can't imagine you with a Dublin accent.' Norah has that lovely soft Leitrim accent, the sibilant 's', 'allus' for always, 'Char-less' for Charles.

'God, I got terrible teasing for it, Tom's sister Carmel and her friend, Anna Hanvey. They were a right pair! They decided I was stuck up and they were going to take me down a peg or two, so they waylaid me on the way home from school one afternoon. To reach Frank and Teasie's house I had to walk up the field at the back of the school, scramble over a ditch and walk about half a mile up by the river. Boggy old land it was but with lots of hedges and brambles at the river's edge. This day there was a ferocious downpour at going home time. The teacher kept those of us that didn't get the school bus in the schoolhouse until the rain eased off. 'Twas no big deal being a bit late coming home from school then, it would be assumed you were playing or chatting on the way home.'

'One part of the path was narrow and if there were more than one walking it you would have to walk in single file.' Her eyes were miles away, back walking that path perhaps. 'On a dry day it didn't matter so much – one person could scramble up on the ditch, but on a really wet day your shoes and socks would get destroyed in the wet boggy soil. After that day, the day I'm talking about, I wore wellies to school, carried my shoes in my bag and changed at the schoolhouse.' Norah sipped at her tea, wrinkling her nose as if smelling something bad.

'Anna and Carmel were standing shoulder to shoulder at that spot. I can still see Anna Hanvey's ferrety little face.

'Here she comes', she sneered. 'Fancy socks Norah Breslin. How can auld Frank and Teasie Breslin afford them socks?'

I stayed about ten paces away from them, scared. Told them my mother had bought the socks.

'How can your Mammy buy you stuff when she's dead?' Carmel came swaggering towards me. Christ, she was a bitch even then.

'She bought them before....they were for my Communion...for good wear.' I could feel the tears coming but I swallowed them. If those two saw me cry they'd have won.

'Well, there'll be no more fancy stuff for you Norah Breslin. Everyone knows that Frank and Teasie Breslin haven't two pence to rub together. Sure Teasie Breslin has to knit and sew for everyone for a few pound and that auld chest of Frank's makes him useless for work.' Carmel had her arms folded and she leaned forward towards me; she was so close I could feel the spit from her words. I took a step back, right into a huge boggy puddle, the dirty water seeped into my shoe and crept up the sock. I yelped and they laughed. Then Anna Hanvey pushed me and I stumbled, putting the other foot into the puddle. They ran away shouting;

"Norah, Norah with the fancy socks,
Now Norah, Norah has no nice frocks.
Norah, Norah without a Mam,
And no-one, no one gives a damn." She said this in that horrible singsong voice children use to tease.

'The little bitches!' I burned with indignation for little Norah.

She shrugged. 'They were kids, horrible kids, but just kids. Anyway I took the socks off and threw them in the river, ran home with the patent leather of my shoes all mucky and chafing my bare feet. Carmel didn't grow up to be much nicer than the child she had been. Nothing was ever good enough, big enough, expensive enough. The mother wasn't the most diligent so Carmel was often left watching the others, bullied them unmercifully. I suppose its no wonder they all turned out the way they did.'

'How many were in his family' I asked

'Just the three, he was the youngest. Carmel still lives in the old house. I don't know where Fidelma is. She disappeared to England after the mother died and nobody has heard from her since. They weren't close. In fact I think they hated each other. You know the way in some families a problem in the house draws them closer, here they just set against each other, each trying to get noticed in different ways and totally ignored by both parents. Eileen didn't look after them properly, the bottle was her friend and with the few bob they had she could afford it and afford to make things look okay on the outside; so as far as she was concerned her family was a success. The father, Seamus, well.... he just stayed out working, making money and kept his mouth shut – anything for a quiet life.' Norah pursed her lips, finished her tea and pushed away her cup. 'Maybe if he had stood up to her, got her help for the drinking, maybe then the kids would've been different and....oh well, he had problems too and I suppose it's always easy to live others' lives in retrospect.'

I glanced at my watch.

'I have to go back to work. I'll walk you to the bus stop. I didn't put the alarm on. I'll show you all that this evening.' I stood up, pushing a set of keys and a slip of paper with directions to the apartment towards her.

Norah picked up the keys and stood too, looking at the piece of paper.

'Okay. Listen Sinead, I can't thank you enough. I'll pay for lunch. You're so kind. I'm really grateful. I hope I won't be any bother.'

'You won't. We'll get along just fine, particularly if you're going to treat me to nice lunches! Everything will work out, you wait and see.' Impulsively I leaned forward and hugged her.

Norah returned my hug with a pat to my back. 'Oh don't. You'll set me off crying again and the whole of Dublin will be looking at me.'

'Believe me Norah, the whole of Dublin would only give you a moment's thought if you ran up O'Connell Street stark naked at the height of rush hour!'

Shaking her head in amusement at the image, Norah gathered her bags and paid the bill. I put her on the bus to Glasnevin and returned to work.

Chapter Fourteen

Norah sits on the bus. She wonders is this her first time on a double decker bus. She would have liked to go upstairs. But. She might miss her stop. Maybe she had been on an upper deck before. Maybe her mother had taken her. Would the buses have been different then? She supposes Dublin was different then.

She's glad to be on the bus. Out of the crowds. The bus got fuller and fuller at every stop. People were standing. It had started raining and she could smell the rain off the wool coat of the woman sitting beside her. She counts the stops. That way she would know again. Although maybe the bus hadn't stopped at all the stops?

She glances at the piece of paper in her hand, Sinead has nice writing. Norah's writing is more childish, rounder. She thinks so anyway. She had showed the bus driver the note when she was paying her fare. A big black man. Norah had felt a little nervous of him, it was only the second time she'd talked to a black man. She was afraid she'd say the wrong thing, show she wasn't used to black people and upset him. She wondered was she allowed to call them black people and who could she ask without seeming stupid. The driver had a big ring on his finger with a purple stone, the light caught in it and bounced off the coins she proffered in fare. He pointed to the chute and she put them in. She had laughed nervously and asked again that he tell her when to get off, he smiled and said something in a rolling deep voice that she couldn't understand. She had looked at him expectantly and he repeated it, this time she understood. He would call 'Bons Secours' over the intercom, that was the hospital near her stop. He asked was she on her holidays.

She had just nodded. She supposed she was in a way. The last time she had had a conversation with a – non white person – had been in a hospital. He too had been kind.

The buildings on the street outside were old, like in a film about lords and ladies, one of those English period pieces. She hadn't expected that. She had seen Dublin on the news and in a soap opera on tv but it was different once you were here. There was a lot of traffic and the bus moved slowly. She had been worried that she wouldn't understand the Dublin accent if it was strong, like some of the characters in 'Fair City'. She smiles to herself now. Hardly anyone on the bus spoke English; she heard what she thought was Chinese and maybe Russian. But the rest could be anything. Two girls sitting behind her are gabbing at a fierce rate.

'They seem to be enjoying themselves anyway and they are further from home than me,' she thought, trying to fight the feeling of fear at being so far from home. She is scared. She has been scared nearly all the time since Tom died. A different fear.

'Bons Secours'. She jumps, stands up, sits again and gathers her bags and pushes through the standing crowd to the front.

'Now Lady, this is it. Enjoy your holiday!' His big white teeth wink like the lights in his ring. She smiles and clambers awkwardly from the bus. There is a fine drizzle, drops as fine as the eye of a needle in dim light. The air smells different to home. No turf fires for one. There are petrol fumes and dust and something else. Something she can't name. Norah has a strong sense of smell. Could smell dirt and damp or any nasty odours that exist in any place she enters. She cannot sit easy until she tracks the source, identifies it and eliminates it if possible.

She reads the directions again, looking up the road to see the block of apartments she is to find. They're not where she thinks they should be.

'Lord, maybe I got off at the wrong stop after all.' She feels the panic rising from her stomach, looks wildly around again. Then she studies the note, the ink blurring in the rain. Oh Lord, if she's lost? There's the hospital, the shops Sinead mentioned... there, there's the apartment building! How had she missed it first time around? Exactly as Sinead had described it. Face flushed with pleasure she stuffs the paper in her pocket and hurries towards the buildings.

It takes three tries to key in the combination to the main door and she is starting to fill with frustrated tears when the door finally clicks and she can enter. She doesn't trust the lift, what if it got stuck and nobody came? So she climbs the two flights of stairs and walks the quiet corridor to apartment 15. Her bags feel heavy, that last hurdle she thinks. You always feel you couldn't go even one more minute and then it just ends.

She negotiates both locks and steps into a dim hallway, the waning light from outside peeping through an open door at the end of a short corridor into which are set three other doors, the first one on the right is ajar and it is, thank God, a bathroom.

Norah's muscles are all relaxing and she drops her bags, loosening her clothes on the way through the door and sits with relief on the toilet. The bathroom suite and the tiles are white, a dark blue raised border around the bath and again half way up the wall. It pleases Norah, so modern. The bath needs cleaning and she notices a rim of soap and toothpaste in the sink. She flushes, readjusts her skirt and tights and as she washes her hands for three counted minutes she looks about for a cloth and cleaner.

She spots a cleaning liquid but is afraid to use the cloth, it looks too good. Stepping into the corridor again she opens her holdall and takes out an old pair of pants. She pours a little of the liquid into the sink and scrubs and rinses until the porcelain gleams and the taps shine. 'Good,' she thinks, a small part of her at home.

Taking the few steps past the other doors she pushes open the door at the end of the hallway. The room is dim. Norah finds what she assumes must be a light switch. A circular knob. It's where you would assume the light switch would be. She pushes and bright light fills the room; then she discovers you can twist to dim the light.

'Lovely,' she murmurs. You could make a room peaceful and quiet with these lights, she thought, especially if you could combine them with an open fire in the winter.

The room is pleasant, L-shaped with a small kitchen-cum-dining area in the smaller horizontal. Stepping to the right she is in the larger vertical part of the 'L', the living room area. She is behind a two-seater brown leather sofa which faces a blank tv screen. On the single leather chair backing onto the wall is a highly ornamented throw. The chair faces a set of drawn curtains.

Norah goes to the curtains and opens them. It's almost dark, early December. From her vantage point she can see hundreds of lights from windows, shops, cars. She laughs with quiet pleasure. It's so busy compared to Tibraden; she can hear the traffic even through the closed windows. She stands for a while not thinking, just looking. The view was like a Christmas tree. Tangled fairy lights trailing off into the distance, winking and twinkling.

It sounds wrong; noise outside – quiet within. At home it was the other way, at least when Tom was home. TV, radio, CDs and singing, shouting.

'Do men find it hard to be quiet?' Norah asked shortly after they had married.

Tom had laughed, roared jokingly like a bear, grabbed and tickled her.

Norah feels the salt on her lips. The tears do not surprise her.

She draws the curtains again and switches on the television.

'Tea,' she thought. 'Tea.'

The business of filling the kettle and searching for tea, cups, milk and cutlery soothes her again. Carrying the cup of tea back to the sofa she notices the carpet for the first time. Neutral beige type, bland. Norah sits on the sofa and places her cup on the coffee table. She reaches down to feel the carpet. The same. Norah once had a carpet like this in her own living room. She had picked it herself thinking it would only do until the babies came. Tom had laughed. The babies never came but the carpet went after two years. Those first bloodstains wouldn't come out. One day when Norah came home from a walk Tom had it ripped up and burning on a bonfire in the yard. He fitted a new patterned green and cream carpet the following night. Norah had never liked it.

She touches her cheek, can still feel the imprint of that first carpet there.

She had opened her eyes, the only noise the tick of the clock on the mantle and her breath through her bloodied nose. Her cheek was pressed against the carpet, from here she could see the coir pattern, beige, cream and brown coarse little wool hairs spun around each other, one of the little hairs looked orange, though that may have been a slight fleck of blood on it. She'd never noticed before how intricate the pattern was.

She had tried to move, wondered what the noise was. Then she realised it was herself. Moans. Everywhere hurt, her back and upper legs most. The broken chair lay near the door.

She had fallen in a crouch shouting,

'Stop. Don't. Stop'.

Then she realised it was pointless – he was so enraged his eyes were tiny; she knew she couldn't reach him. So she had saved her energy, arms over her head, praying for it to be over. She must've blacked out, she remembered grunts of exertion from him then nothing.

That was the first time. The first big one anyway. Before there had been a few slaps and pushes, mostly sharp words or, worse, endless silences; then there had been the occasional drink-induced rants. The silences were the worst, the tension of waiting was unbearable. Not knowing what it was she had done wrong. Once he had pulled a handful of her hair out.

That night, the night of the first big beating he had been drinking. Tom normally didn't drink much, not in the beginning anyway; he died with hangovers apart from anything else. She can't remember now what had enraged him that night. Maybe his tea had spoiled in waiting for him. A man should have a decent meal ready when he came home, she vaguely remembered him saying. Maybe that had been another time. But it had been something like that. Something so simple it was ridiculous the rage into which he flew.

Usually it was her own fault, she had learned how to handle him; marriage was never easy – Teasie had told her the first year or two would be about them getting used to each other's little ways. Teasie. Lying on that carpet she had thought,

'I mustn't let her know.'

She had been so ashamed.

That night it had taken Norah an hour to get herself off the living room carpet and into the bathroom. A hot bath had nearly killed her but at least she was clean. The marks on her face weren't bad, a burn mark from the carpet and slight scratches around her eye. The bruising on her back and legs would fade.

As she lay in the bath she had placed a hot cloth over her face to soothe the scratches. The heat of the cloth drew tears from her and her whole body shook silently, displacing water, causing tiny ripples. She could hear Tom snoring in the bedroom. She wondered dare she lie in the spare bedroom.

She decided not, she couldn't take another slap that

day. Patting herself gently dry with the big green bath sheet, she then wrapped it around her. She cleaned the bath and toilet, placed the soiled clothing in the laundry basket and went quietly into their bedroom.

Tom was on his back, mouth slightly open, his torso bare, the quilt strewn across his lower body. Norah left the door ajar and crept to her side of the bed. Tom liked the door ajar.

'Mammy used to close the door when we were small and it would be pitch dark. Carmel allus tried to frighten us. Waiting until we were nearly sleeping and shouting "Boo!". Or telling us horrible tales! It got so I could not, could not sleep unless I knew there was light somewhere. I never grew out of it. I still feel nervous in a closed room at night.' He had looked away telling her this.

'Poor fella,' she had said and kissed him. He had lain his head on her shoulder and fell asleep; she lay still for hours so as not to disturb him. What had happened to that? Where had that gone?

She spread the damp towel on the radiator and slipped into the bed, glad for once that Tom liked her to sleep naked, the contact with the sheets alone enough to make her wince. She lay on one side, facing away from Tom, manoeuvring herself into the most comfortable position. Tom grunted and moved beside her. She stiffened but his breathing was still deep. She lay, dozing ,willing sleep to come, drifting in and out of half dreams, Frank calling her from the gable end of the house, dancing with Tom at a disco in Carrick, laughing at some quick remark Teasie made.

She woke with a start when Tom rolled on his side behind her. His still-sleeping arm clamped on her shoulder, the fingers dangling near her breast. She stiffened and he woke. She felt the change in him.

His fingers sought the breast, stroked then squeezed the nipple. She didn't move, felt his erection push against her backside. His hand moved down her arm to her waist and then her hip. There he gripped. She felt his other hand slip

155

between the hip nearest the mattress and the sheet, he lifted her slightly and she pushed gently backwards. She prayed he would not lose the erection. She kept perfectly still, although the grip on her hip was hurting her. He found and entered her, pushed grunting. She felt him grow, his heart hammering. His leg clamping her in the position he wanted, he thrust quickly in and out a few times and came with a shudder.

He relaxed and released his grip, patting her upper arm as you would a good dog. Still she didn't move, the only indication she was awake the tears slipping down her face.

'Well, you found us,' Sinead's voice calls as she comes in the front door.

'Jesus!' Norah jumps.

'Sorry, sorry,' Sinead came laughing into the room. 'Did I startle you?'

'No. Yes...... I mean...,' Norah laughed guiltily herself, 'I was daydreaming, miles away.'

Chapter Fifteen

Christmas came and Norah and I went to Mullaghadone. Mother happy to have us down for the days between Christmas Eve and St. Stephen's Day. I had to get back to Dublin then as our panto opened on January third and we were full pelt into final rehearsals.

Norah was a great addition to our small gathering in Mullaghadone, her 'ladylike' behaviour endearing her to Mother and her droll sense of humour and simple ease to be around made her an easy house guest. She's a fantastic cook; Rachel and myself were branded 'hopeless' and banned to the living room where we sipped mulled wine and reminisced about previous Christmases, occasionally asking Mother to referee on some item we had totally different recollections of. Mother's recall was usually completely different to both of ours, which served to increase our laughing bickering.

Mother and Norah served up a magnificent meal, leek and potato soup, a goose and roasties and all the trimmings followed by a flaming Christmas pudding with brandy butter. Then Rachel and I took over the kitchen for the clean up (although they were both consummate housekeepers and had tidied up as they went) and when we went to join them in the living room after an hour we found both of them flaked out in front of *Eastenders*. Rachel commented there was enough drama in Norah's life without the doings of Albert Square to contend with.

John and Eoin arrived Christmas night and Norah proved herself to be a daring and more than competent card player. With Rachel and myself we made up a fairly lively table, particularly when there were a few drinks involved. Eoin is a complete rascal and not beyond either the most outrageous bluffs or even a bit of misleading information. I'll not go as far as say cheat because we did have a solicitor at the table who declared there was insufficient evidence to make such an accusation.

Evidence! Who needed evidence with the devil's own gleam in Eoin's eye. I could see why Rachel was mad about him and he her. They couldn't keep their hands off each other, totally unself-conscious little brushes and touches, big bear hugs and tickles, passing kisses and teasing slaps. This would normally drive me mad but it seemed innate in them and not in the least irritating.

There was a big Whist drive organised in the parish hall for St Stephen's night after the 'Echoes o'er the Lough'. This was a tradition that had been abandoned some years ago as older musicians died and younger ones moved away but had been revived the previous year by the community council of which both Rachel and John were leading lights. It involves a group of musicians with fiddles, accordions, squeeze boxes, whistles and even once a set of bagpipes; anything that a tune could be coaxed from gathering at one side of the lake accompanied by the people who lived nearer that side. Another group of musicians stood on the farther bank with their neighbours.

The only rule was no electronic amplification allowed and the first group to play was decided by a toss of a coin in the pub on Christmas Eve. People from adjoining townlands and parishes came in to hear as well and it had been a huge success the last Christmas. A repeat had been demanded by all involved. And even if each tune wasn't great it still couldn't fail to make feet tap for the life that was in it. Sometimes it would bring a tear to the eye of the older people. The slagging and camaraderie was worth the journey out to it, no matter what the weather.

The last 'Echoes o'er the Lough' had been on a damp St Stephen's night and all we could see on the other side had been the headlights of the cars, beaming across the lake, illuminating the needle-fine drizzle; some flickering torches showing silhouettes of the musicians and the faint echoes of the tunes floating across the water. The theory was that your side replied with a tune in a similar vein, so if they had played a carol you answered with one, or a jig with a jig or a plaintive air with one as mournful. Everyone who could get out at all came to it. Then down to the hall for a warming mug of tea and scones and onto the serious business of St Stephen's night, the annual Whist drive.

These were serious card players, ruthless and way above my useless attempts at participation. I could see Mother battling with her desire to show off Norah's prowess as a card player and her fear that someone would connect her with the murder.

'I hope you don't mind, Kate. I have a visitor calling here this evening,' Norah blushed and looked down at the cup of coffee in her hands.

'Mind, of course I don't mind. You're to treat this place as your home place do you hear me!' I could see the look of relief in Mother's face as she gushed a little. Norah stood up and went to Mother, put her arms about her and hugged her.

'You have no idea what this means to me, Kate. All of you. It's like finding family all over again. Something I thought I'd lost forever.'

Mother filled up. Mother! 'Silly girl. Of course we're family. Why if Sean were here he'd.......' Norah just hugged her again; she was child-like in her affections. If I'd been through half of what she had I think I would have been the opposite, built up a roll of barbed wire about me to keep all comers out.

'Who's the visitor Norah? I thought Liam was gone to his wife's homeplace in Kerry.' I was sitting in Dad's chair, still in pyjamas and dressing-gown despite the fact it was almost lunch time, idly flicking through a cookbook Norah had bought my mother.

'It's that man I told you about, Charles Donnelly, the man that was at the house earlier that day...... you know, the occupational therapist that got friendly with us when Teasie was in hospital. He was interested in gardening. I'd root cuttings for him and things like that. You'll like him. He's a nice man.' She was babbling a little and my antennae went up.

'How did he know you were here?' I stood up and stretched, feigning indifference. 'Not that it's any of my business,' I added as she coloured even more.

'T'was Liam contacted him. Charles agreed to come visit me when I was down next. You see, he saw. Charles that is. He saw some of the.. you know.. the bruising... and I think Teasie tried to communicate with him, but her speech was... there was one day...well...Liam thinks he would be a good witness to prove the consistent... abuse.' She stopped for a moment, fingered her hair. 'I hate that word and I hate getting him involved. He's such a nice man. And I'd be worried about his job as well. He has to go all around the county visiting sick people, trying to organise things for them, handrails and easy access showers and the like, maybe some of them would be nervous, like...if they knew....well you know what people are like..,' she tailed off.

'Well, damn to them anyway'. Mother. Mother, font of all that was 'proper'. Norah had certainly wrought a change in her. I laughed.

'Right you are Ma, damn to them all!'

'Sinead. Ma! I despair of you, at your age – I won't even query who you're mixing with in Dublin.'

Norah and I grinned at each other – Mother was such a bundle of contradictions, but at least I could see her for more than the single-minded snob I had seen her as for so many years.

I went off to shower and dress, John and I were going for a run. A challenge made by him after too many glasses of wine when we had folded out of the last hand of cards last night. It had been supposed to be before eleven am but I had pleaded exhaustion and made him agree to one o'clock. Rachel and Mother would be down by the side of the lake at four-thirty for the 'Echoes'; John and I had decided to run to the opposite side to listen. It was about an hour's gentle jogging. We intended having a late lunch in a little pub there and walking back at our leisure. Norah would have the house to herself for her visitor.

Before I left I checked she was alright with this.

'Are you sure you don't want someone in the house when Charles calls? You're not nervous meeting him again?'

'God, no. I could never be nervous meeting Charles,' she laughed. 'He was actually vaguely related to Teasie, I lost track of how but you know the way it is in a small place. So I feel like I knew everything and one belonging to him. I'll be fine Sinead. You enjoy your run.' She smiled, 'John's a nice man, you're obviously really good friends. You tease each other like brother and sister!'

'I suppose I know him a long time too. We went out with each other at one stage. For a long time really. But we were both too young,' I shrugged. 'You know how it is.'

'I don't you see, that's just it. There was only ever Tom. Always only Tom.'

It seemed to overwhelm her from time to time, the enormity of it all. I'd been glad the respite Christmas had given her, she'd really enjoyed being involved in the preparing of a nice meal that's appreciated, the bickering and laughing over the cards, the warmth I hoped she could feel from us all. She was so courageous, I thought so anyway, to just keep living, I mean, waiting to see what would happen, knowing whatever it would be would have profound effects on the way the rest of her life panned out.

I hugged her. 'You have me as bad as yourself with all this hugging!' I complained, 'but I suppose you've a lot of hugs to make up for. So do I, come to think of it. Mother wasn't much of a one for hugging and as we grew Dad was far more likely to pat you on the head, or the shoulder depending on your height. Maybe we'll start a business in Dublin. A campaign – a minimum of three hugs a day to keep your head healthy – what do you think?'

'Brilliant, I'm first.' I hadn't heard John come in behind me and shrieked as he bear hugged me from behind. Norah laughed and flapped her hands at us.

'You're as daft as each other – away and run off all that energy. God! I sound like Teasie!'

'Well – 'bye 'bye Auntie Norah, hopefully we'll meet Charles when we come back. Right, Mr. O'Sullivan, let's see how out of condition you are.'

'Not so smart, Breslin! I've been training for just such a challenge,' he mock punched the air.

''Yeah!' I laughed as we jogged out the drive into the cold afternoon mist, 'knocking back good red wine and eating Mother's pudding, dosed in Norah's brandy butter. I saw you easing out that belt a notch at the card table.'

'What were you eying my belt for?' He jogged past me and gave me a gentle poke in the ribs.

'You…!' I wasted no more breath on talking, tailed him for a while, got into stride and overtook him. I stayed ahead of him for about fifteen minutes when I relented and slowed down enough for him to come alongside. I grinned and he grinned back. We didn't bother talking, enjoying the noise of our trainers slap, slap, slapping on the damp winter lanes.

It had been incredibly wet for the previous couple of weeks, even wet enough for hardened old farmers to comment about 'bloody global warming'. But the rain held off that day. It was colder than it had been and misty; good weather for running. You could smell the damp vegetation and taste the peat in the air from the fires in every hearth in the area.

It took us slightly more than an hour, John got a stitch so we had to slow to a walk for the last fifteen minutes. I was good. I didn't tease. Well, not much. Ammunition for another day. I really liked the way things were 'developing' between us, working on our friendship, working together for Norah.

And maybe more. I kept pushing it to the back of my mind but it was always there. Evil, gorgeous feeling that it is! Desire. I had admitted it to myself. I still liked him, More. I lusted, fancied, whatever. Shit. I was thirty-six, was I still allowed feel like this? And what do you do about it at thirty-six? The same as at seventeen, or are you more sophisticated? Are we ever more sophisticated when it comes to like, like a lot, lust and love?

We were glad to get into the pub, shed some of our layers and both drained pints of water before tucking into two bowls of seafood chowder with home made brown bread, followed by a pot of tea and apple crumble and custard.

'We just destroyed the benefits of that run, didn't we,' I said, mopping up the last few crumbs of crumble from his plate.

'Breslin, you've never learned, you'd get so much more gathered up if you wet the tip of your finger.' He demonstrated and I laughed.

'I really enjoyed last night and the jog/walk whatever. Despite my stitch. Will we go out for a drink later? Finish up Christmas properly. Maybe Norah and her friend would like to come.' He looked at me. 'You're back to Dublin tomorrow aren't you?'

'Yes, smack bang into the mentality of panto rehearsals. I'm prop and wardrobe mistress and everyone turns into a child that thinks they have absolutely no responsibility for anything that they might need on stage. It's a case of 'Sineaaddd! .... Where's...whatever.' Reminds me of being a kid and always assuming Mother and Dad knew where everything I had mislaid was.'

'You seem to be getting on so much better with Kate. I'm glad. I still can't handle that 'Mother' thing despite all the years I've listened to you saying it.'

'It started as a kind of a joke when I was about fourteen and it stuck. I feel funny calling her Mam or Mammy now.

I only do it in moments of regression! Seriously though, I am getting on better with her. I've stopped bristling every time she tries to find out about my private life and bewails my lack of advancement in the world.' I paused, looking into the fire as I contemplated my life. 'I have a steady number in the Service, fairly decent colleagues, pay is plenty for my needs and the hours and holidays are to die for. If I accept it she'll just have to. What more could a modern girl ask for! I suppose I should stop calling myself that.'

'What? Modern or a girl?'

'Girl of course!' I mock kicked him under the table.

'You look all woman from my vantage point,' he grinned – opening gambit.

'John, let's not do this. Not yet. OK? Let's just have a laugh and enjoy it and well, see...' Oh Christ what had I said? I hoped I hadn't overreacted to what was probably a perfectly innocent flirty remark. No. Thank God. He put his hands up, palms forward.

'Your rules, Sinead. Always. C'mon lets go and hear this 'Battle of the Bands!'. We relayered ourselves in outdoor clothes and set off for the lake's edge. It was a perfectly still night; there had been a full moon on Christmas night and it was still large in a cloudless sky, almost as bright as day.

Our side had won the toss on Christmas Eve and had pulled out all the stops, hauling a piano down on the back of a trailer. They had a saxophone and a trumpet plus guitars, bodhrans, a piano accordion and four fiddles that I could count. At five pm our group led off with a reasonably melodious *Good King Wenceslas*, the last verse sung unaccompanied by a boy aged about twelve, a voice as pure as water from a spring.

I was blubbering at the silence when he finished, then a moment's pause and the applause from across the lough echoed back. We clapped too. Then silence and the strains of *We Three Kings*, drifted across. I think we won round one with our boy soprano though. Then there followed a lively exchange of jigs and reels, John trying to explain the difference to me.

'Listen woman listen! The reel goes round and round.'

Yes, I could hear that – and then there came a jig which he said went up and down. It was all diddle-i-aye to me, but God it was great. Some of the older people were performing elaborate series of steps to some of the tunes.

'I wonder will all this be lost?' I mused.

'What do you mean?'

'Well, do you know any of those dances?' I asked him.

'No. I could make a shape at one or two of them but.... no.... I see what you mean. It will be an awful pity if the Irish dancing brigade with the ringlet wigs and false tans are all that's left of the dancing, won't it?'

He looked admiringly at Maggie Brady, all eighty-one years of her stepping with glee on the shoreline with her sixty-nine-year-old nephew Tom Cowen.

'There's something for the next Community Council meeting! What about 'Dancing at the Crossroads' a couple of weekends in the summer, maybe monthly initially, get the auld ones to teach the young ones the steps.'

'You'll never get the teenagers to go!' I scoffed.

'Want to bet! You seem to have forgotten that there can be little enough to do about here when you're aged between twelve and fourteen. And the older teenagers might even go if it wasn't in the parish hall. They could hang about on the ditches mocking and flirting! Might be just what's needed. All age groups together, old teaching young, young having a laugh and keeping old young. Sinead, aren't you a clever woman coming up with the idea.' He squeezed my shoulders

'Did I? I didn't realise....,' I laughed. I felt happy, good, being here in this lovely place standing in the warmth of neighbours, having fun with music and dance and being with someone I was truly fond of. I wrapped my arm around his waist as we tried to identify the strains of the latest tune floating across the still black water.

Chapter Sixteen

The Breslin house in Mullahaghdone is quiet by five pm. Kate and Rachel gone to join neighbours for the 'Echoes o'er the Lough' and Sinead and John have been out all afternoon.

Norah has the radio off, enjoying the silence of the kitchen, the ticking clock, the noise of sods of turf shifting in the range and the click of the oven as the temperature changes. The room is filled with the smell of baking. She has bread and scones in the oven and stands at the sink washing the utensils singing softly to herself. She realises it's a long time since she has sung aloud. She always sang, particularly when she baked or in the garden but it irritated Tom – her humming half-remembered tunes under her breath so she had learned to keep it in her head, prevent it from whistling through her lips even when he wasn't around.

Now she lifts her voice – a soft act of defiance and lilts out *Fairytale of New York*, an old favourite. She laughs when she's finished. Maybe she is mad. She wrings out a cloth and wipes the surface of the oilcloth on the table. She loves this kitchen. If she ever has her own home again she will have a kitchen like this. She stops, surprised, on the way to the bin. That's the first time she thought of anything good beyond the minute. A future – at some stage – after her punishment. It's good. A good feeling.

She finishes the dishes, sweeps the floor and wonders

from where the tinny Caribbean music she can hear is coming.

'Shag it! That's me – my phone!' She runs to the living room where the tiny black and silver phone is dancing around the coffee table.

'Hello, hello. Oh Lord… which button? Hello?'

'Norah? It's Charles. I got your text with directions but I think I'm gone astray somewhere.'

'Charles! 'Twasn't me did that texting, I never had a mobile phone before. Sinead did that for me last night and I don't know this place well. I know Sinead's number though so I'll give you that and she can direct you.'

'Text it to me.'

'Charles,' she laughs. 'You might as well ask me to fly to the moon. We'll have to do this the old fashioned way. I'll tell you Sinead's number, you repeat it twice then hang up and ring her and get directions. Then when you get here you can give me a lesson in mobile phones!'

'We'll try that so! I don't think I'm too far away. I can see lots of lights around a lake nearby and music. Sure I can look for directions if all else fails.'

She gives him the number, he dutifully repeats it twice and laughing he hangs up.

She admires the phone again. A gift from John.

'You're going to need it when you're gadding about in Dublin. And it's impossible to get Sinead; her phone is always either engaged or off – she could blether for Ireland that woman. So I'll be relying on you to keep me informed as to her movements!'

'I thought you were a solicitor, not a guard! I'll do no tell-tattling on my landlady. Thank you so much.' Norah had been stunned by all the presents. She had brought gifts, naturally as a guest, but hadn't expected anything herself. She had felt so content all day yesterday; that same warm 'Santa came and brought what I asked for' feeling she remembered from childhood.

Sinead had bought her a beautiful wrap cardigan in the softest of pale green wool and a long denim skirt.

'You look ten years younger,' declared Rachel. 'I bet you look fantastic in jeans.'

Norah never wore jeans after she had married, after she started going with Tom really. Tom hadn't liked them, he was very old-fashioned about clothes.

'Men's workwear,' he had called jeans. Sounded like one of Eileen Furlong's prejudices.

She admires herself again in the long kitchen window. Her hair is newly washed and Rachel had blow-dried it that morning, giving it body and bounce. Rachel had insisted Norah leave it loose, she couldn't get over the length of it – it is almost down to Norah's waist. Rachel and Sinead had talked to her about ways of having it cut up and maybe coloured. Norah wonders is she ready for that yet; it has been long for years and years. Too long maybe. They had had a lovely girly morning. All of them. It was like having sisters – proper ones, not like Carmel and Fidelma.

The women had tried to persuade her to use make-up but she only gave in to eye make up, the mascara making her eyelashes long and the same colour – not so pale. It made her eyes seem bigger, brighter. She laughingly submitted to a little lipstick. Yes, the result is definitely pleasing to the eye.

Tom had loved her hair long and hated make up on her. 'Beautiful, natural. My Rapunzel,' he would say in tender moments. Unlike Rapunzel's prince he had pulled too hard on her long plaits, almost pulling them out. Climbed into her brain in the process.

She hears a car pulling into the drive way and peeps through the living room curtains to ensure that it's Charles before unlocking the front door.

Charles is a huge man; much bigger than even Frank had been – over six foot four. A little overweight Norah supposes, he says he is anyway, but she likes that on him, he can carry it. He used to blame all his clients for his weight. Once on a visit to Teasie he had mock moaned about it.

169

'Honestly ladies, the amount of curranty soda bread with butter and rich fruitcake I've had to eat down the years,' refusing a second helping of Norah's apple pie. 'Every house I go to I have to have a cup of tea and a chat.'

Teasie had smiled and tapped his hand – indicating her approval of his kindness. Her speech was gone completely at that stage, but her brain was still sharp, most days anyway. Norah had known that the series of mini strokes Teasie had endured over the years were just a warning for the big one. She prayed it would be an enormous one and take her completely. Teasie had been so independent and it frustrated her terribly being dependent on Norah. And she didn't like living with Tom. But where was the choice. A home? No way would Norah leave her to that.

So here he was – big Charles Donnelly, bending his head and pulling off his woolly hat as he came through the door, over twenty years of knocking his head on lintels making it an automatic gesture. He bent to peck Norah's cheek, thrusting a poinsettia and a bottle of wine at her.

'I know it's late but Happy Christmas, if that's a suitable greeting in the circumstances. Oh God, I shouldn't have said that should I,' he stammers.

Norah laughs at his hang dog anxiety. 'It is a suitable greeting and a happy St Stephen's Day to you. Thank you for these. It's so good of you to come.'

She leads the way down the hall and settles Charles into the big chair by the range as he explains how he had gone astray.

'That music down by the lake. What's that about? I stayed for a short while, 'twas great and there seemed to be musicians on the opposite side playing as well.'

Norah explains to him about the 'Echoes' and they fall into easy chat about different traditions throughout the country.

Norah lifts the bread and scones from the range and Charles groans. 'Norah, that smells so good, please tell me one of those scones has my name on it.'

'It does indeed, with – if I remember correctly – your favourite blackcurrant jam, home made by Kate of this house and topped with fresh whipped cream.' She busies herself with delph, cutlery, a pot of tea and finally sits down in the chair nearest to Charles.

'You are so-o-o bad for my waistline! Ah well – New Year is coming,' he says, moaning with pleasure as he sinks his teeth into the warm crumbling scone.

'Norah, you'll make some man a fine wife.....' he has the decency to choke; giving Norah leave to get up, fetch tissues and a drink of water.

'Jesus, Jesus. I can't believe I said that. I'm around old people too much, I think I can say what I like without considering the consequences!' Charles dries away the tears streaming from his eyes and the mucous from his nose.

'Please forgive me, again. I'm such a bloody eejit. I should just keep my mouth shut, that way I'd lose weight and never say the wrong thing…what…what…'

Norah is in hysterical laughter looking at his woebegone face. She can't speak for a moment or two and eventually he joins her laughing.

Then he says. 'Actually can we just start all over again?'

She smiles. 'Of course we can. Wouldn't it be lovely if we could – we all could – every time we make a mistake. So that will be my Christmas present to you. Out you go to the kitchen door and come back in again.'

Charles laughs, stands and heads to the door, then he comes back and takes the plant and bottle of wine off the table.

He goes out and closes the door; a moment's pause and then he knocks.

'Norah, Norah Breslin! Can I come in?'

'Come in, come in and welcome,' Norah sits at the table, smiling face propped in her hands.

The door opens and in he comes, gifts thrust ahead of him again, a big grin on his face.

'Now, a happy Christmas to you and yours and let me at that scone!'

'Sit down, ye big eejit – you could draw laughter from the gloomiest man in Ireland. Teasie used to love to see you coming. I'm sure all your clients feel the same.'

They sit and chat about some of his clients. Poor lonely men and women – some old, some younger but very ill, almost all living alone in isolated areas. Some communities and families are great but others ignore, deliberately or just through lack of time and thought, the needs of these lonely people.

Sometimes, Charles says, a simple rota of a visit a day could make the lives of those men and women a little easier.

'They're not easy, a lot of them. Jesus, some of them can be fierce contrary. But I think it's deliberate – you know, they've been so independent all their lives and then something happens, a stroke or a fall or something that robs them of independence and they push people away from them. They don't want to be a burden is part of it and then of course nobody can do it right! It's partly pride, partly irritation at themselves. I have to say I love it though. I get frustrated with families and with the system but in general I usually succeed in making lives a little easier for people.' He taps his spoon against his cup 'That's a good feeling, making a difference, however small.'

'You certainly made a huge difference for Teasie. Organising all the stuff she needed and all the advice you gave me about handling her. It was great. We used to look forward to your visits, you'd put her in good form and give me a laugh.' Norah gets up to make more tea then hesitates.

'Maybe you'd prefer a glass of wine? You're not driving for a while are you?'

'You know – I'd love a glass of wine. I'm in no rush, and we've a lot to chat about, don't we?' He looks slightly nervous.

'Yes, yes. Liam – my solicitor – he talked to you didn't he?'

Charles nods.

'Here, will you open that?' She hands him the wine and a corkscrew and goes looking for glasses. 'It's about what you saw and what we talked about. Earlier, a while back, when Teasie was alive and then later. Those last times. And that time Tom threatened you. He did threaten you, didn't her? I can't remember, sometimes I think I've imagined things.' She comes back to the table, places the glasses in front of him and he pours them generous measures of the deep red wine.

'He certainly did. He. I suppose you could say stalked me.' Charles cocks his head and strokes the side of his glass, trying to find the right words, words not to give offence.

'It was near a client's house, he must've followed my car. Pulled ahead of me and parked across the road so I had to stop. It was mad. Honestly Norah, I had never seen anyone so incensed, he was almost foaming at the mouth. That's what he reminded me of at the time, this old dog we had that got some disease, not rabies but something like that where he would crouch and growl at you, these thick dribbles of saliva dripping from his jaws. He went feral and my Dad had to hunt him down and shoot him. Poor bugger; he had been a great dog all his life. Horrible way to end.' He sips at the wine, looks gravely at her.

'Norah, I don't know how or where he got the ideas he had. They were paranoid thoughts. All I wanted was to be your friend. Especially after Teasie, you had been so good with her; a closeness I didn't see too often. And your garden of course – God I love that garden. Remember at that time I had just bought my own place and I was trying to develop my own garden. You were the only person I knew with such a keen interest in their garden. But Tom seemed to think………well, you know what he thought. So he accused me of all sorts. At first I was going to placate him, afraid he'd take his madness out on you. I'd seen you other times.' He pauses; he looks in her eyes then away. 'I often felt guilty that I didn't do more, didn't try harder. I certainly feel guilty now. Liam gave me a brief account of what happened after I left that day. Was it anything to do with me being there?'

She nods.

'I'm a patient man Norah; you have to be in my job but I'm bloody glad now I stood up to the little weasel back before.' She winced a little and he coloured.

'Sorry but that's what he was that day. Accusing me of mad things, impossible things. Sex and dates and things. Jesus, he kept you locked down more than a.. a.. a hamster.'

'A hamster?!' She grins despite the topic. 'Why a hamster?'

'I don't know,' he laughs too.

'You don't look like a hamster or anything – well you have nice hamstery eyes. Oh Jesus! I'm doing it again. No wonder I never manage to keep a woman for longer than a couple of months.'

Norah is surprised. She doesn't know why but she had always assumed Charles was gay. Nothing specific; just he was different to every other man she knew. Then he was in a job mainly held by women and at one stage he had referred to his partner and because he said partner she assumed it was a man. Then his interest in gardens and flowers and plants. She feels embarrassed about her assumptions. Typical her. Stupid. They were sort of stupid reasons to presume to know someone's sexuality. She had never felt threatened by Charles and barring Frank and recently Liam and John she had always felt nervous around men. Charles was like a big bumbling boy – nobody could possibly be nervous of him.

'So I – now excuse the language – told him to move his fucking car off the fucking road or I'd ram right through it. And I had no interest in his wife other than feeling sorry for her being married to a crackpot little bully. And I would stay away, but I fully intended reporting him to the police for harassing me and suspecting he beat you. I totally lost it actually and I'm not proud of it but I told him I could make life difficult by filling out a report saying I suspected he abused Teasie – if I said he did, they would have to investigate. All this at my full height roaring down at the little fucker. I'm sorry I didn't hit him a slap. But it's just not in my nature. Violence never solved anything,' he takes a mouthful of wine, 'except on the football field!' Then he grins ruefully, trying to lighten his tone; but his face had darkened as he remembers the encounter.

'He never touched Teasie, I wouldn't have let him.' Norah moves her hand in a weary dismissive gesture. She finds this conversation so incredibly tiring. 'That much he knew. Sometimes he might say things but....... anyway Denis Bradley called, the sergeant. But I said you were mistaken, that what you had seen ...oh I can't remember what excuse I made. Denis knew our story. There had been a time when Teasie had tried to report Tom to him years ago and there was another time Denis was involved and maybe one other, I don't know. They're all mixed up in my head. I just kept saying Tom never meant it; to everyone and most of all myself. I was always going to make it better. On my own. Love him more. Cure him of whatever it was. Be better myself so he wouldn't feel he had to treat me like that.' Norah twists the wine glass in her hand, staring into it as if the ruby-coloured liquid could give her answers.

Charles touches her wrist. 'You couldn't cure, change; whatever – you know that don't you?'

'So everyone keeps telling me.'

'You have to look forward Norah. Not back. You're here, you're breathing. You seem to have a really good solicitor. I'm ready to help you. That Sergeant Bradley too and now these cousins of yours. Let us help you. You don't have to be on your own anymore.'

She can feel the tears coming and she cannot speak. Then this big awkward bear of a man does the right thing; he moves to the edge of his chair leans in towards her and

175

gives her a clumsy hug. So she pulls the tears back, nods her head fiercely and gives him a watery smile.

'That's it woman. I'll show you what having a good full back line on your side can mean!'

Chapter Seventeen

Back to Dublin after Christmas and I was thrown full pelt into the panto rehearsals and then our run of shows. It was performed in a small community centre in North County Dublin where Rob was from originally. He had founded the musical society with the help of an enthusiastic local school teacher. We put on two or maybe three other shows in the year but the panto is always our major production.

We're always able to run the show for a week and play to full houses, mainly because a lot of the local school children and leading lights in the community get involved, so you got big audiences. It also drew people from bigger towns in the area; people love to see friends, family, neighbours and work colleagues in a different light.

Rob's energy was unbelievable; he always managed to pull off the whole event successfully without alienating anyone no matter how disastrous dress rehearsals seemed to be. I dragged Norah along with me.

'C'mon it'll do you good. The kids get so excited I need someone calm to keep them in order before they get on stage, plus we always need a hand with last minute alterations for costumes. You can sew can't you?'

'Yes, I was always handy with a needle and knitting too. Old-fashioned me you know. Home Economics was the only subject I got an honour in in the Leaving. As Tom never tired of pointing out, 'all you're fit for is cleaning and cooking' – even though he left school at fifteen to serve his apprenticeship!' Her face had darkened as she spoke, her lips pursed in annoyance.

This was a recent development and one that pleased me. Her counselling sessions seemed to be moving her on from grief and regret to anger. Eventually I hoped she would come to acceptance and peace. Bloody bastard. The more I heard of him the more of a monster he became, what she didn't tell me Liam or John would. His petty cruelties, apart from the physical beatings, were enough to drive anyone insane. It was a wonder there was any more than a shell of a human being left in Norah.

Half-way through the run of the show I rushed in from work one evening to change and collect Norah. There was a strange woman sitting with her back to me at the kitchen table.

'Hello?' I said and squealed in fright and delight when the woman turned towards me.

'Do you like it?' her hand shyly up to a chopped and highlighted pixie-like hair cut.

'OhmyGawd! Norah! It's fabulous. Jesus, turn, turn – let me get a proper look. Stand up woman!'

The transformation was unreal. She looked child-like and sophisticated at the same time, the cut flattering her delicate features; she looked like a strawberry blonde Audrey Hepburn.

She twisted and turned for me, laughing at my reaction.

'Cut it off,' I said. 'All of it.' The hairdresser kept asking was I sure. I think she was afraid I'd hate it after. I got loads of compliments in the salon and every time I passed a shop window on the way home I'd have to do a double-take. I hardly recognised myself. Do you like it?'

'I LOVE it! More to the point, do you like it?'

'I do. I think. It's strange, I feel like me inside but I'm changing on the outside, the clothes you got me for Christmas, the bits and pieces I've bought since, the little bit of eye make-up and lipstick, now the hair. I feel…. lighter somehow.'

She brought her hand up to the bare nape of her neck.

'I'm sure you do, you probably lost about five pounds weight in hair! It's fabulous! Lord, look at the time. Come on or we'll never get the curtain up on time.'

Norah was a huge hit with the kids. We had put her in charge of them backstage where she gently steered them into position for their entrances and ushered them back to the dressing room when they were finished. Not one costume, or worse, a child, went astray all week. She amused them with stories and songs between their entrances and exits and both boys and girls were in love with her by the end of the week.

We wrapped up the show for another year on the Friday night and the children voted for their annual excursion treat due on the Sunday. The previous year we had gone ice skating, which I hoped wouldn't happen again. I almost broke my ankle and my behind was sore for a week from the tumbles I has taken. This year they plumped for 'Funderland' a big funfair that visits the RDS, a show centre in Dublin, every year.

'Oh Jesus! High things, fast things! I feel sick on an escalator – you won't get me on those yokes.' I moaned when told of the plan.

'Don't be such a wuss! You have to come, I need all the adult hands I can get to both ferry them there and then keep an eye on the little monsters.' Rob gave me that 'I won't take no for an answer' look and I sighed. I had learned long ago that what Rob wanted Rob generally got. He turned to Norah who was quietly folding and packing pixie costumes.

'Norah, you'll make her come won't you? And you have to come as well.'

'What is it, this 'Funderland'?'

'Ireland's low-grade answer to Euro Disney,' I muttered, placing props none too gently into a packing case.

'A funfair? With rides and bumper cars and candy floss!' Norah's eyes lit up.

'See Breslin, your cousin is a woman of courage with a spirit of adventure. Now stop being a grouch and tell me how many kids you can load into that sexy little Mini Cooper of yours.'

'Three max, I'll have Norah as well.'

'No, not me,' said Norah. 'I mean I'd love to go and all but Charles is coming over on Sunday to see me, he's on a course in Beaumont Hospital for the week.'

'Is he driving?' asked Rob as he stacked chairs.

'Yes, he has a fairly big car, one of those four wheel drive things.'

'That's settled, if Charles has no objections and you go with him you'll be able to fit either four or six into an SUV, Sinead can take four – biggest in front. I can take five max with two in the one belt and that's the lot. Sorted. Oh I love it when a plan comes together!' Off he twirled pushing an enormous sweeping brush in front of him to gather up the debris of our last audience.

I raised my hands in mock resignation.

Norah laughed. 'Is he always like that?'

'Pretty much, it's easier to go along with him because you'll never win. But there's no way I'm getting up on one of those rollercoasters. I'd puke!'

'I went on one of those big swing boats once, when a funfair visited Boyle. I thought it was brilliant. I felt like a bird, never wanted to come off. A big gang of us went from school – Tom too of course. 'Twas a great day.' She paused, 'Sinead, do you think it will be alright for me to be looking after children?'

'What do you mean, haven't you been escorting them all week! They're all mad about you!'

'Yes, but there were parents in and out all the time. I feel guilty deceiving their Mams and Dads; shouldn't we let them know what's hanging over me? I mean, they'll find out eventually when it goes to court, there'll probably be photographs in the papers and that. People out here will never trust Rob and yourself again.' She looked wretched, haunted.

Christ – she would carry that man's ghost around with her for the rest of her life.

I called Rob over and we discussed it.

'I see what you mean' said Rob 'but fuck it – Norah, the parents know you at this stage and trust you. In fact the fact that you finally protected yourself against a lunatic should stand in your favour in the eyes of any parent.'

'I don't think they'll quite see it that way.' Norah pursed her lips.

'Ok. Look – it's just logistics. Would you like to go?' Rob's eyes were soft.

'I'd love to, just to see the place – it sounds great – and only if Charles wants too that is. I'm sure he will, he's like a big child himself.'

'Right, well if it makes you feel better we won't actually place any kids in your care and I'll get one of the parents to draw the short straw and ferry the last bunch out. So yourself and Charles can join us if you can. Sorted.' And with a grin off he skipped to whatever his next task was. No wonder I loved that man. Nothing was a problem; not only did he think outside the box he redesigned the box to suit whatever it needed to hold. Irrepressible.

Exhausted, I decided to cry off the cast's wrap party that night. 'Unless you really want to go Norah, a nice bottle of red in front of a DVD is more what I'd be inclined towards tonight.'

'Oh Yes! My thoughts entirely, perhaps preceded by a nice hot bath?' she grinned at me.

'Norah, you can see into my soul! Come on, we'll leave the rest until tomorrow.'

We said our goodbyes and were home within three-quarters of an hour. Norah won the toss for the first bath and I opened the wine and sat it on the coffee table to breathe as I arranged the sitting room for a night of comfort.

'I've a surprise for you,' I said when she came out in dressing gown and slippers.

'What?'

'That book you asked me to get for you when you were in hospital, *Precious Bane*? They made a BBC drama of it in the late eighties and,' shaking the box at her, 'I finally tracked down a copy of it!'

'I don't believe it! I never knew it was a movie. Sinead!' She squealed and hugged me so hard it hurt. 'Oh go on, hurry up and have your bath, I can't wait. Did you read the book?'

I admitted I hadn't finished it, I'd tried but I had found some of the dialect hard and the complete servility of and submissiveness in the lives of the female characters in the early 1900s depressed me, made me glad I was a female a century later. However where the book excelled was in its wonderfully sumptuous descriptions of the Shropshire countryside and characters. It's primarily the love story of hare-lipped Prue Sarn, for a travelling weaver Kester Woodsheaves. It reminded me in parts of Hardy's *Far from the Madding Crowd,* although Bathsheba was a far cry from the timid Prue. Mary Webb, author of *Precious Bane*, had Thomas Hardy's talent for drawing nature, making you stop and read slowly, inhabit the landscape, see the trees and the hedges and the old stone walls and feel the wind blowing or the rain on your head or the sun on your face. I suppose in ways it reminded me of the wonders of nature in my rural homeplace.

I had a quick bath as instructed and we were curled up on the sofa with the big fleecy throw over us, bottle of wine and two glasses in front of us just as the clock struck midnight. The DVD was a poor bootlegged copy but that didn't diminish the beauty of the film. It was incredibly sad in parts but it had a happy ending made stronger by the difficulties the lovers had to overcome to reach it. The costumes, settings and acting were superb. We both blubbed throughout and when Kester hauls Prue up in front of him on his horse despite her protests that

'You mun marry a girl like a lily. See I be hare-shotten'.

He pulls up the horse sharply and looks at her with a 'No more sad talk! I've chosen my bit of paradise. 'Tis on your breast, my dear acquaintance!

That finished us; the combination of wine, warmth and the happy ending had the two of us in floods, we both went to bed red-eyed and happy.

I spent the following day over in the community hall finalising the clean up and getting my list of the little darlings I had to ferry to Funderland on the Sunday. I did try to moan my way out of it again but Rob promised me a long boozy lunch some time within the next fortnight with all the juicy details of the new man in his life. How could I resist?

Norah was making dinner when I got home and Charles was ensconced on the couch watching sport.

I'd met him in Mullaghadone on St Stephen's night; he seemed to be a nice man, a bit awkward and I thought him a tad innocent, naïve, but he was fully willing to appear as a witness for Norah and John felt his testimony made a much stronger case, so that made him a good one in my book.

'Hi Charles, h-m-m, something smells good!'

'Will I include you in the pot for dinner?' asked Norah.

'No. Much as I'd love to collapse and chill with you for the night I'm only home for a quick shower and change, and I won't be home tonight either. I'm drinking so I'm bunking down in my friend's house.' I raced off to the bathroom but Norah followed.

'Sinead, would it be alright if Charles slept on the couch tonight? He came up a day early so he could be here on time for the Funderland trip and his B and B isn't free 'til..'

I put my hand up to stop her in full flow.

'Norah, I told you. This is your home, you can have over who you want when you want. Of course it's alright, provided he promises to give me a dig out with my squad of kids tomorrow.'

'Thanks. How many thank yous can I give you?'

I shooed her out of the bathroom. 'You might not thank me after a day in this hell hole tomorrow!'

Norah lies in the spare room of Sinead's apartment. The room that she now thinks of as 'my room'. She's close to sleep, warm and comfortable and smiles at the rumbling snores from the sitting room. Charles had warned her of the power of his nocturnal breathing, particularly after food and wine. They had talked about going out, maybe to a movie, but it was raining and dull outside and they got comfortable. They had chatted about music, film, books; Charles was as avid a reader as Norah and he recommended several he thought she'd enjoy. He was like a big kid about the funfair tomorrow.

'I always felt deprived as a kid. I never got to go on a rollercoaster or any of those yokes. My mother was convinced I'd fall out and the annual visit by the funfair to Sligo became a battle ground between us. In the end my Dad bribed me not to go; actually, it was worth it to see the relief on her face. She was a real old worry wart my Mam.'

'Is she still living?'

'She is but she has MS. It was diagnosed in my last years of school. She's not too bad, been good really the last three years. It was her illness pushed me towards O.T. really. I thought if I could make some difference, well you know. Dad's hale and hearty, he's retired now and cares for Mam on a full-time basis. I see a good bit of them both, go for a few pints or go fishing with Dad the odd time.' He smiled.

'I used to fish with Frank, Teasie's husband. Nothing fancy in the way of rods and lines but I loved it. Just being with him, sitting in the silence, listening to the water, trying to hear the fish. We often caught a nice tea! Seems like a lifetime ago.'

'Tell you what, next time you're down my country I'll take you out on the lake, we'll take a picnic and make a day of it.'

'Thank you Charles, that would be lovely. But you don't have to, it's enough that you're just helping me in the case.'

He colours, 'I know I don't have to. But I want to – anyway I have to pay you back for fulfilling my childhood dream of going on a rollercoaster tomorrow!'

'You mightn't feel that if I puke on you!'

And so the night had gone by in easy conversation, some serious, mostly light, and when she sorted out bedding for him before she went to bed he had stood and planted his hands firmly on her upper arms and pecked her cheek.

'You're a lovely woman Norah Breslin, and never let anyone tell you different.

She'd pecked him back shyly. 'Funny you're the only one that's called me Breslin in years. Just curious, why? I suppose I better get used to it again anyway.'

'I don't know, Teasie Breslin I suppose. And then you were just Norah, so Norah Breslin just seemed natural.'

She runs the conversation through her head. She's starting to feel like Norah Breslin again; it's as if Norah Furlong has died along with Tom. Her eyes fill and she takes a deep breath, concentrates on her breathing as she has been taught.

She feels herself drifting into sleep as she thinks about Frank, the first time she met him. Charles in some ways reminds her of Frank. His gentleness and awkwardness. She resolves that tomorrow will be a good day, an ordinary, special day to remember on all the bad days that still must come.

Chapter Eighteen

It is the noise that hits Norah first. She thought she had gotten used to the noises of traffic and the throngs of people about Dublin city on a busy day.

But this, this is different. There were all the people first, chattering and laughing and squealing, then the music. Hurdy-Gurdy music. Loud pop music from the various rides and over it the noise of the machines, a constant whirring, swishing noise. And the lights. Whirling, swirling, flickering like a million sets of fairy lights combined with a fireworks display. And this just from the outside rides. The light drizzle doing nothing to dampen the palpable excitement in the air.

They had agreed to meet the others in the café in the inner area and as they queue to enter Norah nudges Charles to point out the young boy of about eight in front of them who can barely stand till. He hops from one leg to the other, does some strange martial arts type moves and keeps bumping into his younger sister – a princess in head to toe cream and pink.

'Ma, he did it again! He's doin' it on purpose. Jason stoppit,' the whine in her voice at odds with her fairy-like appearance.

'Jason, take it easy. We'll be in in a minute. Will yeh mind!' The woman turns to apologise as Jason bumps back into Norah.

'Not to worry, it's not every day there's a Funderland

to go to,' Norah smiles as the boy moves shyly away.

'It's not just Funderland, that fella can't stand still. This is the highlight of his Christmas, so I suppose I can't blame him.' The woman grins as the boy moves a few steps away, craning to get a better look.

'Da! Can you see it, dat's the Waltzer, dat is,' he turns to Norah and Charles. 'Were yiz ever on dat! Mega it is! We did dat one tree times last year, didn't we Da? Megan wouldn't do it. Megan wouldn't do entin' 'cept the bumpers and even then she cried.' His eyes huge.

'I only cried 'cause you bumped real hard in the back of me and I banged me head! Ma, tell him he's not to do that again. An' I was too small for some of the rides last year. I'm going on the Waltzer and the Flyin' Carpet this year and Ma's comin' with me, aren't yeh Ma?'

Ma nods with a nervous grin. The father starts to laugh.

'If she gets on anything faster than the merry-go-round Ireland will win the next World Cup!' He dodges away from her aimed thump.

'Smart-arse, wait and see. You were fairly green yourself last year after that bleedin' Rollercoaster.'

'Yeah Da, remember, we had to stop the car on the way home 'cause you felt dizzy,' Jason crows.

The father laughs. 'Jayz, yeah – that was weird. We were stopped at traffic lights and I was daydreamin', then I felt like the road was tilting away from me, like being at the top of the rollercoaster; just when it seems to stop before it swooshes down. I had to pull in and Bernie had to drive the rest of the way!'

'He put the heart crossways on me, I thought he was having a stroke or something!'

'Same thing happened to me after climbing a mountain in Donegal once, about a week later I was driving along thinking about it and I had to pull over too, get out and take a couple of deep breaths,' says Charles. 'I actually felt sick as well. It's something to do with your vision and the sensory nerves in your joints being out of sync; it can even happen to people who are used to heights, the memory of the sensation can hit them later.' Norah feels proud at Charles's knowledge.

'See, I'm not a wimp – it's a well-known condition!' the man delightedly tells his wife. They chat to the family as the queue moves. Norah asks about Santa and the little girl goes into great detail about every present she received, most of them things Norah never heard of and all to do with something called 'Bratz'. 'Kinda like Barbie, only better' the child informs her, 'an' I got a 'Bling bling Barbie Stylin' head – but Ma keeps playin' with that.'

Norah smiles, enjoying the normality, but a thought at the back of her head nips her. Would this family even consider talking to her if they knew what she had done? Was she condemned to feeling this for the rest of her life?

They locate Sinead sitting in the restaurant with two over-excited boys who crow with delight when they see Norah. Sinead looks stressed already.

'I swear Rob owes me a weekend away for this. I'm ready to thump one little bugger in my group,' she hisses. 'But his mother is my other adult so I can't really – well, not when she's looking!'

Charles laughs 'Sure, we'll give a dig out – what about it lads? What's the best thing to start with?'

The boys get into excited discussion with Charles, and Sinead's face lightens. 'Would you? Are you sure? I'd be eternally grateful, another pair of willing hands would mean I could go over to the brat's mother and help her with the smaller ones –I can cope with trampolines and bouncy castles. But some of the other stuff! And they all get so hyper, I swear I don't know whether I'm terrified I might lose one of them or whether I'd be delighted.' She sits back in her chair, grimacing at watery-looking tea in a paper cup.

'Anyone any Valium on them?'

Charles and Norah laugh at the expression on Sinead's face and stroll towards the Waltzer with the boys whilst Sinead goes in search of the rest of her group.

Norah isn't too sure about her agreement to go on the

ride as she watches the previous one coming to an end.

'Oh Lord! I don't know. It looks a bit fast!'

'C'mon Norah you have to. I swear it's deadly – me and Sean did it already; it's a bit fast but not mad high or anything.' Niall jumps up and down beside her

'Yeah, and if you hold your arms up and scream or sing it's even better – you two can sit in the middle seats – it'll make you feel safer.' Sean condescends.

So they pay their money and sit into the semicircular unit, Norah and Charles in the middle, the two experts taking the outer spaces. Charles pulls the safety bar down over them and the car starts to move almost immediately and Norah lets fly a few 'Jesus's', then apologises to the boys.

'That's nuttin' Norah, we're only moving up so they can fill the other cars. We'll get goin' when they're all full.' Sean wriggles beside her.

'Anyway, my Mam says much worse curses than that when she's driving,' pipes up Niall from the other end.

Charles laughs. 'You're gas men.' The Waltzer lurches upwards again. There is a pop song playing and the boys start to belt out the lyrics. By the time the Waltzer is fully loaded and ready to go Norah and Charles have the hang of bits of the song and they too sing out the chorus which involves a series of ah-ha, ha – ah ululations,

And then the ride begins it earnest.

'I don't know why they call it "the Waltzer," roars Norah, 'it's nearer to a jive! Oh Sweet Jesus!' She screams as the centrifugal force pushes her head against the back of the seat.

The boys are howling out the song now, thrilled by the speed and the danger. Norah has both hands firmly clamped on the safety bar, half-laughing, half-screaming. She is conscious of Charles's big frame squeezed in beside her shaking with laughter, and he too lets fly a few choice swear words. In one of the lurches he leans further in against her and clamps his left hand firmly over her right. She feels sick, but good sick – excitement sick. For the first time in many years she feels happy, then buries the thought. How in the name of God could she be happy? After everything that has happened? After what she's done?

But she can't help it – so she just accepts it gladly.

When the ride finally stops and they get off laughing she feels weak at the knees; the ground seems uncertain so she walks slowly for a few minutes taking deep breaths.

Charles's face is bright with excitement.

'That was brilliant. Will we do it again?'

Norah cries off and stands and watches Charles and the boys as they whirl through over and over again.

'He looks so right,' she thinks. 'A child on either side. Like he was born to it, born to be a dad.

'C'mon Norah, we'll do the dodgems now, me and you against Charles and Sean.' Niall bounces off the Waltzer. 'Can I drive?'

'You can indeed. I don't know how to drive an ordinary car let alone a bumper!'

'Norah Breslin! You can't drive. Jesus, how did you survive all those years in the arse hole of ……' Charles voice trails off as Norah goes bright red. The boys race ahead to get in the queue for the dodgems.

'He told me I couldn't. I'd never learn. I was too stupid. I did try a few times but it always ended with him screaming blue bloody murder at me. It was a row I could do without and I just dropped it. I had a bike for a while but I stopped using that too, Tom would go on about the danger of being out on the roads on the bike. I suppose he was really trying to keep me isolated at home. But it never seemed like that, I just thought he was over protective. Oh, let's not talk about Tom today, let's just have a "fun" day.' She smiles and waves at Niall and Sean jumping up and down in the queue.

'Agreed. I'm going to bump the living daylights out of you now and tomorrow you're starting driving lessons with me.' He places his hand on her shoulder and instead of stiffening she turns and says in horror.

'In that big yoke? What if I crash it? You'll be out of a job or maybe even a life.'

'Listen, she handles like a baby's buggy – dead smooth, automatic gears and power steering – it'll be a piece of cake to you.'

'Promise?'

'Promise.'

And she believes him.

The dodgems go well, Norah and Niall claiming victory, scoring at least three bumps into the back of Charles and Sean. Sean argued that the last bump shouldn't have counted because it was only as a result of a pile-up caused by one little girl who seemed unable to get her car moving. So they finally agreed on a draw, two hits apiece.

They went to one of the shooting ranges where Charles showed himself a fine marksman, winning an enormous stuffed crocodile which he presents to Norah.

'Now, Charlie the Croc will look after you when I'm not around!'

'Sinead will move me out if you win anymore like this. We'll need an extra bedroom,' laughs Norah.

The boys take a couple of pot shots with balls towards buckets and managed to win smaller teddies apiece.

'You'll have to find girlfriends now to give them to,' teases Charles

'No way!' says Niall 'I'm never havin' a girlfriend, I have three sisters and they never stop fighting and being in the bathroom for ages and sometimes when I'm absolutely burstin' my Mam lets me go out the back to piss – except she says piddle, not piss!' Charles and Norah laugh at this tirade.

'Well, you might change your mind in a few years and if you only have one girlfriend you could buy a house with two toilets and that would solve the problem,' Norah suggests.

'Oh yeah! Cool. Is Charles your boyfriend? 'Cept he's not a boy, he's a man. Do you call him a man friend then or is it still boyfriend?' Niall rattles on and Norah blushes as Charles throws back his head and guffaws.

'Niall, you're a great fella. Yes, I am a man and I am Norah's friend so I'm a man friend, amn't I Norah? I don't think I'm her boyfriend boyfriend. Not yet anyway.' He spared Norah a reply by shouting.

'Who's for candy floss?!'

'Me, me, me' the boys raced ahead towards the candy floss machine.

'Kids. They're gas, no hang-ups – say the first thing that comes into their heads.' He puts a companionable arm around her.

'Charles…I…I don't know that I…' Norah doesn't stiffen but much as she likes him, she's not ready for him. There are too many other things happing. She can't confuse herself with Charles in a different role than the one he's had up to this.

He places his finger on her lips. 'Not to worry, you're the boss. But I'm here. Really. As your friend or as – whatever you want me to be. I don't just feel sorry for you Norah… although I do because no human being should have had to go through what you went through. But I like you as well. For yourself – your way of looking at things; your gentleness despite everything.' His voice thickens. 'Plus, whether you know it or not, you look great – I liked the look of the old Norah, the one that nursed Teasie in a shapeless cardigan and long skirt, but I love the look of the new Norah, with her pixie face and sexy jeans. You even have matching eyelashes now! And they make your eyes look so big and soft.'

'Stop now! You're embarrassing me! Do you know I've never tasted candy floss.' Norah blushes but smiles at him.

'Let that be remedied forthwith. *Barbe à Papa* it is! Four please,' he asks the young Asian man at the machine.

'What's that? I want candy floss' says Sean

'It's the French word for candy floss. 'Papa's beard' – see?' Charles holds the pink cloud under his chin, looking like a Santa Claus that was put through a whites wash with a red tee shirt .

'More like Barbie's beard,' laughs Niall. 'I wish they made candyfloss in a different colour, it's very embarrassing having that girly colour near your face.'

'Listen here young man, there's nothing wrong with pink on a man. I have at least two pink shirts that I wear to work all the time. I even have a pink tee shirt. But I only wear that one around the house. Or under a jumper. Somewhere where no one can see. What do you think Norah?' He hands her her candyfloss.

She wonders how to approach eating it, then follows the boys' example and just sticks her mouth in and sucks. As the sweetness mixed with the stickiness melts in her mouth she gets an almost immediate sugar rush.

'I think,' she says through the next mouthful, 'that it doesn't matter what colour you like to wear and that candyfloss is about the funnest thing I have ever tasted'.

'Funnest? Funnest? That's not a word, is it?' says Niall.

'Well, it should be. We just made it up. We're going to have the funnest day so far this year,' announces Charles.

'That won't be hard – it's only the eighth of January!' crows Sean.

'Right, c'mon let's have a go on the 'Power Wave'.' Charles moves in the direction of the ride, the boys hip-hopping about him.

Norah sits this one out too, smiling and waving as the boys dip and rise in front of her.

'Hey!' Sinead tips her from behind. 'How are you getting on?'

'Great, I even did one of the rides. Although I'm not sure I'll ever do one again! And look,' Norah holds up the empty stick. 'I had candy floss for the first time ever. I feel twelve or maybe fifteen again. Even better than that.'

'Good on you. Charles is certainly enjoying himself,' Sinead shouts over the swoosh of the 'Power Wave' dipping down again and the boys singing out

'Ah-ah, Ah-ah, Ah-ah, Aaah-a!'

'Listen, we're finished in here and heading outside to do one or two more rides and then, thank God, we bring the little monsters home. And we're going to the pub for well-deserved pints. Rob is buying and he bloody well better buy me plenty.' Sinead waves and joins her group leaving the indoor arena.

When the 'Power Wave' finishes, Norah, Charles and the boys join the queue outside for the 'Wild Mouse Rollercoaster'. It looks tame enough and the fact that they are allowing even the smaller children on it reassures Norah that it can't be that bad. It isn't, just a bit scary, but exhilarating, and a camera flashes at one point and takes their picture. Charles buys key rings for the four of them with their photo in it, showing them in varying states of fear and excitement.

'Norah, look at you! Ye mad thing! You look so-o-o-o-o scared Charles.' Niall studies the photo.

'Me? Scared? – not at all. I was just pretending so the rest of you wouldn't feel like babies. Now last ride, who's going to do it and what'll it be?'

Norah bowed out again. No amount of pleading would make her do the bigger rollercoaster or the huge ferris wheel.

'The flippin' ferris wheel stopped last year or the year before and people were stuck up on the top of it. I remember it on the news, so I think it'll have to be the rollercoaster lads.' Charles laughs as their charges career ahead of them to get places in the queue.

'You're brilliant with them,' says Norah.

'Sure, have you not noticed? I am one of them. I never grew up, never want to.' Norah smiles and shoos him ahead of her. He has grown up though, she thought, he has grown up into a very fine man.

195

Chapter Nineteen

By the end of February I was exhausted, the running around for the panto coinciding with tax year end meaning work had been very busy. So a heavy cold confining me to bed for two days was a blessing in disguise. I slept and slept, occasionally wandering out for drinks or paracetamol.

Norah took care of me. Normally I would have found this an irritation but she was so sweetly unobtrusive that she was a huge bonus.

On the Friday of that week I felt definitely better so got up and dressed. When I went into the living room Norah had the TV on but was listening to it with headphones plugged in. I laughed, tipped her shoulder to attract her attention.

'What are you doing? I've never seen anyone watch TV that way!'

'I was afraid I'd disturb you.' She pulled the headphones off, 'you look much better, still pale but your eyes aren't as feverish looking.'

'Yes, I think I've knocked it on the head. I'm even hungry.'

She hopped up.

'Well, sit you down and I'll make us both some lunch.'

'Norah, you have me thoroughly spoiled.'

She busied herself in the kitchenette and within twenty

minutes had produced scrambled eggs, bacon, toast and big mugs of tea.

'Delicious.' I pushed the plate away from me. 'I think I'll have to adopt you, move you in permanently.'

'I wish you could, I've been so content here – despite everything. But you'll never guess Sinead. I've lived around this area before!'

'What do you mean?'

'You know how I walk most days for a few hours? In general I walk towards Phibsboro and the city but the other day I decided to walk in the other direction.'

'Oh, up towards Ballygall and Finglas?'

'Yes, yes.' Her eyes were sparkling, whether with tears or excitement I didn't know. 'And I found my house – the house of my parents. At least I think it's my house. I certainly found the road I used to walk up after school. I remembered the way it curved towards the left and had two storey semi-detached houses on it, not like the bungalows on my road. So I followed it up and there it was. Definitely. My road. Our road. All bungalows in a crescent around a green area, and each set of six bungalows of a slightly different design.' Her hands were moving at a fierce rate, I'd never seen her so animated.

'So I counted down. I remember we used to count the houses – Mammy and me – and from the corner it was nine houses down to our gate. And the old gate is still there – if it's the right house. When it's closed it looks like a setting sun. It's awful rusty but it was tied with a plastic bag as if there were children in the house that might be out playing and needed to be kept safely in. The windows are all different and the garden looks different but I'm nearly sure it's the house I was first raised in.' She was flushed, her words tumbled from her.

'Surely there's an easy way to check. What about your birth cert? If your parents were living in the house when you were born the address will be on it.'

'I think they were, why didn't I think of that?'

She ran to the bedroom and returned with an old, much

folded yellow document. 'Here it is – 1968, February fourteenth, Rotunda Hospital. '

'Valentine's Day. You were born on Valentine's Day!' The lovers' day had fallen the previous week and she hadn't told me.

'Yes, so I always got spoiled. Tom would …well…I always got lots of presents.'

'Norah Elizabeth – Female. Name and Dwelling Place of Father – Daniel Francis Breslin, 45 Willow Park Crescent, Ballygall.' That's it, that's the name of the road I saw! Oh Sinead. I have to show you!' Her hands shot across the table and gripped my arm.

'I could do with a brisk walk after my time in bed, so why don't we set out now?'

'It's cold and damp out, would you be able for it?'

I laughed. 'Positive Mammy. I'll wrap up well and the cold air will kill off any lingering bugs.'

Leaving the apartment we walked up Ballygall road and as we passed the church Norah stopped.

'I don't know. That church wasn't there. The church we used to go to was a little blue tin church'

'A tin church?'

'Well, it was that whatchacallit – corrugated iron – they were always collecting extra money to pay to build a block church. My Dad used to grumble about it. 'All them fellas in Rome in fancy palaces and houses and they want us to build a block church for them'. Mammy would be mad with him and tell him to stop that talk in front of me and I'd keep quiet and say nothing so they wouldn't argue. Isn't that funny, remembering that. I always thought of us all being perfectly happy, but I'm sure there were rows. We all have rows, don't we?' She was walking fast and talking a blue streak.

'We wouldn't be human if we didn't. John and I certainly did.'

'Not now though.'

'No, not now. Maybe we're just older or don't care as much anymore.'

'Or maybe you care more and realise what's not important enough to row about.'

I laughed. For a woman whose emotional range had surely been blunted if not broken by her bastard husband, Norah had enormous insights into what made people tick. She had a child's intuition helped by an adult vocabulary.

'What about you and Charles? Do you argue?'

'No, how could you argue with Charles? Anyway it's not the same – I mean he's not like – we're not, you know, well we're not like you and John.

'And what way do you think that is?'

'Sorry,' she blushed. 'I thought... well it looked to me and Rachel as if you two might be, you know – getting together again.'

'Are you two talking about me behind my back?' I must have sounded annoyed because she started to backtrack – badly – but in all honesty I was more amused than anything.

We came to a roundabout at the intersection of Glasnevin Avenue and Ballygall Road.

'I think we can get up to it by going straight up that road,' she pointed ahead. 'But I turned left here the other day, up the rest of Glasnevin Avenue until I came to a set of shops. That was when I started to recognise things.'

'Okay, let's do that.'

It had started to drizzle and we put up umbrellas and commented on the gardens of the houses on the way up. Norah's interest in gardening showed, she could rattle off the names of shrubs and flowers – both Latin and popular names. I can barely tell a daffodil from a crocus; in fact I think I called the crocus a pansy, which raised a laugh.

We came to the intersection of Glasnevin Avenue and Grove Road.

'This is where I got bit confused,' she pointed. 'There were shops there but not those ones – or not the way I remember them. And see,' she pointed further up Glasnevin Avenue to a junction that had Ballygall to the left and Finglas straight ahead. 'Those traffic lights, I think

200

there was a whachacallit, a zebra crossing there. You could get to the school by crossing there and then down to the left and up a laneway. There was a horrible dog in that lane. We were all afraid of him. But this is it.' She turned right up Grove Road and I followed her.

She yammered on nineteen to the dozen, describing different days she had walked the road with her mother, helping to push the pram with her baby sister in it and they sang songs, played counting games, talked about school and what was for dinner.

When we got to the top of Grove Road we turned right again and it was as Norah described it. A crescent of semi-detached bungalows around a green area.

'I think there used to be a low wall around that open space. I used to sit on it in the summer when we were out playing. I can't remember the names of the kids I played with. I remember one of the neighbours. Mrs. Corry or Corrigan, yes Corrigan that was it. I think I played with her children. There was a Valerie, or was it Andrea?' She was flushed with everything – the remembering, the excitement; the sadness too I suppose.

She stopped at one of the gates. It was as she had described, rusty with the original white paint flaking off and tied with a plastic bag. There was a pink child's trike in the driveway and a toddler in a snowsuit waddled towards us.

'Hiya. Hiya. Hiya lady.'

She had a big grin and a snotty nose.

Norah crouched down. 'Hello. What's your name?'

The toddler said something unintelligible then pointed towards the bungalow.

'Nanny, Nanny,' she said.

'Is Nanny in the house?' asked Norah.

I started to feel uneasy, talking to any unattended child was an almost arrestable offence.

A grey-haired woman in slippers and wearing a pink fleece zip-through appeared in the driveway and walked towards us.

'Nanny, Nanny!' called the child, running and holding up her arms.

'Well, Nelly Jelly Tot. Who are these ladies?' She lifted the child and raised her eyebrows inquiringly at us.

Norah started to babble so I interrupted and told her story as concisely as I could.

The woman knew the whole story. She and her husband had bought the house when it came on the market after the deaths of Norah's family, reared their family there and now she looked after two of her grandchildren whilst her oldest daughter worked.

She insisted we come in. 'We built on a small extension as the family grew but I'm sure the house is much the same as you remember it. Except we eventually added oil central heating, new windows and the usual redecoration over the years'

She took us around to the back of the house and Norah immediately burst into tears.

'The swing, the swing is still here. I can't believe it. Is it the same one?

The woman patted her arm.

'The frame is the same, we've had to replace the swing a few times. We were just talking about getting rid of it when this little one's big brother was born, so there it is. It's stood the test of time. They made things to last back then. Come in, come in – this is the extension now. Small enough but it gave us extra living room. Invaluable when mine were teenagers!' She laughed. 'I'm Maighread by the way. I'll put the kettle on and you can ramble about. Don't take any notice of the mess. It's hard to keep things tidy with small ones about the place.'

The woman busied herself with kettle, teapot and cups as the toddler grasped Norah by the hand and pulled her through to a living room area strewn with toys where a muted television was showing some children's programme.

'This was the kitchen!' exclaimed Norah and she moved up the hall, pointing at doors 'Louise's room,' to the left. 'My room,' to the right, 'the living room,' the next door on the right hand side, then a t-junction in the hall, a left hand turn to the front door with the bathroom and a cloakroom beside it. 'And up there,' she pointed to the top of the hall, 'Mammy and Daddy's room'.

'No!' said the toddler 'Nanny bed! Nanny bed!' and she bustled ahead of us and threw open the door to show us our mistake.

Norah could barely speak. She walked around the house touching walls; seeing it I'm sure with her seven-year-old eyes. Seeing it with different wallpaper, carpets, curtains. Reclaiming memories, good ones this time.

The woman stood at her kitchen door watching us with smiling eyes.

'C'mon. You'll have a cup of tea now. You look like you could do with plenty of sugar in it! Are you alright love?'

Norah nodded and sat at the kitchen table. She opened her mouth but no words came. I thanked the woman and chatted to her, explaining how Norah had moved to relatives in Leitrim of whom I was one. The rest of it was too complicated and scary for a friendly suburban kitchen on a February morning.

The toddler wandered out with a bottle demanding 'Doose' which Nanny kindly interpreted and supplied a drink of juice. The child then turned to Norah and held up her arms. Norah lifted her automatically, kissed her ginger curls.

'Will you look at that! She's normally shy with strangers. It's like she knows you belong!'

'Is there a Mrs Corry, or Corrigan still living on this road?' Norah stroked the toddler's head that lay totally relaxed against her shoulder.

'Pauline Corrigan! No, I'm sorry love, Pauline died six, or is it seven, years ago. Cancer. Poor Pauline, she was young – early sixties – my age now. Cormac, the husband died a year or two later. Heart. The family were grown and gone so they sold the house. There's a young couple in it now; they've done a lot of work on it and have two little ones. It'll be nice for Lisa here when she gets a bit bigger, have someone to play with on the road. I've missed that the last few years, little ones on the green playing.' Maighread sounded as if she could talk for Ireland. There aren't many people would take in two complete strangers with a weird story and let them wander her home.

'Look at that,' Maighread laughed. Lisa was fast asleep in Norah's arms. 'You surely have a knack for it. Have you kids yourself?'

'No, I.. I mean we couldn't.... my husband...well.' Norah's whispered voice tailed off as Maighread lifted the toddler and gently placed her on the couch in the living room covering her with a blue and yellow fleece.

'Flat out. Wouldn't you envy her. And there she is, like the rest of us – in a mad rush to grow up and do it all. Now. Now. Everything Now.' Maighread turned towards us and smiled.

I stood. 'Thanks so much Maighread, Norah is still a bit stunned. But it's meant a lot to her. Far more than you'll ever know.'

Norah grasped Maighread's hand.

'Thanks. I... Just thanks.'

Maighread gave her a hug. 'I don't know you from Adam, Norah. But my granddaughter's trust in you is enough to convince me you're a good 'un. You're welcome to call anytime. I'll see if any of the other neighbours remember you. I think maybe Mick McMahon up the road was here in your parent's time. Who knows, he might even have photos or a few yarns about you as a child. Leave me a phone number where I can contact you.'

'Would you. Oh that would be... here,' Norah scribbled her phone number on the back of an envelope on Maighread's kitchen table.

We left the house and walked further along Willow Park Crescent, turning right at the t-junction at the end of the road and the roundabout on the intersection of Glasnevin Avenue and Ballygall Road was in sight again.

Norah was very quiet on the way back to the apartment, so I kept up an inane stream of chatter about our morning.

When we got back to the apartment she said,

'I can't go back.'

'What do you mean?'

'Even if she, Maighread, rings. I can't go back, not without telling her.'

'About what?' I stupidly asked.

'Tom, of course. Killing Tom. Oh Jesus. If she knew that the woman her little granddaughter trusted so much...' she was growing hysterical. Perhaps only the second time I had seen her like this.

'Norah. Listen. Listen to me now. Yes, you killed Tom. But it was half accident, half self-defence. Maighread and any other decent human being will feel nothing but sorrow and pity for you. Nobody, with the exception of Carmel Furlong – who is certifiable anyway – blames you for what happened. And any judge or jury worth their salt will forgive you and let you go. And you have to, have to, have to do the same for yourself. Else you might as well have died with him.'

She stared at me, eyes streaming. For the third time that day she couldn't speak. She just indicated her room and I nodded.

I heard her sobbing for ages afterwards but didn't go near her. Her tears were important too.

Later I made tea and tapped on her door, no answer so I gently opened it and peeped in. She was fast asleep, curled in a foetal position, her thumb touching her lips. I could feel a lump in my own throat. I threw her dressing gown over her and left her to sleep, hoping that her dreams were of sunny summer days in the gardens or green of Willow Park Crescent.

Chapter Twenty

Liam rang Norah fairly regularly, keeping her updated on the progress of the case. The majesty of the law. The cogs and wheels grind incredibly slowly in civil cases and convoluted tribunals on misdemeanours in business or political life. Norah's case seemed to be galloping along, a date in early November had been set for the case. Barring the original charge and the granting of bail Norah had had no previous involvement with the courts and the atmosphere in them really intimidated, dwarfed her. Norah's plea would be guilty to manslaughter in self-defence.

Carmel Furlong had been kicking up a bit of a stink. Insisting that the police and prosecution investigate Charles Donnelly; the fact that Norah stood to inherit a substantial sum of money and land and businesses did strengthen the prosecution case. It supplied a motive for premeditation re Tom's death. The fact that Carmel was a paranoid and deeply disturbed woman somewhat diminished her assertions. But the smokescreen she was creating was causing something of a fire with the DPP.

When Norah had been examined by the police doctors there had been no marks of a recent beating, but Liam and the barrister felt there was enough evidence to substantiate their plea in the photographs taken of her on arrest and of her garden after Tom had wreaked havoc with the digger.

There was also substantial evidence obtained from medical records in Sligo, Leitrim and Donegal.

The deviousness used by Tom Furlong to disguise his abuse of Norah was incredible. When he calmed down after a beating he would usually help her clean her up and if he thought she had broken bones he would take her to hospital.

One Saturday in March Norah told me how Tom had changed hospitals after a concerned doctor queried her third visit to Leitrim in eighteen months.

'He was foreign, maybe an Indian or Pakistani or something like that,' said Norah. 'A young fella, his hands felt very cool; he had long dark fingers, the skin on the side of them cracked and stained the colour of black tea. He was very gentle, soft spoken. Two of my ribs were cracked and when he looked at my file he saw it was the second time I'd come in with cracked ribs. Then there was the broken thumb in the previous year.' She held up her right hand, the thumb was crooked. 'It never set properly, Tom left it for two days before he brought me in. I think he only brought me in because I cried in pain when I put pressure on it trying to lift a pot of potatoes off the cooker.'

'This doctor – he had a funny name, his surname and first name were the same. Sahid Sahid.' She smiled. 'It sounded so...I don't know...strange. Like a name in a fairy story. I was in a lot of pain when he examined me. I felt weird, a bit spaced out. He started to ask questions; we had prepared stories for them all but he was suspicious. This was maybe four or five years after we were married. I was starting to feel strained at that stage and he must have picked up on it. Tom nearly died; he got me out of there as quickly as possible. The next time I needed a hospital he took me to Sligo General, told staff there we were visiting family in Sligo town.'

'That's where Charles works isn't it?' I placed part-skinned chicken breasts in a casserole dish to marinate. Liam and John were both in Dublin and were coming to dinner. Norah was at the sink peeling potatoes, her back to me. 'Yes, he works out of the Occupational Therapy unit there. Are you doing separate vegetables or are you putting them in with the chicken?'

Norah was a great cook. I don't think I'd ever eaten so many lovely home-cooked meals. She preferred eating in, seemed to be uncomfortable with people waiting on her. Mother had given me gift vouchers for a restaurant of a higher class than I would usually frequent for Christmas. Norah and myself went along one gloomy February evening. When the waiter shook out Norah's napkin to place on her lap she jumped like a startled hare. Catching my eye she blushed, laughed when he went away.

'Lord, I didn't know what he was going to do.' We giggled but after that she hesitated any time I suggested eating out.

Initially she had kept out of my way in the evenings, going for a walk if it was dry or to her room if she couldn't get out. She said she found the noise of the traffic and the busy suburban streets a bit alarming after the peace of rural Leitrim. She often spent time in the local library. She talked about joining a book club they were running but was hesitant. I felt for her. She couldn't even commit to something as innocuous as that, fearing that her cover would be blown.

I broached this with her that evening.

'Honestly Norah, that library is in Phibsboro, almost the city! Most of the people who use that library are either students or people renting houses and flats. A passing populace. Your picture never appeared in the paper and unless you were unfortunate enough to bump into someone from home you could be anyone. Actually,' I laughed, 'you could have a bit of fun, make up a whole new persona for yourself, wear a wig, buy new clothes, change the way you look. You've an ideal opportunity to be anyone you want to be.

'I don't even know who I am anymore, let alone pretend to be anyone else.' She shook her head. 'I couldn't. I just wouldn't feel comfortable. I'm not like you.'

'Believe me Norah, once I had as many... What? Can I call them hang-ups without insulting you.'

I looked at her.

She coloured, looked at me with hurt eyes.

'Sorry, I'm not trying to offend you. Tact was never my strong point. But all the things you feel insecure about, I felt too. It's only in the last five or six years that I've had the courage to take my life in my own hands, be responsible for my own happiness.'

'You sound like that America fella off the telly!' she retorted. 'That Dr. Phil! Is that not all a load...Tom used to say it was rubbish, people like him and that Oprah making money out of ordinary people, using their unhappiness, putting it on the telly, making them into freaks. Telling them they can change things. No thanks. I'll stick the way I am.' She pulled her cardigan around herself, twisted her lips. 'There are no mirrors in prison!'

She could be a little odd. She spent a lot of time cleaning, was a bit obsessive about things being straight, clean lines, that sort of thing I got used to coming home to a spotless apartment. I wouldn't have thought of myself as a total slattern, I'm a bit untidy but I do get mad fits of energy and tear into the housework, but Norah was unbelieveable.

'I like things nice,' she said when I told her she didn't have to bother. 'I'm here most of the day and it keeps me occupied. Tom was so fussy....' She stopped and turned away, straightening some books I had dumped on the coffee table.

'And..?' I prompted.

'Nothing, I just got into the habit of tidiness. He couldn't bear anything to be out of place. The first time he, you know, lost his temper, it was over a mug I hadn't dried properly before I put it back in the press. I didn't do that again. I learned to be really, really tidy. I do like it like that myself though,' she added quickly.

'It wasn't really over a half-dried cup though Norah was it?'

'What do you mean?'

'I've been doing a bit of research, the Internet is brilliant. Christ, if my boss discovers how much time I've spent searching it I'll be fired! I'm no psychologist but Tom just used getting mad about stupid things like half-dried cups to punish you, make you see he was in charge. It's all about power, control. It's what they do.'

'Who do?' She had been slightly red about the neck.

'People who abuse other people, dominate them, use force to make them do what they want.' I was in full flow.

'I don't know what you're talking about. You and Liam and John, even Charles. Those people. They're not Tom. Tom was my husband. I did love him. I did. He was good most of the time; he tried so hard. I'm not stupid. I wouldn't have stayed if I didn't love him, think I could help him. I had to. There was Teasie you see. Maybe you'd be better off reading a flippin' crime book instead of trying to see what made me and my husband tick.' She threw a damp cloth she had been dusting with onto the table and she half-ran to her room.

I sighed, gave up. It was frustrating. I'd grown fond of her in the time she was with me, she was quiet and unobtrusive. When she'd cut her hair and started to come out of her shell I had hoped it was the beginning of a new life for her. But I wasn't going to change a lifetime of habits and her way of looking at the world in my ham-fisted way. Hadn't Tom tried to mould her to his way of liking too? Was I guilty of the same thing?

'Norah, Norah!' I called after her, 'I'm sorry, I was just trying to help, to understand…' I leaned against the wall in the corridor to her room.

Silence. I walked down, knocked softly.

'Norah, please. The last thing I want to do is upset you.'

'I'm not some kind of a freak, you know.' Her voice muffled by both tears and the door. 'I didn't just lie down and let him do it. He couldn't help himself, he didn't used to be like that, in the beginning he was mostly gentle and kind. For God's sake I wouldn't have married him otherwise. I'm not stupid.'

'I know, please. I'm sorry. Look, I'm going out for a while for a run. The lads will be here in about an hour, I'll be back before that.'

Silence. 'Norah?'

The door opened a little. Her pale and puffy face appeared in the jamb.

'Okay. I'm sorry. I know you're all only trying to help. It's just...' she left it unfinished. ' I'll look after the casserole.'

I placed the palm of my hand on her face and she flinched slightly.

'I really am sorry, Norah. Typical me, barging in, over-enthusiastic. It was one of the things John and I argued about most. What he saw as interference in others' lives I saw as interest in them. There you are. 'Marry a cat of your own kind and it won't scratch,' my Dad used to say. Mind you he hadn't taken his own advice; himself and Mother were totally different.' I gave her arm a squeeze and went to my own room.

I pulled my running gear from the wardrobe and started to change, thinking about what I had just said.

I was glad Liam and Norah would be there that night. I didn't know if I was ready to be completely alone with John, to start re-examining what had gone wrong with us all those years ago, to look at what I had probably let go. No probably, I knew I had let the love of my life walk out of it. No, I had virtually kicked him out the door. As I started my run in the damp March afternoon I wondered did he think about that also and was he ready to come back in that door again.

Chapter Twenty-One

It's April and Norah's sessions with the therapist have hit an impasse. Norah is struggling, deeply depressed, so he refers her back to a psychiatrist to review her medication. He suggests they take a two week break and recommence then. Recommence, talk it all out, make everything alright. Most days she opens her eyes and feels 'Christ, not again.' And then there is the day to be crawled through with unbearable slowness before she can climb back into the bed and wait for blessed, numbing sleep to take away the loneliness and horror of her life.

'This I understand,' says Sinead. 'Just be, Norah; all you have to do today is "Be".'

'What does that mean!' Norah is snappy.

'Look. I know the way you feel. I've been through something like this. I know how you feel. Not fully, but I have an inkling. Believe me. It will pass – just keep going Norah, get up and be. You don't have to do anything else. See the psychiatrist; give the therapist a break for a while. Just take the next breath; I won't talk unless you want to. I'll just be here for whenever you need me. But breathe Norah, just concentrate on the next breath, the next step.'

Sometimes Sinead talks a lot of touchy-feely crap. But this makes some sense. So she tries. Not to think, not to do anything, but be. But some days it's hard. Because some days being is the one thing she doesn't want.

No matter what she does, what she says, what she

thinks, nothing can change the fact that she took Tom's life. She doesn't care what anyone else says about Tom. John and Liam and their attempts to justify what she did, find a defence for her, 'battered wife syndrome', provocation, self-defence. They're just excuses. All excuses. What the therapist and psychiatrist said about forgiving herself and moving on. She took Tom's life. And she knew, in that very minute she knew what she was doing.

It had been a bright, warm day, one of those pet days that October can throw at you, lulling you into thinking that winter is still far away. Norah worked all day in the garden, deadheading dahlias and roses, weeding, mulching. She had cut the lawn, potted on some cuttings.

The sound of tyres crunching on the gravel at the front of the house surprised her, Tom had said he'd be later than usual. She sighed, wondering was he starting up his obsessive checking on her again. Things had been quiet, calm between them for the last couple of months. As she washed her hands at the garden tap the sound of the doorbell ringing surprised her more. Someone other than Tom obviously. Someone lost perhaps.

'Just a minute. I'll be with you in a minute,' she shouted.

She was sitting on the back door step pulling off her wellies when the big smiley face and ginger-topped head of Charles Donnelly appeared around the gable end of the house.

'Might have known where you would be. God Norah, you have it absolutely beautiful. That's some kind of dahlia isn't it?' He pointed to her pride and joy, an enormous dahlia still bearing deep wine-coloured dinner plates of blooms. The summer had been kind to the plants, their well-sheltered position combined with good staking and an almost religious fervour when it came to watering and protecting them from marauding caterpillars and slugs meant they still looked good.

They had rambled around the garden, she showing him additions to it and changes made since he had last seen it, he asking questions and admiring her handiwork. She was pleased that someone was so appreciative and understanding of what she had done; to Tom it was simply a garden, a place to sit and read the paper on warm summer evenings. She glanced at the sun in the sky, it was still early.

'Will you have tea?'

'Is there apple tart?' An old joke.

'No, but I think I still have curranty bread left.'

'Oh, even better,' he moaned in delight.

She led him in through the back door and the utility room to the kitchen and they sat and chatted. He had been calling in on clients about five miles away and decided to call, see how she was.

They talked about his garden, how it was developing and what plans he had for it. They reminisced about Teasie.

'So many of my clients just want to curl up and die. But not Teasie, she was some lady, a real battler.'

'She was that alright. Frank used to call her a Jack Russell when she got the bit between her teeth over something. She would never give in without a fight.' Norah's eyes had filled for the loss of her beloved Teasie. It still hurt, even three years after her death she missed her every day, would talk to her in her head as she worked in the house and garden. She pulled the tears back and blew her nose.

'Now, all done,' she said. 'Teasie would've been the first one to dust off her hands at the graveyard, say that's that – now we must get on with it. The dead wouldn't want us wasting time grieving, would they? They would give anything for the one thing we have that they haven't.'

'She was incredibly wise.' Charles patted Norah's hand.

'Look, take some of the cuttings I made this morning. I've far too many.'

She stood up quickly and disappeared out the kitchen door.

Charles lifted the mugs and plates and placed them in the sink and was waiting for her at the back door when she reappeared from the shed. Walking around the house towards his car she had explained what to do with the cuttings to give them the best chance of survival.

'And will you come gunning for me if they die?'

'Yes, I'll hear them screaming from forty miles away.

'Norah, save us Norah, he's crucifying us,' she responded.

He carefully placed the cuttings on the floor of the front passenger seat.

'Speaking of which, how are things with you and your husband?'

She flushed then went pale. No one, except occasionally Denis Bradley, was this direct about Tom, or rather her and Tom.

'Oh you know. Good. Good most of the time.'

He raised his eyebrows.

'Look, honestly it's okay. You're not married are you?' She felt embarrassed and a little angry also.

He shook his head.

'Well then, every marriage has its ups and downs. That whole time with Teasie being ill and all. It was tough on all of us. Tom just felt neglected and sometimes he took it out on me. But everything is fine now.'

'Okay. If you say so. I know its none of my business but… well look, if you ever need to talk you can ring the hospital and leave a message and I'll contact you.'

'It's really not necessary but thank you anyway.'

He nodded and climbed into the car, drove away with a wave out the window.

She raked through the gravel, eradicating the signs of a car being parked in an unfamiliar spot, then went indoors.

She switched on the TV in the living room and sat on the sofa, she felt a little tired after the gardening and the discussion with Charles about Teasie and then Tom left her feeling a little strained. It had gone cool, the living room faced east and was always a little chilly in the evenings. She pulled the tartan Foxford rug from the back of the settee around her and half-watched the inane chatter on some afternoon magazine style programme. She soon drifted into sleep.

When she woke Tom was standing over her thrusting two mugs towards her.

'Oh, hi! Is it that time? Sorry. Lord, I must have fallen asleep. It won't take long to do dinner though; it just needs heating up…'

'Who was here? Drinking tea in my kitchen with my wife?' His eyes black pinpricks in a tightened face.

She opened her mouth to speak.

'Don't bother your head telling me. He was spotted you see. Him and his bloody big tank of a car. P.J. Cunningham stopped into the shop wondering were you sick that you need an occupational therapist calling.'

He hadn't showered, she could smell raw meat on him.

One of the mugs smashed against the wall behind her, the other came crashing down on her skull.

'You're such a fucking bitch, a stupid lying fucking whore. I fucking warned you. I fucking warned him to stay away. Oh Jesus, Jesus what did I ever do to deserve this? All I've ever done was work hard to provide for you and those other fucking bitches. And this is how I'm repaid. Well, you won't make a fool of me lady. No. No more. Tom Furlong says no more. You'll not make me a laughing stock….'

She pulled the blanket over her head, muffling his words to a roaring wave and hoping it would help dull the expected blows.

But he left the room. He left the house. Pulling away from it with a screech of tires and a shower of gravel.

She fingered her skull, no blood. An egg of a lump was rising. Picking up the shards of ceramic she went to the kitchen and binned them, then got a packet of frozen peas from the freezer and held it on the lump until her head felt numb. She went back to the living room, straightened the rug on the back of the sofa and switched off the TV.

She washed the two plates and cutlery, wondered whether to put the spuds on. Most likely Tom had gone to the pub and it wouldn't be food he looked for when he came home. Maybe she'd just heat the stew and have some with bread. But maybe not. Her stomach felt sick, she knew a big beating was coming. It had been ages. Months. She had even dared, yet again, to hope.

She tried to plan escape strategies, routes. Debated with herself whether she should hide in the shed, or walk the five miles to Carmel's house on some pretext. He seemed reluctant to touch her when Carmel was about. Was Carmel the lesser of the two evils? No, if she was missing when he came in it would make it worse in the long run.

She wondered would this time be like the last one. She didn't think so. Last time he had simply fallen asleep on the couch. He had been contrite the next morning, not remembering if he had anything to be contrite about. But this time he had a grievance. She was very afraid.

'Fuck.' Her voice startled her. Apart from what she had said. She rarely cursed.

It was the waiting that was killing. She decided to do something, keep busy and then she wouldn't think. Maybe she'd turn out the hot press. The bathroom could do with a good thorough clean. Yes. The bathroom.

Norah had been on her knees with an old toothbrush scrubbing the grout between the tiles when she heard the rumble outside. She stopped, head cocked, listening. It was some type of engine, but not the car or the tractor. Whatever it was, it was rumbling up the side of the house.

She slipped into the kitchen, almost dark at this stage and through the window she saw Tom in the seat of Josie Diver's battered mini digger. She was about to wonder what he was at when it struck her. Her garden.

'Ah Jesus, Ah no.' She thought her legs would go from under her, but she gathered herself together, ran through the utility room and wrenched open the back door.

'Tom, please. No Tom. Please. Oh Jesus.' The lower

teeth of the digger were burrowing under the roots of her long-established weigela, gnawing and tugging until it started to fall in on top of the digger.

Tom reversed and moved further down the garden, the caterpillar wheels crushing smaller plants as the teeth smashed and devoured larger shrubs. Above the rumble of the digger he roared,

'Now. Now we'll see. Fuck you. Fuck you. What did I ever do? There. See. See what I can do.'

Her roses, her beautiful roses. The peach rambler planted in memory of her parents, the yellow floribunda for her darling Frank and the newest a beautiful ivory tea rose for Teasie.

'Tom, Tom,' she screamed again, 'Stop, please stop.' She ran out towards the digger, not thinking of her own danger, intent on deflecting him from his rampage.

'Fuckin' whore. He'll not come calling anymore.' He was laughing and shouting at something she couldn't see. His face was red and sweating, his eyes wilder than she had ever seen.

'Tom. Please Tom. Not my garden. Not my garden.' She was crying.

'Your garden? My fucking garden you mean, your grave. I'll bury you in the fucking thing. Your bones will make great fertiliser.' He grinned manically, a laughing parody of every mad man in every stupid horror movie she had ever seen. He turned the digger in her direction, revved like a boy racer.

She started wildly to run but then twisted, which way? He anticipated her path to the house and reversed to block her. Panicked she ran towards the shed, fumbled at the bolt as he bore down on her.

'You fucking idiot. Always and ever a fool. Think that bit of wood will keep you safe?'

She jumped into the shed and before the door could bang shut behind her he had stopped it with the arm of the digger and forced it away from its hinges.

'Oh Jesus, Jesus.' It would be her coffin.

He was cursing, manoeuvring the digger into the best position to mow her and the shed down. She could go nowhere. She wet herself.

'Oh No. Not like this. Jesus, Frank, Teasie, Mam, please help me, help me. No. Tom. No.' The jittery mumbling from her rose to a scream as with an almighty cracking the wall caved in towards her and the roof shifted and started to fall. Initially she crouched, hands protecting her head, then she threw herself flat.

When the world stopped shaking and she was sure she was still alive she crawled towards a shard of dusky light knifing through a gap in the collapsed wood. She almost lost an eye when her face came in contact with the sharp end of the garden shears and she grasped them and dragged them with her, twisting away from the sound of the digger coming again towards the flattened shed.

She freed herself from the wood and crawled behind the overgrown moss rose which normally semi-camouflaged the shed.

'Jesus. Sweet Jesus.' Her heart was pounding so hard she thought something in her somewhere must burst to relieve the pressure.

'Now. Cunt. Fucking useless dried up cow. Now. Where's your big man now? Stupid bitch.' On and on he roared, fouler and fouler.

He was insane.

Then it had all stopped. The engine, the shouting, the sound of cracking wood. A thick, waiting silence.

She had bitten on the sleeve of her cardigan to muffle her racked breathing.

Tom started to cry, tear-laden words tumbling from him. 'For fucksake Norah. Why? All I ever wanted was you. This shouldn't have happened. It shouldn't have happened. It's all ruined now. Ruined.'

He sat for a while weeping and mumbling.

Then he had reversed the digger and left the engine running, throwing light on the heap of wood as he started to pull at it, calling her name over and over.

She had to move. Or did she? Adrenalin dictated yes. Peering through the dense shrub she tried to place him. His back was to her and he was lifting the side of the shed, looking for her, calling her name. She made a run for the open back door but she tripped and sprawled across the lawn. He heard and sprinted towards her arms outstretched, pleading,

'Norah, Norah. Aw Jesus, Norah'.

'Get up! Up! C'mon! Up! Up!' She ordered herself back on her feet and just made it through the back door into the utility room before him. She backed her way through the room, pointing the shears at him.

'Tom. Enough. Tom. Stop. Please - just STOP MOVING!' She screamed in fear and rage.

He stopped, wary, surprised. He had never seen her, she had never felt like, never reacted like, this. He took another step towards her, arms out, placatory.

'I won't touch you. It's over. Over. Look. I'm sorry. Norah, I'm sorry. It'll stop. Never again. I'll stop.' His eyes glittered with tears, face pleading. She saw the little boy in that face.

She let the shears dip slightly and stepped backwards up the step into the kitchen, pushing open the kitchen door with her elbows.

'I can't take anymore Tom. I can't. I have to go.'

'No! What do you mean? Stop. Where can you go? Don't go. Norah. Norah.' He was crying, something in her different and something in him saw it.

She was crying too. 'We're bad for each other. I just... Just let me go.'

'No. Why? I'll stop. I'll change. It'll be different. It was good wasn't it, this last year? When it's just you and me. I'll stop drinking completely. It's only been then hasn't it, these last two years.' He was inching forward, his right foot reached for the step into the kitchen.

'Stop Tom!' She raised the shears again. 'Please. It's no good. We're no good.'

'I won't let you. You'll never get away. I'll find you.

You can't leave me.' His voice rose to a panicky scream.

His left foot was moving up onto the step and it was a split-second decision. But it was a conscious decision. He was right. She could never leave. He would never let her. And he would destroy her and she would let him do that and in doing that destroy them both. So she raised her arms and with all the strength her years of digging and weeding, clipping and cutting combined with a vicious wish for all the hate and pain to stop she drove the slightly opened shears at him.

The breath came out of him in a long, exhaled 'umph'. He stumbled back into the utility room and tried to lift his arms up to the shears lodged in two places in his chest.

'Norah? Norah?' He looked at her in surprise, a trickle of blood came out his mouth.

Then his legs went and as he started to fall forwards he looked at her, his eyes pleading. The handles of the shears had prevented him falling fully face downwards and by the noise he made she knew the tips were being driven further into his body with impact. He rolled on his side, his left hand curled around the handle of the shears, staring at her without seeing her, opened his mouth but only gurgled.

The light in his eyes faded and he quietened very soon.

Hands by her side, breath ragged she stood watching, waiting for him to move again. Then she realised she felt cold and suddenly weak. She half-closed the kitchen door and moved towards a kitchen chair.

The intercom buzzer goes. Norah ignores it, but it's persistent. Then her mobile phone rings. Charles's name pulsing on the little green screen. She answers it and starts to weep as his big warm voice washes over her.

'Norah? Hey Norah? Are you in the apartment? It's me, love, it's me. Open the door, let me up.'

So she does. And he comes up and he sits on the sofa with her and holds her and lets her cry, lets her tell it all, everything. And he doesn't tell her it's all going to be alright. He doesn't try to make her think or accept herself, he just keeps stroking and murmuring and she knows that with him she'll never have to think before she talks or moves. And it doesn't matter if she doesn't accept herself and what she's done. Because he accepts it and her. And how did he tell her all this without saying anything?

So she starts to laugh at herself, at him, them, through the snots and tears and he laughs too, without any idea why he's laughing.

'Why are you laughing?' she asks.

'Because you are. And it's a great sound. Even if it is a bit watery.'

So she laughs more. Then in a while he gets serious and tells her everything he had already told her without saying it.

'Come on,' he says after an hour or so, standing up, pulling her off the couch. 'Wash your snotty face. We both need some air. So does Slippers.'

She stops on the way to the bathroom.

'Who or what is Slippers?'

He throws his eyes up to the ceiling.

'It's a long story. To do with aging parents, a fool of a brother and me running out on an elderly spaniel. Come on and I'll introduce you to the new female – bitch actually – in my life.'

When they go outside a lunatic barking is coming from Charles's jeep.

'Be quiet you fool.' Charles opens the rear door and a golden bundle of muscle and paws and tail throws itself kamikaze-style at Charles then turns and leaps at Norah, tail wagging furiously, eyes bright with excitement.

'Oh Lord! She's gorgeous. Hello, hello. Aren't you gorgeous?' Norah grapples with the beautiful golden retriever as she tries to slather Norah with affection.

'My brother, David, decided the parents needed a dog to keep them company and bought them this lunatic. She had them heartbroken within a week. Chewing everything in sight and throwing herself at all callers. She destroyed Dad's garden too. But the last straw was when she knocked down two of my nieces in her excitement. I don't know what David was thinking of! Retrievers are definitely a pet for someone with plenty of room and energy. So I swapped my poor auld spaniel Lady for her. Get down girl. Slippers! Here – fetch.' He throws a tennis ball from the back of the car across the car park and the dog charges after it. He takes out a lead.

'Are you okay for a walk?'

'Yes. A walk would be good. We could walk in as far as the canal, let her have a run there. It won't be busy now. I never even asked. Why are you up?' Norah smiles as Slippers gallops back at full speed, drops the ball at their feet and barks in delight.

'Sinead rang me. Don't look like that. She was worried about you. So I took a few days off and I'm going to mind you. If you'll let me.' He looks at her.

'Charles, are you sure? I'd love to say I don't need minding, but it's really great you're here.' Norah blushes and places her right hand on his upper arm. 'I feel so safe when you're around. And it's a long time since I felt safe.'

Charles takes her hand in his and rubs it gently.

'Norah, darling...you do need minding. I'm here because I want to be. I was going to say 'wild horses couldn't have stopped me' but I proved the saying by bringing a wild dog instead.' This as Slippers is twisting herself and the lead into a knot about Norah's legs.

She laughs and disentangles herself and they set off on their walk. Slippers is definitely in charge, straining at the leash, barking frantically at a plastic bag that skitters ahead of them in the breeze; it takes all of Charles's strength to keep a modicum of control on her.

Norah takes the lead at one stage and is amused by the power of the animal. She talks about the different dogs in her life in the past. Her fear of them years ago when she lived in Dublin, then having pups to care for when she arrived at Tibraden and growing up with them. The fun she had had with them, the ache in her heart when one had to be put down. She would have loved a dog in recent years but Tom thought of dogs as working farm animals not pets. He had a lovely collie to help him with sheep but she was kept up in the shed beside the old house. She wonders now is Carmel still looking after the dog. Probably not – the poor animal.

At the canal they let Slippers off the lead and try to wear her out by throwing sticks and the ball. She is indefatigable. They're tired long before her and sit on a bench enjoying the early April sun glinting on the grey-green water. A family of swans are moving in slow and stately procession up the canal. Slippers spots them and stands stock still, tail straight and nose quivering as her eyes follow their progress.

Then she's off. Launches herself into the canal, intent on making new friends.

'Jesus! This is going to end in tears! Slippers! Slippers! Come here girl, good girl come on.' Charles stands up and moves to the edge of the bank, crouches down, clicking his fingers and whistling at the dog.

Slippers has no intention of coming back; the water's lovely and she wants to have a chat with the cygnets. She doesn't take into account their overprotective parents. One of them, Norah thinks it's the pen, stretches her neck and hisses at Slippers. The dog stops for a moment, treading water, then lets out a friendly bark in return. That does it. Both cob and pen spread their wings and hissing and flapping drive the misfortunate Slippers towards Charles and relative safety.

The dog scrambles onto the bank and immediately drenches Charles as she shakes filthy water from her coat. The swans retreat, still hissing.

'Slippers! You twit!' Charles grabs her collar and reattaches the lead.

Norah is crying again. But this time with laughter.

'Look at you, you're soaked. Poor old Slippers. Did you get a fright, you silly dog?' She rubs the animal's sodden fur, shrieks with laughter and jumps back as Slippers shakes herself out again.

'Poor old Slippers? What about poor me? What did I ever do to deserve this eejit in my life?' Charles pulls a self-mocking face.

'I bet she's the best thing that's happened to you in a long time. A bit of life. You'll need to put in a dog run at home though. I don't want to hear she's ripped up all the lovely plants you've put down. Come on, let's get home and dry you both out.'

Charles says something about the dog being the second-best thing. But Norah shushes him and changes the conversation back to inconsequentials. That's what she likes about him, he can chat about anything and he follows her lead. He hasn't disguised his feelings for her in any way but is not forcing the issue. He's waiting for her. And she's not quite ready yet. She will be soon she thinks. She knows now that what Sinead said about 'being' is true. Right now, this moment it feels good to be. And she will enjoy right now, this minute and then maybe the next minute or the minute after that might be bearable as well.

Chapter Twenty-Two

One glorious day in that unusually sunny June, Rob and I sprawled on the grass in the park in Mountjoy Square. Rob was a bit uncomfortable – he's neurotic about Weill's disease. He always carefully wipes the top of a longneck or a can before he drinks from it.

'Do you know how many rats there are in Dublin?' he said, irritated at my slagging.

'No, but I've a feeling you're going to tell me.' I took a bite from my ham and cheese sandwich and stuck a cheese and onion crisp in my mouth to enhance the flavour.

'In urban areas the ratio of rats to humans is roughly 5:1, so that makes – in the city alone – roughly two and a half million rats? It's the thoughts of the little buggers pissing all over the place. If I even think I'm developing 'flu-like symptoms I'll be down to the doc double quick.' He shuddered.

'Never knew you were a hypochondriac Rob, I can't remember the last time you were out sick.' The watery latte from the machine in the local Spar was disgusting so I discarded it and popped a can of Coke, wiping the lip of before I took a sip.

'See, you're doing it too! I'm not a hypochondriac. I just don't like bloody rats!' He turned his face up to the sun and we ate in a companionable silence layered with the rumble of traffic and the lazy chatter of other people doing as we were. There was a playground opposite where we sat. We had a bit of fun trying to match child to parent of the few families in it. Rob won – getting two definitely right when the mother he had selected for a boy and girl on the see-saw shrieked,

'Darren – ye thick ye – don't bang Leona down so hard. She'll only start her whinging.'

I failed miserably – Rob told me I just wasn't observant enough, couldn't read body language, etcetera.

'Yeah, yeah, okay Mr whatshisname, the manwatcher fella. Oooooooo!' I stretched like a cat, moaning with pleasure as the sun warmed through to my bones. 'I think I'll move to the South of France or Italy. Imagine having this all the time.'

'Mr whatshisname is Desmond Morris – ye thick ye. As to the sun, we'd probably get fed up of it, the continentals all stay indoors sensibly sleeping in the siesta. Isn't it only "mad dogs and Englishmen that go out in the midday sun" – who said that?' His eyes were closed, face upturned.

'Noel Coward – ye big jackeen thick. Shit – look at the time, it's twenty past; we'll have to run if we want to make the clock.' I started to gather our rubbish together.

Rob groaned. 'Let's take a half day. C'mon, please. We owe it to ourselves. It is our duty to enjoy the sun when it shines in this country. I think that should be written into our Constitution – yeah – all office workers can have halfers on sunny days.'

'We'd have to have another bloody referendum though. You know, you're right. I'll text Les now and tell him I'm taking leave – there's nothing urgent on anyway.' I pulled my mobile from my bag.

'That's one referendum there would an overwhelming yes to. I'll ring my gobdaw in about an hour, make up a sick aunt or cat or something.' His boss, Daithi, is the original twit and worse still one of those twits who considers himself highly intelligent. Management had sidelined him into the place he could do least damage and rotated staff under him every six months or so. Rob was considered a saint because he had put up with him for over a year. He said that fact better be taken into consideration the next time a promotion prospect arose. We bitched about him for a while.

'D'ye remember 'The 'A' Team?' asked Rob.

'God yes, Hannibal and Murdoch and Mr 'T'. What was the good looking fella's name?'

'"Face" or "Templeton Peck" – take your pick. Do you know he was the first man I had a crush on. All the other kids wanted to be Hannibal or Mr T. or Murdoch. Me? I was happy with the suave "Face". That's when I started to realise I was different. Remember what Mr T. used to say about Murdoch?' He adopted Mr T.'s gruff voice, '"the man's a fool Hannibal!"'

I laughed, 'You have it to a 'T', okay okay, poor pun!' This for his pained expression.

'Well Mr T. always said that phrase with a certain amount of gruff affection for Murdoch but I say it without the slightest affection and great vehemence for our revered Daithi.' He stood up. 'Feck it, let's get pissed! We haven't had a jar together since January.'

'Ah Rob, I'm not going to sit in a pub, it's too gorgeous out here.'

'Not a pub, let's be teenagers, I'll go down and buy a flagon of cider. They keep it in the fridge in Spar. Are you on?'

I pulled a face. 'I'd feel a bit common drinking in a public park'

'Are you turning into your Ma? Sure, people would just think you're Eastern European.'

'That's racist and Motherist! Alright, but make sure you get plastic cups, I'm not swigging it by the neck, I do have some standards.'

So he did and he brought back Pringles and cashew nuts and we slowly drank our way through the afternoon. We solved all the conundrums of the world, talked nonsense about our 'Sunshine referendum', I argued for the 'No' side on behalf of employers and people who already worked outdoors, but lamely admitted I would be a 'Yes' voter.

By five o'clock we were both well oiled and mellow and had dissected the characters of all our colleagues. My face and arms were a bit sunburned. Rob has sallow skin so he had just toasted himself a delicious golden brown.

'I bet you've no protection on – you look like a lush – your face is bright red!' He touched my already peeling nose.

'I beg your pardon Mr. Cleary. I always use protection, I just didn't think I'd be out in the sun so long.'

'Speaking of protection, how are things with the lovely John O'?'

I groaned. 'Oh, I need more drink to discuss that one.' I proffered my plastic cup. 'Fuck it Rob, I think I love him. Think I've always loved him but I think we're starting to dance about the playing for keeps stage now. I'm happy but I'm scared. What am I going to do?'

He poured the last of the cider into my cup. 'Drink that, I'll go back to the off licence and we'll meander up towards your place via the canal and finish the discussion there. I assume it's alright if I pass out on the sofa?'

'Of course. Even if Charles is there, he seems to have moved from the sofa into Norah's room.'

'What! You never told me!'

'I was afraid to. It's so recent and delicate, I'm afraid if I talk about it something will go wrong. Imagine in the middle of all she's going through she finds love. John and Liam are a bit worried word will get out and it'll look peculiar considering Charles was in Norah's house earlier in the day Tom died.' I paused. 'The Gardai were never fully happy with Norah being the culprit, despite all the evidence. She's so slight. But she says she did it and the pathologist said it was possible. Jesus, if Carmel Furlong gets wind of Charles and Norah being together she'll go to town altogether. She's making a terrible nuisance of herself, even though Liam has written to her and assured her that the house will be signed over to her. Norah's wishes. I'd give the witch nothing. At least the DPP seem to have her measure – according to John it doesn't look like they'll put her in the witness stand.'

'Jaysis, nobody in their right minds could believe Charles had anything to do with a murder. It's just not in the man's psyche. Mind you I'd say the same about Norah. No, I think them getting together is a great development. He's so good for her, they just seem so right together. They're both kind of childlike, trusting.' He got to his feet and walked, admirably straight, out of the park.

When he came back the bag looked suspiciously bulky.

'What did you get?'

'Vodka and a two litre bottle of coke. We're going the whole hog on the teenage front. See, when we get halfway through the vodka we pour the rest of it into the by then half-empty Coke bottle and innocently walk around with it. We might even be allowed on a bus if we can't face the full walk.' His eyes were dancing.

I'd love to see Rob play Puck in *A Midsummer Night's Dream*. I suggest at least once a year that the society should try a straight play, but then I made the mistake of mentioning the play I want to do.

'Shakespeare's too heavy'

'It would put people off.'

Most of them associated it with slogging through texts in a heavy handed way for exams in school. I couldn't convince them that Shakespeare's real genius lies in his comedies – he knew how to make ordinary people laugh. The ease and the flow in the musicality of the lines with all their wonder, poetry and magic. Rob was so physically perfect for Puck and it was well within his acting range. Secretly I fancied myself as Titania, Queen of the Fairies, beautiful and mysterious and wise, but was more likely to end up directing – afraid that someone else wouldn't show MY *Midsummer Night's Dream*.

I tried to bring up the subject again as he poured the first of the vodka and cokes.

'Now, now Breslin. This is not an E.G.M. of the

Musical and Dramatic Society – hold your fire until the yearly planning meeting next month. If you're a good girl and give me the complete low-down on yourself and the wondrous Mr O'Sullivan I might even support you. Shit, I have to ring Daithi.' He pulled out his mobile and made a ludicrous phone call to his paper boss.

'We could even find a part for Daithi in it. There's loads of half-eejits in the play.' I would love to say that I sipped from my cup, but I was at slugging stage.

'No way, it's enough having to work for him. Even the thoughts of spending time with him outside of work makes me feel sick.' Rob narrowed his eyes and examined the mixture in his cup.

'The nausea would have nothing to do with alco…alcol…the jar would it?' I lay on my side pulling at bits of grass. My words were definitely slurring and the grass seemed intensely green in the sun.

'D'ye know, I think we better walk a little. Buy some bread and ham, find a nice bench on the canal to eat some of it, feed the ducks with the rest and then consider whether we'll continue drinking,' he started to pull our bits and pieces together.

'You're probably right. I think that park ranger is starting to look funny at us anyway!' I sighed, pulling on my shoes. 'Oh I'm so glad I didn't wear heels today. Hey listen aren't we being too sensible now? I thought we were going to be teenagers?'

'We are. But there are some sensible teenagers. I was one. Bet you were too.' He stood and offered me a hand to pull me up.

I waved my hand in a 'so so' gesture and let myself be helped to my feet. 'It depends on who you talk to. I thought I was extremely sensible in that I always knew when to stop, but my mother thought I was the spawn of the devil, mainly because I would be deliberately awkward about things just to irritate her.' We passed the park ranger with as much dignity as possible and a friendly 'Lovely evening!'

'Oh Lord, I'm sure he knew what we were up to.' I felt like a child on the mitch.

'He's not bothered, he's far too busy looking out for drug dealers and people trying to fall and put in an insurance claim to worry about a couple of respectable office workers drinking out of plastic cups.'

He was probably right.

We rambled out towards Dorset Street and chatted, taking in the early Friday evening atmosphere. Smokers gathered outside pubs, glasses of beer in hand eying members of the opposite sex.

A raucous gaggle of young girls in varying shapes and sizes walked towards us, all scantily clad and fully intent on a good night out. I didn't know whether to be revolted or impressed by the sight of rolls of pale, slightly sunburned Irish flesh revealed by hip hugging shorts and skirts and slinky tops worn at half mast. I think once I overcame the 'yeuuch!' factor I was impressed at their confidence. They were flaunting it, whether they had it or not. Better than hiding it under a baggy tracksuit and staying indoors.

We sat on the first free bench we found on the canal and watched the antics of a gang of young lads in their early teens jumping, diving and pushing each other into the water.

We ate the sandwiches we had bought on the way down. Did you know that vodka and Coke goes very nicely with a cheese sandwich on white bread? I tried Rob's egg and onion but thought the mix not as good. I visualised the egg and onion coming up again later. Perhaps that was what put me off.

'Now Breslin. Give.'

'What do you mean?'

'You. John. Story?'

I groaned again. 'Story. I wish I knew. I'm more confused now about our relationship, don't you hate that word, well, our whatever it is. I can't go back to the carefree person, child, I was years ago and I worry that

that's who John is still in love with. Or maybe it's the idea of us being soul mates and always together no matter what difficulties there are that he loves.' I swirled the diluted Coke around in its plastic container, then proffered it again for a refill.

Rob did the honours. 'Ok. pros and cons.'

Typical bloody book-keeper – everything in columns.

'I'll do the pro's,' he said. 'From the outside looking in. Then you can argue them if you want.'

I laughed and waved an indulgent hand at him to continue.

'1. You love John.

2. You have always loved John.

3. No matter what happens you will continue to love John.

4. John loves you.

5. John has always and will always love you.

The rest of it is just a matter of logistics. My argument is completed m'lud.' He stood and bowed.

'But it's not that simple Rob.' I was already feeling dizzy from the drink, his stating bald facts that I was shying from were not doing anything to improve my dizziness. Facts and alcohol do not mix well. Flights of fancy are far better.

'It bloody is, Sinead. And you know it and you'll never forgive yourself if you allow that man to walk out of your life. He is the other half of you. I bet the sex is great as well. You just… what's the word…tessellate.'

'Wha'?'

'Tessellate. It means fit together the way little pieces of mosaic do, exactly –leaving no spaces.'

'Tess-ell-ate' I tried it out. I liked it, it described the way I felt about John and me, or rather how I felt we could be. At the moment I felt like the exposed edge of the mosaic, the bit that's not quite finished, waiting for the border to be placed. But what would finish our mosaic? Make the picture whole? Shit. I was too drunk to think about it now, but Rob had given me the nudge I needed. I knew whatever happened between John and me would have to happen soon now. I had to either piss or get off the pot, not string both of us along like I had been doing.

'Y'know. You could be right Roberto, you could be right. 'Nuff about me, what about your own love life?'

'No love life to speak of. Sex life is deadly though.' He laughed and went on to describe in graphic detail an encounter he had with a rather large Russian gentlemen who was somewhat confused about his sexuality at the start of the night but in no doubt whatsoever about it at the end.

I thought I would wet myself laughing. No one can paint pictures with words the way Rob can.

'C'mere, d'ye want a love life? Or are you happy enough with life at the moment? Is that the last of the vodka? God we're awful alcos!'

'Do I want a love life? Yes, of course, eventually. I mean the crack is great and all that when you're single but I'd love to meet someone to share life with. The whole bit – house, garden, trips to Woodies and the supermarket, arguing over which washing powder we should buy, whose turn it is to empty the dishwasher. Contentment enhanced by passion. And yes, that is the last of the vodka and I'm taking you home. C'mon.'

'Ah Rob! Can we not have a swim first? Look at those lads, they're having a ball. And I'm hot and sticky and my feet are sunburned.'

The look of sheer horror on his face was worth the suggestion and he nearly had heart failure as I started to pull at my blouse in a pretended effort to take it off.

'Stop that! Sinead! Are you mad! If you didn't drown you'd surely pick up some weird disease or at the very least a virus.'

'Not at all, not at all.' I continued my faux undressing. 'Sure look at those young fellas, healthy as horses.'

'Ah Sinead c'mon now, stop the messing. They're probably immune to anything that's in the water. Honestly Sinead, please don't. I'm afraid you'll get into trouble in the water and I'd have to go in after you,' he shuddered.

'Would you do that for me? Ah Rob, I think I'll dump John and turn you, make you my boyfriend. We could have lots of babies and rear them as free spirits.' I tucked my blouse back into my skirt and gathered up my bag and shoes with as much dignity as my inebriation would allow.

'I cannot imagine a worse fate.' He put his arm around me 'Much as I love you Sinead dear, having to live with your myriad irrational insecurities would drive me to drink. If you were gay you'd be camp, hysterically camp. And sex. With a woman! It's not natural' He shuddered and I laughed.

'I'll be a good girl and do as I'm told on one condition.'

His relief was palpable, although he eyed me dubiously and asked about the condition.

'A little teensy, weensy ducking of feet in the canal. Both of us together. Like a baptism of happiness – that our feet will then choose the right path for us no matter what our brains tell us.' I walked to the bank and plopped myself on the ground, legs and feet stretched in front of me ready for dipping.

'Aw, Sinead. What about rats?'

'Rob, the canal is full of young fellas swimming and larking about. No self-preserving rat would come within an ass's roar of them. Shoes off,' I commanded. 'Now socks and trousers rolled up.'

He did as he was told, sensing I wouldn't budge until my silliness was complete.

'Right, are you ready? On the count of three.' We wriggled forward until our legs dangled over the edge and "One… two… three..." slipped our feet into the delicious coolness of the water. We sat and chatted a while, nonsense mostly, gently splashing each other's legs.

'Jesus!' Rob pulled his feet out and started to dry them with his socks. 'I felt something! Honestly Sinead. Shit, what if it was a rat?'

I pulled my own legs out. 'Rob, you're such a city boy,

or worse a girl. I must introduce you to the wonders of the countryside some weekend soon. Show you some of the more unusual sights. Like Paddy Devanney up the lane de-balling some of his rams. Or the vet with his hand halfway up a cow's ass trying to release a blockage.' I was being deliberately OTT.

'De-balling rams! Have you really seen that? And why?' He shivered as he rolled down the leg of his trousers, drawing his knees together instinctively.

We strolled, or half-stumbled, up the rest of the canal bank towards Phibsboro as I enlightened him about some of the lesser known practices of animal husbandry. Duly exaggerated of course. It was a beautiful evening, the sun going down in a blaze of glory against a salmon pink-tinged sky – a promise for tomorrow.

We debated getting more drink and decided against it. There was a bottle of white in the fridge at home; that should surely be enough to knock us out at this stage. We were allowed on a bus, mainly because we held our breaths and tried not to titter as Rob valiantly counted out change into the fare machine's chute under the bored eye of the bus driver. When we got to the apartment I rang for a take-away while Rob showered to scrub away any traces of rat urine. He opened the wine while I showered and had the dinner set out on plates when I came out of the bathroom.

We finished the bottle in front of the telly, slagging off every programme we flicked onto.

I woke in the early hours my legs on Rob's lap and a crick in my neck. When I moved it exacerbated the thumping in my head and I groaned, drank a pint of water popped two paracetamol and threw a fleece over Rob's sprawled body before I crawled into my own bed.

'Tessellate,' I murmured as I dozed off. 'Like that. Tessellate'.

Chapter Twenty-Three

A swarm of starlings swoop through a grey sky, a rolling, dark, fragmented wave coming to crash on a stony beach. They rest sporadically on treetops, roofs, telephone wire, then up in flight again at some signal unknown to duck and dive, swerve, leapfrog, a rolling path. Norah stands at the living room window, fascinated. It's the numbers that stun her. She laughs suddenly.

'Rats of the bird world.' Teasie would grumble when the family that nested in the eaves every year had shit yet again on her kitchen window. She tried everything to stop them; she had Frank up with chicken wire one year but the 'little buggers' still got through it.

It's a Thursday in late August and Sinead is on holiday, herself and John gone for a fortnight to Italy. Charles will be up on Saturday morning and has next week off so they're going to spend it together.

'Let's be Yanks' he had suggested.

'What?'

'Do the whole Dublin tour bus thing, hop-on, hop-off. Go to the Abbey and the Gate. Do a Saturday night "genuine" Irish music session in a "genuine" Irish pub.'

'With "genuine" stout I suppose,' Norah had smiled.

'Oh, we'd have to give it a whirl. And go to the Guinness place and the whiskey distillery. I think I see an alcohol-themed week here,' he said.

'I'll go along with the alcohol if we can do a day in some of the fabulous gardens that are open at the moment, here and say in Wicklow.'

'Deal negotiated with no difficulty,' he had proffered his hand, they shook on it and then sealed it with a kiss.

She puts her fingers to her lips. They tingle when she thinks of their kissing, their lovemaking. Sometimes after they are both sated her lips will feel swollen, pulsing and bruised from all the kissing and being kissed. She never thought. Really. Never ever imagined that it could be like this, that this kind of love could exist outside the pages of a novel. She loves Charles with all of her. He is everything she ever wished for.

'My beautiful Charles,' she had murmured to him at one stage. He had laughed, said he could never be called beautiful and was she sure she was still taking those tablets the psychiatrists had given her? She smiles, he makes her laugh, he holds her when she cries, he accepts her and all her frailties and she adores him for it. She feels part of him, naked without him.

She spends a lot of time in wonderment at all that has overtaken her in the last ten months. She realises that she never knew what love was until recently. The love for Frank and Teasie totally different to this all-encompassing desire and acceptance. What was it she felt for Tom? She had called it love in the beginning, the feelings she had for him because he said so often and with such vehemence that he loved her that she was sure what she felt must be love.

After she had rescued him from the dry toilet that day he had become her constant companion in the school yard and out in the fields. There had been a childish affection for him which grew as they grew into fondness. A general acceptance by classmates that they were 'together'. She never questioned it. She had also felt a pity for him as he had to suffer the merciless tongues of the Furlong women. Perhaps too she had been flattered, only Tom had ever shown any real interest in her. Towards the end she thought now what she felt was a fear of and a sorrow for what Tom had become. A sorrow for his insecurities that ate away at him. Whatever the feelings were they were as nought to the way she felt about Charles. She shakes her head, she may never know, may never understand.

The only thing from her former life that Norah misses is her garden. Even that last horrible day can't take away the joy it gave her. She opens the french door and steps out onto the narrow balcony. She had made up two window boxes and a planter for Sinead. But she looked after them herself. Sinead didn't know one end of a plant from the other. Norah deadheads the white and purple petunias, the slight crushing releasing their sweet fragrance, tidies up a straggling geranium and waters the containers. She stands for a minute enjoying the sun.

She glances at her watch, the Botanic Gardens will be open for another hour, she'll run around. The Rose Garden is beautiful at the moment.

As she walks down the steep slope of Washerwoman's Hill thinking about roses a big yellow JCB digger rumbles in first gear up the hill. She has to stop, her legs feel weak and she thinks she's going to vomit. It's the first time the memory has caught her unawares, overwhelmed her. In all its completeness. Every goddamn, bloody horrific minute.

'Are you alright, love? Whoops, there we go.'

She stumbles into the arms of the passing stranger. To the physical fright the sight of the digger had given her is added the sensory shock of contact with thin curly-haired male arms and the faint smell of male sweat.

'Now. Are you with me? Yes. Good woman. Come on now, here we go.' His accent is familiar, assaults her ears. She opens her mouth to scream for help but only emits a low moan.

She tries to pull away, but can't. The elderly man manoeuvres back the few steps to the doors of the 'Tolka House' and shoulders open the double doors of the pub. He half carries Norah through and sits her on a high-backed seat.

'Head down, love.' He pushes her head gently down towards her lap. 'That's it. Good woman. Hold it now.' The good Samaritan disappears for a moment or two, returns with an anxious lounge girl bearing a pint glass of iced water.

Norah's head is starting to clear. She still feels nauseous, is now embarrassed at her public display of weakness.

'Will I phone for ambulance?' The beautiful young barmaid with the big eyes and Slavic cheek bones crouches beside Norah, her hand on Norah's back. The man is hovering behind her.

'No!' Norah half shouts. 'No, sorry. I'm fine. I don't know what came over me. The heat I suppose. Honestly I'm fine. I'll just sit here a while. If that's okay?'

'Yes. Yes. I will bring tea, yes? And you sir?'

The man orders coffee and moves to sit opposite Norah.

She smiles at him and starts to thank him.

'Now, save your words and your strength. Just sup that water there and then good sweet tea and we'll get you sorted.' He takes a cloth handkerchief from his trouser pocket and blows his nose noisily. 'It'll be the heat of course. Us Irish aren't used to it. It has me half-killed. You're not ill or anything, are you? Are you sure we shouldn't get a doctor now?'

'No. Thanks.' She still feels a little out of body but the nausea is lifting.

The lounge girl returns with the tea and coffee and hovers for a moment. The elderly man asks how much he owes and the girl blushes,

'Nothing, sir. Of course, nothing. Anything you need you ask for.'

He laughs. 'Well, be Jayminnity God, there's one for the books, eh! Only joking love, only joking.'

The girl retreats, abashed.

'Think I embarrassed her, didn't mean to. It's just the first time I ever got something for nothing in a pub.' He gives a little laugh. 'I don't think she gets the Irish slagging. Now, sip at the tea until you're sure you feel alright. Is there anyone I can ring for you?' He pours her tea with a slightly trembling hand.

'No. Honestly, I'm fine. You're very kind. You must have other things to do. Please, don't let me delay you.' Norah's voice has strengthened.

'Me! Lord not a thing. Retired I am. I was just out for a ramble around the Botanic Gardens and was going to come in here and treat myself to my tea and maybe a pint and a chat with someone at the bar.' He smiles. 'You'll always find another auld codger at the bar to have a good moan and a laugh about today's world with a fond smile about yesterday's.'

Norah sips the tea, the horror of the yellow digger receding. She shudders slightly and her sharp-eyed companion notices.

'Are you chilled? Are you sure you're not sick? Maybe we should get you to a doctor.'

'Honestly, I feel much better. It was the heat and... I was just thinking of something and it... I just felt weak.' She finishes lamely.

He nods and pats her hand again. 'Ye'll be grand now in a minute. Then we'll get you home. Do you live near?'

She tells him where she is staying.

'Sure you're only up the road. I'll be walking up that way meself. You're not a Dublin woman though, are you?'

'Well, originally yes. But I was reared in Leitrim.' The dizziness is gone and the cooler air in the pub and the tea are helping eliminate the nausea

'I thought so, I recognise the accent. Sure amn't I a county man of your own! Originally Shancurry, 'tween Drumshanbo and Leitrim village. Do ye know it?' Norah shakes her head, she knows of Shancurry; she was never there but Tom's second shop is in it. She is terrified that the conversation will now turn around to him trying to name someone she knows or vice versa.

'I'm out of it these fifty years. No one belonging to me

243

there anymore. Haven't even been back for the last ten year. Be Jayminnity God! Isn't that a good one, hah! So few of us in the county in the first place and here's two exiles running into each other by chance on a Dublin street.' He shakes his head, smiling with delight.

Norah laughs at the man's enthusiasm. She hasn't heard the 'Be Jayminnity God' in twenty years, it was something Frank used to say also. Whatever about this man being her good Samaritan, she feels she may have made his day.

He spends the next half hour telling her about his family and being reared the third of a large family in Leitrim of the thirties and forties. His parents scratching a living from the poor soil.

'I suppose I look back with rose-tinted glasses,' he says, 'but summers seemed sunnier and the freedom from fear, except of the schoolteacher and the parish priest was great. There was never a door locked morning or night in Shancurry. There was nothing to steal, nobody had anything! Mind you there weren't too many houses anyway. But what there was we were all reared in and there was a great camaraderie between young and old. I suppose the poverty was rough on everyone; the women in particular had a hard time, too many children, too little in the way of food and education to pull those children out of the trap they were in themselves. Then what were they rearing us for? Sure there was no work about there, the farms were small enough and poor enough without splitting them down further amongst sons. As soon as you could you were away looking for work and adventure. But they were great women, my own mother was always laughing and she had little enough to laugh about. My generation had it easier and no disrespect dear, but your generation have it easiest of all.'

Norah starts to laugh and can't stop. The man looks at her, a worried expression on his face.

'Oh, I'm sorry,' she gasps. 'It's just... I've been through a bit of a time... and you saying I had it easy. I suppose. It just puts things in perspective. At least I think it does.'

'Well, there you are. Are you married?' He looks at her ring finger. She had removed her wedding ring but her finger was still dented from the years of wearing it.

She hesitates. 'Widowed. Since last October.'

'Aw Lord save us, may God be good to your poor husband. Well, I see what you mean about having a bit of a time. I lost my Mary eight years ago and honest to God I still miss her every day. I just live up there in Ballygall and I ramble down to the Botanics on any dry day. Loved flowers and plants, she did. So I sits meself into the rose garden this time of the year and chat to her, tell about our lads, what they're up to. Always feel better after.' He pours more tea.

'We had our ups and downs, money worries, I probably drank too much and gave her a hard time on and off. And she had a right little temper on her!' he laughs. 'But I did me best and so did she and we grew up together, learned to accept each other, warts and all. And we were great pals by the time it came to her going. Bit unfair really, just when things were getting easier for us she was taken. Ah well, mysterious are the ways of Nature and God, eh? Sure you're only a young woman. It's probably hard on you now, but believe me love, life goes on and some day you might find someone else to share it with. Too late for me. Would you listen to me blethering away, typical grumpy old man eh!'

Norah looks at the man's well-lined face, the broken veins of the habitual drinker and his slightly filmed eyes tell their own stories.

'You've been so kind. Honestly, everyone whose path I've crossed since my husband died…I never knew there was such caring left in the world. You hear plenty of complaints about how people don't look after each other anymore. I can't agree to that. I have had nothing but care and kindness from everyone I've met in the last year. You're right, life does go on and once there are people like you about to help the likes of me it will continue to go on.' This all came out in a rush and she's embarrassed by it, covers her confusion by excusing herself to go to the Ladies.

She goes to the toilet and washes her hands for several minutes. Then splashes her face with some cold water and pats it dry with paper towels. She studies her pale face in the mirror. She has put on a little weight in the last three months and she thinks it suits her, softens her angles. She's no longer as stickishly gawky, her haircut she describes as 'grown-up' and she has taken to wearing eye make-up and a little lipstick. She looks like a real person.

For so many years she would look in the mirror and see Norah Breslin, Frank and Teasie's niece, or Norah Furlong, Tom Furlong's wife. Now there is just Norah and she likes this Norah. A Norah who finally knows what she is doing, no longer drifting through each day trying just to get through it, responsible for her own life. She smiles at her reflection, she's starting to analyse things like Sinead. And maybe that's not as bad a thing as she thought – in moderation.

When she comes out her white-haired knight in baggy slacks and short-sleeved check shirt awaits her.

'Now, dear. Will I ring a taxi to take you up the road or would you rather walk?'

Norah insists she is fine to walk and Gerry Gallogly, for such is his name, insists on accompanying her.

'You could come over weak again and fall into the road. I'd never forgive myself if such a thing happened to a fine young Leitrim woman. I'll walk you up and then ramble down again for my tea.'

She offers to make him something to eat and he declines.

'Well, now if you see me walking about the place raise your hand to me and stop to have a chat. And if you're ever in the Rose Garden say hello to my Mary. And sure if I ever see you in the pub we can have a pint together and I'm sure we'll find someone between Shancurry and

Tibraden in the County of Leitrim that we both know!' If he'd been wearing a cap, which she felt he probably did on cooler days, he would have tipped the brim to her.

The apartment is peaceful and feels like home and she gladly sets about preparing a meal for herself. She thinks about dishes she can make for Charles next week and plans a trip to the supermarket to pick up supplies. An ordinary woman planning ordinary things to do for the person she loves. At last.

Chapter Twenty-Four

John and I came back from a wonderful holiday in Italy with it decided that we were 'officially' an item. That was as far as I was ready to commit at the time. I did promise to enquire about a transfer to Sligo and he said he would look at some practices within commuting distance of Dublin.

So things more settled, both of us inching towards a happy medium.

'I don't know where you got the idea I'd never leave Mullaghadone,' he said. 'I'd prefer to live there but not above living with you. Mullaghadone and you would be fantastic but if it comes to a choice it's you one hundred percent. And you know we can afford you not working.' He spotted the obvious tension in my face at that suggestion. 'It's just another option, you could complete your degree, do a different degree – anything you want to do, just don't leave it out of the equation. But you're the boss, your terms.'

Why was he so bloody nice? Of course his leaving it all up to me made me want to please him, do what he wanted. Was he being devious? Stupid thought, John didn't have a devious bone in his body. Some days it went round and round in my head until I felt dizzy. Why couldn't I just close my eyes and leap? How in the name of God does anyone ever make a decision to marry? Does everyone go through this blur of feelings? Love, fear, excitement, anticipation, or was I the only one in the world? It seemed to be simple for John, he knew he wanted to be with me and I said I wanted to be with him so the rest of it was just detail.

Apparently that simplified things but not for me. It meant I had to make choices. I hate making choices, afraid I'll make the wrong one. It happens invariably in little things, the queue I join in the supermarket, assuming it to be shorter, ends up with being the one with the cranky or inept cashier who manages a dispute with each customer or runs out of till roll or change or something and every shopping basket in the queue I considered and rejected as being too long has been barcoded, bagged and cashed up successfully. Grass is always greener, etcetera. And this choice was a lot more life-changing than a supermarket queue. And I'm hopeless with change. I dig my heels in, I know I do. Fear.

I had Norah and Rob worn to a frazzle analysing every possible combination of options. Rob said if I let John go this time he would never talk to me again. I retorted that I might hold him to that. I was joking of course. They were invaluable, both of them in different ways. Rob's strategy for dealing with me was the 'you need a good kick up the behind and I'm the one to do it' attitude, whereas Norah just listened and suggested some of the techniques I had been trying to get her to adopt in relation to her own life.

'Just Be…Just Be…' she kept saying, half slagging me for my cack-handed attempts at helping her through her darker moments.

'Sinead a stór, I don't know why you do it. You have yourself exhausted, all wound up over the whole thing; you're like a silly dog chasing his own tail. What does it matter where you live once you're together? Of course, maybe you don't really love him, in which case the whole discussion is irrelevant.'

This conversation one Wednesday evening as I painted her toenails.

Norah, giving me advice! And short, punchy, good advice. How much she had grown.

I hugged her.

'What's that for?' she asked smiling.

'Nothing. For being here, for listening to me ramble on ad nauseam about John and me. For being so wise. How did you get to be so wise?'

'Wise? Am I? I don't think so. I just know that if you feel for John half of what I feel for Charles I can't understand you bothering to try and understand it. It just is. And it's the only thing that matters, everything else will click into place, some of it quickly, some slowly. I may have to spend time in prison, but it will be bearable because I will have Charles to come home to afterwards. I know I can stick anything once that reward is at the end of it. John rang me earlier, my date came in.' She wiggled her toes, admiring the ruby-coloured nails.

'Your what?'

'The trial date, it's been brought forward.' The original date had been expected to be January.

'Christ, when?'

'October, provisionally the 22nd, it may change.'

Silence. I felt humbled, bleating about the decision I had to make, Norah's future about to be decided by strangers.

'They're dry, aren't they? Will I make tea?' She stood up, slipped on flip-flops.

'Yes. Fuck, no. Not tea, we need alcohol. Open a bottle of wine. Jesus, how can you be so calm?'

'Sinead Breslin, if your mother could hear you! Your language is foul.' But she laughed and moved around the kitchen – glasses, opener, wine. 'As to my calmness, I suppose there really is nothing I can do about it. It's inevitable. I know the best and the worst result there can be. And the worst result isn't any worse than anything I've already been through. All I have to do is wait. And for the first time in a long time I'm not waiting on my own. I have a whole team of people waiting with me. That makes it all bearable. I suppose that's why I can't fully understand you holding out on making that final leap to be with John. Imagine having someone as loving and strong as John on your side all the time. Why, you could do anything!'

Do you know? I agreed with her and it was that more than anything that made me throw caution to the wind and decide that what would be would be and I would stop procrastinating and be proactive. Of course I didn't say any of this, Norah would have rolled her eyes around and told me to stop watching Dr. Phil.

The fact that the court case was now looming made every moment spent with Norah more precious. One way or the other after the trial she would move on. Either to prison or into a place of her own or with Charles. I would miss her. Living with her had been extraordinarily easy (plus a lot tidier and more organised). She had brought John back into my life and Mother too in a way. She made me appreciate what I had in the way of family and friends. But most of all I would miss her own gentle sweet self. Her general air of stillness and acceptance. There was never, and could never have been, any badness in Norah Breslin.

Charles had a friend with a house near a village called Kilcar in South West Donegal. Norah and he and his mad dog were to spend a weekend in it towards the end of September. Despite Donegal being so near to home I had only been in it once or twice. And it had always been wet, even wetter than Mullaghadone, so that put me off.

When I mentioned I hadn't visited it much I was immediately invited along, as was John. Then Rachel got wind of it and herself and Eoin were included too. The summer had been a good one by Irish standards and September was still mild. It would be nice for us all to spend time together before the court case. A sort of charge the batteries, prepare for battle.

The house was an old two-storey restored country house which had originally belonged to the local cobbler. The business had been run out of a little stone-built shed beside the house. The shed was ramshackle but the old equipment was still in it. It felt funny standing there, imagining the relatives of people of the area who had tramped in and out here with worn out or broken shoes, asking for the cobbler to mend them so they could get another winter out of them. The place was an anachronism in today's world, a reminder in our throwaway society of a bygone era where the last bit of wear was eked out of everything. I'm not sentimental about Ireland's rise from poverty but there are times when it feels we have lost as much as we have gained.

Norah and Charles in particular loved the ambience of the house. I'm more of an en-suite mod cons type but even I had to admit this place had a certain charm. Built some time in the 1940s it had been restored with a careful eye and the best of its architectural features had been retained. High ceilings, picture rails, deep windowsills. It had a comfortably furnished and stocked big kitchen, the range was still in working order but it was also equipped with a gas cooker, fridge, microwave and all the conveniences of modern life. There was a large living room that ran the width of the house, one wall with floor to ceiling built-in white book shelves, all fully stocked. An open fire, two large comfy sofas and several small tables adorned with lamps created an atmosphere of comfort and love.

Upstairs there were three big double bedrooms with, thank God, the most comfortable of newly-sprung mattresses on the beds. Rachel squealed with delight when she saw the bathroom. A big claw-footed standalone tub was the main feature.

'Bags we first to use that. Look at the size of it!'

'What's with the "we"? Too much info! And if you do use it when the rest of us are here please do remember the bathroom is directly over the living room. So don't make too much noise.' I felt like Mother; I could almost hear Mother's disparaging sniff and winced.

Of course they not only made too much noise, but caused water to splash over the edge of the bath and drip through the floor and ceiling below it onto my unsuspecting dozing head. Large amounts of hilarity all around. You couldn't be cross with Rachel and Eoin. I told Eoin he was like Slippers, a big, affectionate, sloppy eejit.

He was delighted with the compliment and drove me mad for the rest of the evening by letting the odd appreciative bark out of him if I was nice to him in any way. And every time he barked Slippers took up the chorus.

We walked down to the village that evening and split our custom over the street's four pubs.

John Joe's was the liveliest of them and the man who had sold us groceries in the shop earlier now sat on a small rostrum with a guitar and entertained us all. There was a bit of a free-for-all at the end and several people got up to sing, each one better than the one before. Give the Irish a drink and put a mike in our hands and you have a country full of entertainers. It must have been almost three a.m. when we walked back up the hill to the house, Eoin and Charles singing a filthy version of the Fields of Athenry which described a rather dubious encounter after a rugby international between a pyjama-clad inner city young one and a brandy swilling, D4 rugby gobdaw.

When I opened my eyes the next morning the sun's fingers were pushing through a gap in the curtains, illuminating John's sleeping face. He has an eerie way of sleeping, his eyes seem to be half-open and to be peering down his nose at something. I waved my hand over and back in front of his face. He didn't stir. I admired him for a while. Watching him all my worries disappeared. I knew we'd be okay, that we would always understand each other, that our conversations would contain as much in the silences within them and pauses after them as what was said by either of us, that we would never be at cross purposes, that I would always tell him the truth in future as he had always told me, no matter what I thought I should 'protect' him from.

Whatever that sun showed me I saw. I knew I would

spend the rest of my life with him. I shook him awake to share the good news.

I think he was pleased.

Eoin was in charge of the fry-up. It was a glorious day and Norah, Rachel and I sat outside the house drinking coffee and enjoying the sunshine. Trees from around the house had been cleared, leaving a breathtaking view up the glen and in the distance the mountain we were to climb after breakfast. Norah sat in 'the throne,' a seat cut out of the stump of an enormous tree, looking up towards the mountain that dominated the landscape. There was a slight breeze and small clouds scudded across the sun.

'Look at the way the colours on Sliabh Liag keep changing,' said Norah. 'Every shade of grey, purple and green you can imagine – pulsing one into the other.'

'Pulsing?' smiled Rachel. 'Yes. Haven't you a great way with words. That's exactly what it's doing.'

'Grub up,' called the chef and we all went indoors for the full Irish.

Norah insisted we clean up straight away and I have learned life can be easier, well tidier, with her 'clean as you go' policy. Despite that we still managed to be at Bun Glas, a plateau about half way up Sliabh Liag, before one o'clock.

It was, is, one of the most beautiful and unspoiled places I have ever been. The drive up to it from Teelin had been scarily breathtaking. I was in the front passenger seat of John's car and on some of the bends I was convinced that I had to be hanging out over the cliff edge, flying on two wheels above the restless Atlantic far below.

We parked the cars at Bun Glas and got out to stunning views of cliff and sea, mountain and sky. Charles pointed out two enormous rocks jutting out of the sea in the inlet below.

'They're known as the 'Giant's chair and table'. You can just imagine a giant lumbering down the mountain to sit and eat his dinner at them!'

It looked like the giant had first discarded his cloak to

cover the mountainside in shades of purple heather. We slogged and slagged our way towards the summit, scrambling over rocks, pulling our way through brittle scotch grass and moss, on hands and knees in places. Charles knew the names of the various peaks and ridges from land some 2,000 feet below but was confused by them up closer.

It felt good being up there, all of us together. Nothing to explain or excuse. We stopped several times, it would have been foolish not to take our ease and admire, let the eye take in and the brain to register the wilderness, the richness of colour of the rocks, ravines and precipices, then the sight of the cliffs plunging to the hungry ocean.

We stopped at the summit for almost an hour, absorbing the clean, ozone-laden air, listening to the silence.

'Something else, isn't it,' said Charles. 'Last point in Europe, the highest sea cliffs, the battering Atlantic. Christ, it could turn you into a poet.'

'Wouldn't go that far,' laughed Eoin. 'Might make you believe in a God though.'

'Where's this infamous "One Man's Pass" then?' asked Norah.

Charles turned and pointed at a rocky knife-edge rib about forty feet long and a yard wide at most. It wasn't called 'One Man's Pass' for nothing. A yard sounds a lot when you're standing in your living room, plenty of room to stand on, but this yard was stuck up in the air and nothing Charles had said had prepared us for the verticality of the cliffs on either side of the Pass. The drop to the Atlantic on one side is practically sheer whilst the drop to the valley on the other side, whilst not as steep, was certainly heart-in-the-mouth stuff.

'Will we do it?' Norah broke the studious silence.

'I'm game if you are,' said Charles.

'Couldn't be any worse than Funderland I suppose,' she said.

So they all inched out onto the pass, Rachel on hands

and knees. I chickened out, I was really afraid that I would look down and feel the pull of gravity too much for me. The desire to let go, to feel like a black-headed gull hovering on the thermals, then to plunge freefall into the steel grey sea, where the hypnotic pull of the white-capped waves would wash all traces of me away. I shivered, the place was magnificent but scary, a reminder of what little dots we all are on this great big planet of ours.

Exhilaration had obviously overtaken the gang out on the pass. John shouting 'Top of the world, Ma. Top of the world' at the uninterested gulls gliding above his head. Eoin was whooping with delight. Charles had managed to sidle in slightly behind Norah and was holding her around the waist whilst she peered down the cliff. She looked like a figurehead of a ship, I couldn't help thinking of the Di Caprio and Winslett montage from 'Titanic'. I daren't tell them that of course, the teasing at me turning sentimental wouldn't be worth it. But they looked so good together, they could have been carved into the rock face and looked as if they belonged. Only poor Rachel looked terrified and she was the first one to make her way back to me by a series of crablike movements alternated with sliding on her bottom.

'Jesus. No words can describe that.' She looked very pale. 'I have never, ever been so terrified.'

'That was one of the best experiences of my life.' Eoin bounded over to us like a young goat.

'God, if you could bottle the feeling you get out there and sell it you could make a fortune!' John squeezed my shoulder, eyes lit up like a child who has scored his first goal. 'You should really try it, Sinead.'

'It's alright,' I said. 'I'll take your word for it.'

'We better start moving folks. I don't like the look of the front that's moving in. If mist falls we may have to stop until it lifts. It would be too dangerous.' Charles led the way and we trailed in his wake.

Within twenty minutes the mist had caught us and within another ten Charles called a halt. I couldn't believe how quickly it had rolled in. It was terrifying, you couldn't see where you were placing your foot.

I sat on a damp rock and huddled close to John for heat. His hair was beaded with droplets of mist. I knew the others were within a couple of feet of me but I couldn't see them, in fact if John pulled back his head by more than a couple of inches I couldn't see him.

We chatted desultorily for a while, but the disembodied voices soon put paid to any banter. The mood grew as grey and clinging as the all-pervasive fog.

Norah started to speak. Haltingly at first, she told us in detail what had happened the night Tom Furlong had died. Charles and John knew the story already but she had never given Rachel and I chapter and verse. Her voice grew steady and firm, it was like a voiceover of her life.

'And I wish I could say I'd change the end if I could, but I wouldn't. I might have changed the beginning. With the wisdom of hindsight I definitely would have changed the beginning. Maybe I could have saved both of us if I had gone for help years ago.'

I tried to interject, to object to her blaming herself in any way. But John squeezed my shoulder. 'Sssh. Norah needs to do this. Go on Norah.'

So I let her pour it all out. She told us of the good times in the beginning, the way he used to make her laugh, shower her with presents and affection, the way he would make the sign of the cross on her pillow at night 'to keep you safe for me 'til morning. My wife, my life'. She told us of his seemingly never-ending paranoia, his determination to keep her for himself. Tom told everyone that she was agoraphobic, this had - according to Carmel anyway- become much worse after Teasie's death which is why Norah was rarely seen about the village. She described in some detail the increasingly frequent bouts of jealousy and violence, followed by tears and contriteness on his part until eventually he would twist the episodes to make her in some way responsible.

'About six months before that last evening he came

home drunk, not roaring drunk or even angry drunk. He just stared morosely at me for a while then told me to go to bed. I did of course and prayed he would fall asleep on the sofa. He did and some time very early next morning he came up to bed and…..' She gave a peculiar little laugh, muffled by the moisture of the mist.

'This is difficult – and I can only say it like this. It's so personal, the mist is allowing me say it really.' She stopped again and the stillness of the mist seemed to make solitary pods of each one of us. It reminded me of that little wait in confessional boxes I had frequented as a child – that moment just before the priest slid back the grille when I felt utterly alone- fear and anticipation in equal measure, convinced I both needed to tell the truth and be forgiven and hide my shame at whatever misdemeanour I had committed. Norah spoke again – her voice definitely thick with tears.

'I need you all to know…and I may never be able to refer to it again. But I have to tell it, let it out…to you – only to you. There is one thing I haven't told any of you – it felt too personal – but I cannot find peace until I have told everything, every last little thing, to someone to make sense of it all to myself really – and who better than the people who love me best.' She paused and I think it was Charles who cleared his throat. I hoped he was near Norah – ready to hold her if it all became too much.

'The only time Tom could…oh God, I feel like I'm betraying him……he couldn't maintain an erection long enough for him to… ..ejaculate…not unless he had been drinking heavily and slept before he wanted to……… All the radio and television programmes and magazine articles I had heard, watched and read about the problem - I never discussed them with him, he couldn't bear any discussion of our private life, said that alcohol had the opposite effect. Poor Tom. He couldn't even be 'normal' in his dysfunction. When he finished he fell asleep and started to snore. It was bright and I decided to get up. I went into the living room to open the curtains and I stepped in a puddle just inside the door.' She gave a little snort.

'I knew immediately what had happened, he often walked in his sleep and if drunk pissed in any corner he could. I got a basin of soapy water and cloths and newspaper to absorb it from the carpet. As I kneeled to clean up the mess something stopped me, I realised that I shouldn't have to do this. One human being should not have to clean up another human being's piss unless that person is too young or too old or too ill to do it for themselves. I stared at that puddle of piss and I felt something harden in me. I know now that that night was the beginning of the end. A tough, wizened little walnut of bitterness settled in me and it grew and grew until I could free myself, free us. I think that night I knew, knew in some deep corner of me, that the next time – the next beating or roughness or unkindness would be the last, one of us had to stop the way we were living our lives. It seems insane now – all of it - but maybe I was insane then. I wish I had walked away that night – not waited until it was too late.' Her voice hardened.

'Instead I bent my nose into the puddle of my husband's piss hissing through gritted teeth; "Who's the dog? Who's the dog?" My inability to do anything about our problems made me as guilty as him. And for that I can never forgive myself or pay a high enough price.' She fell silent.

I found it hard to breathe, and the others seemed to be holding their breaths also, caught in the horror her words had woven through the mist. A sheep or goat nearby was bleating plaintively. I shivered and leaned back against John's knees, he put his arm about my shoulders. I was glad of the fog because it disguised the tears pouring down my face. I could hear Rachel sniffling too. Even Eoin could be heard clearing his throat. It felt lonely, like maybe the last time we would all be together.

A half an hour later the wind changed and the mist thinned, giving enough visibility for us to descend safely to the car park. It was after eight o'clock and we were half frozen. *The Rusty Mackerel* pub was a welcome sight on the road back to the house and the place was hopping when we walked in. An old woman, her face as lined as corduroy, was belting out a song in *sean nós* style, investing it with all the feeling that only someone who has lived as long as she could.

Bowls of chowder, brown bread and two drinks later we felt warm enough to continue back to Kilcar.

We didn't leave the house again that night, curled up in the living room and watched TV. The three men fell asleep and Rachel recorded them snoring in concert on Norah's phone. Then set it as her ring tone.

'Now even if your phone is bringing you bad news it will make you smile first'

Norah hugged her, then me.

'Again. Thank you.'

'Gerroff!' I growled, 'I can't take any more tears or emotion today. You're not in prison yet Norah Breslin and you won't be if my man has anything to do with it.'

'My man!' Rachel laughed, so she got a punch.

'It's like having sisters,' said Norah. Then we all did cry.

Chapter Twenty-Five

October 2006

Norah sits in the small ante room off the court. The jury have been out for nearly two hours. She has been looking out of the little window high up in the panelled wall, it has a wire mesh over it. She wonders why. It's not likely that anyone, barring a very small child, could wriggle their way through. Perhaps the window can be opened and the mesh is to prevent city pigeons or seagulls coming in and frantically flapping against the old oak wainscoting. She wonders how many people, guilty and innocent, have sat in this room down through the years. Maybe some great, great ancestor of hers had been caught for some misdemeanour and had sat waiting to hear their fate just as she does.

'I think we'll go for some lunch Norah, the jury will be breaking for something to eat soon too. We'll just go down to the restaurant for a sandwich, what do you think?' John. John O'. What a wonderful man he is. He's been there all the time, never faltered, even though he didn't have to be, didn't have to do anything for her.

'John. I want to...I want to tell you again... how much. You know don't you, you know how much it means. All of you, Sinead and Rachel, Kate, Liam and you. And then finding Charles as more than a friend and all Sinead's friends. No matter what happens today, a new life has started for me, a better life. Far, far better than anything that's gone before. A grown-up life I suppose. I went as a child to Frank and Teasie, stayed as a child with them and then let Tom treat me as a child who needs affection will.

He takes her hands and squeezes them.

'Norah, we did what was right by you that's all. You have nothing to thank anyone for. You would be the first to run to someone's aid if they were in trouble'

'Yes, but you have such busy lives all of you. I'll never ever be able to repay you.'

Liam comes into the room accompanied by the barrister.

'They're back.'

'Jesus. That was quick, or was it? What does that mean, Liam?' Norah stands.

'I don't know Norah, I wouldn't pre-empt any jury decision. But whatever it is it must be unanimous because it's been so fast and I feel that's a good sign. Come now, come and we'll find out.'

The court clerk is at the door. 'Your presence in court is required Mrs Furlong.'

Norah nods, takes a step or two forwards then stops, puts her hand to her stomach, her mouth in an 'oh' of surprise.

John comes quickly to her 'Are you alright?' She looks up at him, then at Liam and the barrister and opens her mouth to speak. But she closes it again and shakes her head, then nods.

The life she feels fluttering inside her for the first time can remain her secret for a little longer. Hers and Charles's, their littlest matyrushka doll, nestling at home where it ought to be.

She smiles weakly and steps forward again, steadier, stronger.

'I'm fine, and I'm ready. With all of you - I'm ready.'

THE END

Acknowledgements

I would like to thank Emma Sherry (www.capitalletters.ie) for her sterling work in editing this work and Catherine Ryan Howard (www.catherineryanhoward.com) for her advice on self-publishing. Thanks also to Andrew Brown of www.designforwriters.com for his cover design, using an original photo by Kenneth Walsh.

I couldn't have completed and published this book without the constant support and encouragement of friends and family.

Thank you - each and every one.